TOCK TICK

How not to do time travel

TOCK
TICK

How not to do time travel

Steven Scott

First published in Great Britain in 2024

ISBN is 978-1-0687170-0-0

For all the amazing members and staff at
Centre 81, Great Yarmouth.

Sincere thanks to Peter Woods,
Harry Day, Nick Marshall and Linda Scott for proofreading, editing,
fact checking and generally saving me from embarrassment.
Any errors are down to me.

The excellent cover design is by Nick Marshall.

Bigby – 1719

Nobody visits the village of Bigby. Wagons, coaches and carts rattle past on the north-south road - dusty in summer, muddy in winter. But nothing ever turns into the hidden, almost invisible, track that winds like a serpent to Bigby. The village can just be glimpsed from the sea, a few of its houses gripping the sides of a shallow cleft in the cliffs, but there is no beach here, and no jetty, just a clutter of jagged, wave-splashed rocks that deter incurious captains from pausing on their restless journeys up and down the German Sea coast.

The people of Bigby venture out into the world from time to time to sell their merchandise at nearby markets - leather goods, kitchen utensils, tools, cloth, boots, vegetables and such like. But buyers rarely think to ask where these well-crafted items come from, and if they do ask, the information they receive is imprecise, confusing even.

And no one comes to call.

Except early one summer's day in 1719, someone did.

Eli Graves was driving his weather-racked cart along the track towards the north-south road, his head-drooped horse plodding the dappled route with a slow, rhythmic tread. Eli was enjoying the familiar symphony of grasshoppers, birdsong and sissing leaves when his ears detected something else, something unfamiliar on this lonely trail.

Footsteps. Footsteps crunching the dry surface of the path.

His horse halted without being asked and looked up, alert. He too was surprised by the sound, which suddenly stopped. Standing before Eli was a stranger, paused in the middle of the track, observing him and his horse. There was silence between them, until Eli broke it.

'Good morrow young . . . woman?' The question in his tone indicated that he wasn't sure if this particular person was male or female, dressed as they were in dark brown breeches, black boots and a loose-fitting white linen shirt topped by a tan waistcoat. Short-cut raven hair added to his uncertainty.

'Woman is correct, sir. Forgive my appearance, but it makes travelling much less troublesome,' the person said. 'What is the name of your fine horse?' Her voice was confident, friendly.

'Er . . . Clarence,' stuttered Eli. 'After my grandfather.'

'An excellent name,' said the woman.

'And what might your name be, young lady?'

'I am Esmerelda Fortescue-Jackson, but people call me Jax. And you, sir?'

'Eli, a carpenter. Off to market with my buckets,' he said, jerking his head towards the back of the cart and gradually coming to terms with meeting another human here. 'Are you lost?' he asked.

'No, sir. I have business in Bigby. How much further might it be?'

'About another mile or so. But you have business there, you

say? May I ask who with?'

'I'll know him when I see him,' she said with a smile.

Jax adjusted the leather bag slung across her shoulder and walked up to the horse, gently rubbing his eye with the back of her hand. 'Good to meet you Clarence, and you too, master carpenter. See you again soon, I hope.' With that, she walked off slowly towards the village, tugging a stem of long grass from the verge and chewing its moist end. Eli turned in his seat, and as he watched her depart he suddenly realised that he was engulfed by something he had never before experienced on the trail. Utter silence. No birds, no insects, no trees made a sound. Until the woman disappeared around a bend, and the eerie stillness surrendered to the everyday chatter of the countryside once more.

Eli mopped his brow with a scarlet-spotted kerchief. 'Well I'm blowed,' he said to Clarence, because no one else was there. His companion snorted in reply and moved forward, head raised now, just in case other surprises lay ahead.

Enid Whipple, who could cure everything from sprains to leprosy - or at least, said she could - knocked hesitantly on the door of the corner cottage. She didn't like coming here because the man talked funny. He had appeared in the village more than a year ago and nobody was sure how he had got there. One day he was just . . . there, looking dazed, like he had banged his head, and mumbling words that made no sense. And he was naked. The villagers that found him lying under an oak tree covered him with a blanket and took him straight to Enid to be cured, but all she could do was lie him down on some clean straw in the cowshed and give him a sleeping draught.

Enid reckoned he was about 50. She described him to inquisitive neighbours as lanky, taller than Seth the blacksmith, who was very tall, but in need of a good feed. She asked Mags, the widow who lived next door, if she would sit with her overnight in case he was "that way inclined".

The man didn't make much more sense after he woke up the next morning, but at least he had stopped raving. And he thanked Enid for looking after him, which showed he had nice manners. Then he said he would go for a walk around the village to "compose" himself, so Enid told everyone he must be a musician of some sort.

Anyway, here she was knocking on his door, putting her ear to the wood to detect his approach. He startled her by appearing around the side of the cottage with a handful of carrots he had dug up from the back garden. 'Lorks! For a large man you can be awful stealthy, Master Calvert.'

'Apologies, Enid, I will endeavour to make more of a racket when you come to call in future. How may I be of assistance?' He invited her to sit with him on the rough wooden bench outside his front door. 'Tell me all.'

She paused, not knowing where to start. 'I've had a strange feeling,' she said eventually. Calvert put down his carrots. 'I gets them from time to time but keeps 'em to myself in case people think I'm . . .'

'A witch?'

'. . . going funny,' she said stridently. 'Don't you go using that word about anyone. Ever. It could have . . . consequences.'

'Sorry, Enid. Go on, tell me about this feeling.'

She settled herself and straightened her whitish pinafore over her greyish floor-length dress. 'Something's going to happen,' she said. 'Or is happening, or has happened. I'm not sure which. I know that sounds a bit vague but that's how these things come to me. Sort of like a fog seeping into my bones and telling me things. Warning me, but not being very precise about it. Does that make any sense?'

'Of course,' lied Calvert.

'I had the same feeling a few days before Mag's husband fell off the roof and broke his neck, and before the stables burned down. And then when you turned up out of the blue. I daren't say anything in case people think I'm a you-know-what. I think I can trust you because you're a bit strange as well. No offence.'

'None taken, Enid. Are we talking about a cataclysm of some sort?'

'Eh?'

'A disaster? Is someone going to die?'

She looked agitated. 'Oh, I don't know. I just had to tell someone. You don't mind, do you, Master Calvert?' He shook his head. 'Not at all. Us weirdos must stick together.'

'Hmmm,' she said, standing. 'Any of those carrots going spare? The root fly got mine.' He handed her the bunch with a smile. 'Enjoy,' he said. 'And let's keep our wits about us.'

Constable Bartholomew Bartleby, known to everyone as Barty, was sitting on the ground with his back resting against the door of the village lock-up, a one-room stone building with a pitched slate roof that sat next to the village pond and the stocks. Inside was a slatted wooden bench attached to one wall and an earth floor that smelled permanently of stale urine. Also inside, lying on the bench, was Joe Dings.

'Why do you think we are always at war with someone,

Joe?' asked the constable in a thoughtful manner. 'The French, the Dutch, the Spanish and goodness knows who else over the years. It must cost a few shillings, a war. I bet those cannonballs aren't cheap. And men losing legs and arms and stuff. I don't think wars are a good thing, on the whole.'

There emerged a loud snore, which Barty took as a response to his musings.

'If they start it, of course, we have to defend ourselves, don't we? I can see that. We don't suddenly want to be learning French, and having to change all the road signs. And keeping the womenfolk locked away for fear of them being . . . you know, bothered.

'Anyways, I expect you wouldn't mind a good war, seeing as how quickly riled you get when you've had a few. If your breeches hadn't fallen down and tripped you up I might have chucked you in here for more than drunkenness last night. You could have hurt someone. Again.'

Another snort, the sort that announces that someone is waking up from a skinful. Barty got to his feet and dusted off the seat of his pants. 'You've had enough time to sober up so I'm going to let you out. Just go home peaceful-like and try and behave.' He unhooked an iron key from his belt, slotted it into the lock and turned it, pulling the door towards him an inch or two so that he could peer into the lock-up's dark, smelly interior. He couldn't see Joe on the bench so he opened the door a little more. Then he opened it wide, letting light flood the tiny building.

Joe wasn't there.

Barty walked in, hands on hips, puzzled look on his face. Bravely, he even knelt on the pee-infused floor to look under the bench. The place from which snores and snorts had emanated only seconds before was empty. The constable backed out, stopping only when he reached the edge of the pond. He scratched his head and dashed back to have one last look, just in case Joe had managed to find a hiding place in the ten-foot by ten-foot building. He hadn't.

Jax took a sip from her leather water flask as she reached the edge of the forest she had walked through for the past hour or so. The trees, which swept a protective arm around the western side of the village and its verdant fields, had provided welcome shelter from the sun. The remaining journey would be a hot one. The land sloped gently away from the treeline, enabling her to take in the buildings in upper Bigby, with the dip down to the sea beyond. She knew as she stepped forward on the narrow track between two cornfields that her arrival would cause a stir.

'I've been to his cottage. His wife hasn't seen him since last night when he left for the inn, but says she couldn't care less that he's missing. Good riddance, she said. The poor woman had a black eye.'

Barty was sitting in Enid's kitchen, worry etched over his round, weather-beaten face. 'I never wanted to be the constable. I'm no good at it, but you lot insisted,' he said. 'There wasn't even a badge or anything to go with the job.'

Enid handed him a small glass of her notorious home-brewed plum brandy, which he accepted before realising what he had done. Now it was in his hand he would have to drink it. 'I think you're fretting needlessly,' Enid told him. 'He's probably escaped through a hole in the wall or dug a tunnel or something.

Trying to make a fool of you.'

'I've checked. There's no holes or tunnels. He was snoring in there just before I opened the door to let him out. Joe's vanished. Gone. I've looked all over the village and no one has seen him since yesterday. Seth said he would never forget his last sight of Joe, red-faced drunk with his breeches around his ankles and his tackle out. Not attractive, Enid. Not an attractive picture at all.' But she was picturing it anyway.

Barty sipped his drink without thinking and couldn't prevent his face from crumpling under the effect of the brew. 'That'll do you a power of good,' Enid said proudly. 'It's got special herbs in it.'

Barty picked a stalk from his mouth and found he was unable to talk, so he nodded and smiled politely, wiping tears from his cheeks.

'I think we had better go and consult Master Calvert,' said Enid.

They knocked on the door and walked straight in, as was the custom in Bigby in an emergency, despite the fact that people walking straight in occasionally found themselves witnessing things they would find difficult to forget. 'Master Calvert, my feelings have come true quicker than I expected,' blurted out Enid. 'A strangeness has occurred. Constable Batholomew would tell you about it himself but he hasn't quite got his voice back after sampling my latest batch. I might have made it a bit stronger than usual. I'll bring you a bottle to try.'

Barty, standing behind Enid, was shaking his head vigorously in warning. Calvert got the message but thanked Enid effusively and said he couldn't wait to sample it. Barty slumped in despair.

'So what's happened?' asked Calvert.

'A disappearance, that's what. Barty locked up Joe Dings for drunken disorderness last night and when he went to let him out not a half hour since, he was gone. Vanished into the ether. Nowhere to be found,' added Enid with a theatrical flourish.

'He must have escaped and run off. I'm sure it's nothing more sinister than that.'

The constable found his voice. 'I was leaning on the door talking to him,' he croaked. 'Heard him snoring inside the lock-up but when I opened the door he wasn't there. I even knelt on the floor to see if he was hiding under the bench.' Enid and Calvert pulled a face and studied the officer's damp knees with horror.

'Why would he escape when he knew I was going to let him out? It don't make sense. What's happened to him Master Calvert? Is he dead?'

Enid jumped in. 'I wouldn't be surprised if he'd died in there, the stench is something fearsome, but there's no body. No Joe. If he has gone for good, though, he's not going to be missed, least of all by his poor wife. He was a lazy beggar, and too eager with his fists. Bigby will be a more restful place without him.'

Calvert rubbed a hand over his stubbled chin. 'It's a mystery for sure but there must be a logical explanation. Do we need to report it to anyone?'

'I'm not sure what we would report exactly,' said the constable. 'He could hardly be considered a dangerous escaped criminal when he'd just been locked up for the night for being drunk.'

'I'll have a look at the lock-up later. In the meantime, spread the word around the village to see if anyone has seen Joe.

Perhaps check the rocks on the shoreline.'

Calvert closed the door behind Barty and Enid and sat at his kitchen table. The relaxed demeanour he had shown his visitors had been replaced by a look of concern and he quickly made notes of the details the constable had provided. He then headed to the lock-up, securing his front door as he left.

The iron-braced oak door of the tiny gaol was unlocked, and it swung towards him when he twisted and pulled on the heavy metal ring. The door groaned on its hinges as the lock-up's distinctive odour assaulted Calvert's nostrils.

'You can smell that place a hundred yards away,' said the voice of a young woman peering into the darkness over his shoulder. 'If that's not a deterrent to a life of crime, I don't know what is. Dr John Calvert, I presume.'

He turned around slowly, hardly believing his ears. A voice from his past. And his future.

A tall, lean woman with a handsome face knew who he was. And he knew her. 'Oh my god, Jax!' He reached out awkwardly as if to shake her hand but abandoned the idea. And then, without thinking, he hugged her. 'You're alive! You're bloody alive.' He continued to hug her while jumping up and down like a five-year-old at Christmas.

'OK, let me go, John. I'm sorry to surprise you like this but the mobile phone signal is rubbish in the 18th century, and they haven't even invented fax machines yet. Let's go and chat somewhere other than the precincts of what smells like a well-used and ill-maintained privy? What are you looking for, anyway?'

'Erm, a man who disappeared from here a short time ago. Just as you arrived, come to think of it.'

'A coincidence, surely,' said Jax.

The stranger's arrival had not gone unnoticed. Josiah Drake, the landlord of the Rising Sun, spotted her first and rushed, as far as his portly frame would allow him to rush, into the inn to report his observation to his stick-thin wife. Magnolia was wiping down the rough wooden tables with the grey cloth she used to spread the stickiness more evenly around the surface. 'What's up with you, love of my life?' she snarled without looking up from her work. 'Found that farthing you lost last night?'

'There's a woman,' he shouted. 'A stranger, talking to Master Calvert, all pally like. Looks like a man, but pretty.' Josiah grabbed his wife's arm to drag her to the door but quickly released it when he saw the scowl on her face. 'Well, well,' said Magnolia as she stood in the doorway with her husband and watched the stranger and Calvert turn a corner, heading for his cottage. She removed her apron, handed it to Josiah and strode off. 'I won't be long, my sweet,' she said with a bitterness that mocked her words.

'Hurry back, you vile hag,' replied Josiah, but not before she had drifted from earshot.

Magnolia watched the couple enter Calvert's cottage and heard the key turn in the lock. Her face did something it had rarely done since carefree youth had mutated into careworn wedlock. It smiled. And she set off to spread the news.

'People have a habit of just walking in,' said Calvert to explain his locking of the door. 'And we probably need to talk before attempting any sort of explanation to the villagers.'

'Secondary double glazing. Impressive,' said Jax, nodding towards the cottage windows. 'Isn't it a bit risky introducing things like this?.'

'Nearly everyone in Bigby has it. We make it ourselves.'

'You set up a glassworks?' she said. 'That's pretty amazing in a small place like this.'

'These people are very resourceful. They can do almost anything when they put their minds to it. I can't farm, or forge metal or make stuff from wood, so I contribute in other ways. Ideas mainly. This is my home, after all.' He paused and looked intently at his visitor. 'Did we arrive at the same time?'

'I assume we arrived here at exactly the same time. I just plonked down somewhere else. That little incident didn't just affect you, John. There were five of us in there, remember. You're the first one I've found.'

'I assumed that everyone else in the place had been killed, which is why I was so surprised to see you. Do you think the others are out there somewhere?'

Before Jax could respond there was a gentle tapping on the cottage door. Calvert ignored it. 'Master Calvert, I've brought you a bottle of that lovely plum brandy I promised you,' said Enid sweetly. 'I thought you and your . . . guest might enjoy a sip or two.'

'Bloody hell, that didn't take long,' whispered Calvert, getting up and opening the door an inch or two. 'Thank you so much, Enid, that's very kind of you. Much appreciated. I would invite you in but my guest is resting after a very long journey. Perhaps I can take the bottle from you and we can sample some a bit later.'

'You'll have to open the door a little wider, Master Calvert. I'll never get the bottle through there,' said Enid, desperately trying to peer into the room. He opened it a touch more and took the bottle, thanking Enid for her thoughtfulness, before closing the door and locking it again. 'If she knows, the whole village knows. We'll need to come up with a convincing story,' he said.

The sun was casting its final few rays on Bigby when Eli and Clarence arrived back from the market in Crassacre. Although it was just seven miles in distance, the town was a world away from Bigby, which had been transformed since the arrival of John Calvert. Not only had most of the cottages been double glazed, their roofs had been insulated with some of the low-quality wool they had been unable to sell, and doors had been draughtproofed. Drains had been laid in the streets, thanks to the setting up of a pottery that not only made cooking pots and storage jars, but also lengths of interlocking clay pipe and channelling that diverted rainwater into a large clay-lined reservoir to ensure a year-round supply of water for people, animals and crops.

Instead of the muddy streets and uncomfortable homes that most 18th century rural dwellers had to put up with, the people of Bigby enjoyed a level of comfort that fostered a contented community. As a result, they were healthier, happier and more productive than countryfolk almost anywhere else in the land. And regular trips to the noisy, muddy market towns and their grumbling, worn-out, downtrodden inhabitants confirmed how lucky they were in having Master Calvert in their midst.

The price they paid was to keep all this a secret from the outside world. Calvert had made them promise that he would make their lives better if they said nothing beyond the boundaries of the village.

Eli, his cart empty of buckets, settled Clarence into his stall with hay and water, and retrieved from the secret compartment in the floor of his cart the weighty pouch of shillings and pennies he had earned that day. He tucked this away in an iron box Seth the blacksmith had made for him and headed to the inn. The place seemed more boisterous than usual but Eli had hardly planted his 60-year-old backside onto the high-backed pine settle when Magnolia was upon him, depositing a slopping tankard of ale on the table.

'You won't have heard,' she exclaimed with gusto. 'She arrived when you were in Crassacre. A strange woman in the village.' Magnolia could hardly get the words out quickly enough, eager to share her news before anyone else could scoop her.

'Oh, you mean Jax. Yes, I know,' said Eli in a tired drawl. 'I met her on her way here.'

'You spoke to her? You know her name?' Magnolia was crestfallen, trumped by Eli the carpenter.

'She seemed very nice. A bit on the odd side but she was kind to Clarence. I think he liked her.'

'Clarence! What does he know?' Eli smiled to himself as Magnolia stomped off. 'He's a wise one, that horse. He knows things,' he said to himself.

The level of noise in the Rising Sun was surprising given the scant amount of information that was available regarding the stranger's appearance. She had arrived. She had spoken to Calvert. He had taken her to his cottage. So the bulk of conversation was guesswork. Some theorists had her down as a girlfriend or even a wife who had tracked him down after he had deserted her. Others thought she might be a spy from another town or village who had heard about Bigby's fancy drains and windows. A third train of thought was that she had just materialised somehow, like the mysterious Calvert himself. Eli's view was that they would all know in due course.

'I woke up face down in a dark, smelly, muddy alley,' Jax said. 'Well, most of it was mud. I don't like to think what the other stuff was, but there was a sheep's eyeball peering at me and a barrel full of animal guts at the back of what all the evidence indicated was a butcher's.

'Considering, seconds earlier I was in a bright, ultra-clean laboratory in Cambridge it was a bit of a surprise. I stole some clothes - rags would be a better description - hanging out of a window and itched for days.'

'I came to beside a large oak tree,' said Calvert. 'It's possible I banged my head when I arrived and was out of it for hours. Probably had concussion. It was days before I could recall anything about my past. I knew my name but that was about it. I was sitting in the inn trying to decide whether I should risk drinking the ale when I had a vision of a startlingly bright room filled with shiny metal. And walking, talking snowmen with purple hands.'

'White coats and those lovely latex gloves,' offered Jax.

'I felt dizzy and slumped over the table. Someone must have called for Enid because when I woke up her face was a couple of inches from mine. Her breath could wake a dead horse.'

'I look forward to meeting her.'

'As the day wore on I remembered more and more, including the five of us in the lab . . . and that blinding flash. What the hell went wrong?'

'We went wrong,' she said calmly. 'Something happened while we were about to test our temporal superposition theory.'

'Nature telling us to stop meddling, perhaps?' said Calvert.

'Quantum physics, eh? It's always throwing up big surprises. But accidental time travel, that's a whopper.'

'I just hope we haven't destroyed Cambridge and that Jenks, Allstein and Cooper are OK. Can we assume that they're in 1719 too?'

'Well we're both here. Perhaps we can try and locate them.'

'Before that we need to come up with an explanation for your presence. In the time I've been here not one person has visited Bigby. You are big news and my friends here are going to want to know the full story. But not the truth, obviously.'

Enid Whipple doesn't go to the inn. It's not that she regards drinking as sinful. She's not averse to the occasional small libation and acknowledges that people are entitled to enjoy themselves after a hard day's work, as long as it doesn't spill over into fighting and shenanigans. Her problem with the Rising Sun is the landlady who stole from her something precious - her childhood sweetheart and the love of her life, Josiah Drake.

Enid admits that Josiah had always considered her a friend rather than a potential wife, and that Magnolia was a fine-looking woman in her youth. But the whole village could see that what Magnolia truly coveted was the money-making enterprise that was the Rising Sun, which Josiah had taken over from his father. The wedding vows taken, the couple had made it only as far as the lychgate when Magnolia paused and held out her hand for her husband to hand over the keys to the inn. And from that day on she had directed little but spite and scorn towards Josiah.

Enid had twice tried to kill her nemesis, on both occasions when Magnolia had fallen ill. Enid had been called upon to provide healing potions, which she had laced with hemlock. But not quite enough. Magnolia's iron constitution had resisted Enid's efforts.

So Enid was not aware of the speculation going on at the inn and was ruminating on her own thoughts about the stranger when there was a tap at her door. Calvert and Jax had decided to try out their story to see if Enid could spot any holes in it.

'Master Calvert. Miss . . . ?'

'People call me Jax, Miss Whipple. We've come to thank you for your kind offer of refreshment when you called earlier. I'm so sorry I was indisposed.'

'Not at all, miss. Please come in. I would be overjoyed to offer you a little plum brandy, although I think it should be last year's brew rather than my latest one which seems to have caused my cat's tongue to swell up. Please sit a while and tell me all about yourself. Other than Master Calvert, I was but a girl when Bigby last had a visitor - a tax collector, if I recall, who has not been back since. My mother gave him some of her special potion . . . quince preserve, I mean.'

Enid produced a brown glass bottle shaped like a long-necked onion and poured three glasses of a pleasant-looking dark amber liquid. Jax immediately reached for one of the glasses but Calvert touched her arm and looked her in the eye. 'That pleasure can wait a moment. Why not tell Enid all about yourself first?'

'Ooh yes, who are you and what brings you to Bigby?' asked Enid with barely concealed excitement. 'Have you journeyed far?'

Over the next half hour they explained that Jax had travelled from London to seek out her uncle John following the death of her mother, his widowed sister. He had written to her more than a year ago at their last known address but had received no reply and assumed that they had moved. Jax found the letter among her mother's possessions, and having been forced to vacate their lodgings after her death she resolved to travel to Bigby to find her only surviving relative.

Calvert and Jax looked at one another, satisfied with what they considered a simple and coherent explanation.

'How lovely that you have been reunited,' said Enid. 'What work did you do in that there London, my dear?' They hadn't thought of this.

'She was in service,' said Calvert quickly.

'A governess, actually. Not really service, Uncle John. But the children were all grown up so I didn't feel guilty about leaving them to find my own precious family.' She touched his arm and smiled sweetly at him.

Enid had a puzzled look on her face. 'It's a mighty long way from London, Miss Jax. Did you walk?'

'The weather recently has been very clement, Miss Whipple, and many of the people I met on my journey were kind enough to take me aboard their carts. I have enjoyed my travels and met some charming folk along the way.'

'And what a joy it must be to be reunited with your uncle, my dear. I expect his address was in the letter you found,' said Enid, whose face took on a quizzical look. 'But how did you find Bigby exactly? It's on precious few maps, as far as I know, and is a tricky place to find if you don't know where the track joins the north-south road. There's no signs.'

Calvert looked at Jax, wondering if she had an explanation ready. They each took a sip of their plum brandy and shuddered. Jax nodded, as if to say to herself, 'This might do. Let's try it.'

'Well,' she said. 'It was an almighty piece of good fortune, Miss Whipple. I knew roughly where the village was from Uncle John's description of the countryside in the letter. I'd walked some way from Crassacre and the north-south road was eerily quiet. Not a horse, cart or a carriage to be seen, and not a breath of air to disturb the leaves. But there was a faint sound among the trees - the slow clip-clop of hooves and the crunching of cartwheels.'

Calvert smiled. This was good.

'I turned to face the sound and stepped into the woods lining the road, where I chanced upon a track leading east. As you know, the lane is far from straight. It winds around ancient oaks and elms. But as I ventured further into the cool embrace of the trees the sound of horse and cart grew stronger, and suddenly there was Master Eli the carpenter and his handsome steed, Clarence.'

Calvert jiggled in his seat. This was excellent storytelling and Enid was beaming.

'Clarence is a handsome creature, isn't he? And what a lovely tale you tell, my dear. Fortune was on your side, that's for sure.'

Calvert thought he had better jump in at this point. 'My niece will stay with me for a while and I'm sure will be as warmly welcomed by the village as I was. But we must not take up any more of your time, Enid. Thank you most kindly for your generous hospitality.'

He and Jax rose purposefully from their seats and headed to the door, making a swift exit and looking pleased with themselves. 'Brilliant,' he said as they walked away from the cottage. 'I think we got away with it.'

Then Enid appeared in the doorway with her arms folded and a smile on her face. 'That is, of course, a load of old rooster, Master Calvert,' she shouted ominously. 'But I'm sure we'll get to the bottom of all this eventually.' It stopped them in their tracks.

'Shrewd old bird, isn't she?' said Jax when they got back to Calvert's cottage.

'Yes, we need to work on our story. More detail required. She was always going to be the trickiest. Also Eli. Nothing much gets past him.'

'Perhaps we could just tell them the truth.'

'They'd laugh their heads off and then have us in that stinking lock-up before you could say pisspot. Let's stick with the story we told Enid and then fill in the gaps if we need to. I'm sure we'll be able to think on our feet.'

They settled down at Calvert's kitchen table and eyed the bottle that Enid had squeezed through the door earlier. They shook their heads and shivered at the thought of sampling its contents. He produced some bread and cheese from a cupboard and a flagon of ale he had brewed himself in the large workshop he'd built behind his cottage.

'So, double glazing. What else have you introduced here?' asked Jax. 'I thought the first rule of time travel - if indeed there are any rules outside sci-fi films - is that you don't mess with things that could change the course of future events.'

'I'm trying to be careful. I've grown to like these people and life can be pretty hard in rural England in the 18th century. You must have seen that on your journey here. I just want to make things a little easier for them. And me,' explained Calvert.

'I've seen such hardship,' said Jax. 'It's the big landowners who are growing fat on the work of people who barely have enough to feed their kids. Talking of which, who owns Bigby? Friend or foe?'

Calvert chewed a hunk of crusty bread and washed it down with a gulp of sweet-tasting ale, looking pleased with himself. 'Actually, the people of Bigby own Bigby. Sort of.

'Not long after I arrived here I was having a nose around the graveyard of the parish church, St. Martin's, when I literally bumped into the minister, Parson Perkins.'

'Parson Perkins! Wow!'

'And to make things even more wow his first name's Peter. Anyway, he was dashing out of the porch on a mission to deliver the last rites to a farm worker trampled by a bullock when I came round the corner and knocked him flying. I apologised and helped him up but didn't have a chance to say anything else. He just sprinted off like a flapping, earth-tethered crow.'

'The perfect way to make friends,' said Jax. 'What then?'

'I went round to the parsonage later to offer a proper apology. I suppose he's mid-thirties, wiry edging towards bony with a cadaverous face, a generous smile and teeth like porcelain. He invited me in and said he was the one that should apologise. He had forgotten his manners in his haste to get to Edward before he departed this life for the next. The poor parson reached him in minutes but by the time he got there Edward was on his feet and brushing the mud from his woollen waistcoat. Edward swung a boot at the offending bullock but missed and fell over again, this time into a pancake of fresh dung. The parson broke into a huge guffaw as he told me this and reached for a bottle and two glasses on a side table. He told me not to worry, it wasn't Edith's.'

Jax smiled. 'He sounds like a hoot.'

'He's a very gentle man with a great sense of humour, but is terribly underworked. That's why he was so keen to save Edward's soul. He gets very few villagers in his Sunday congregation now that it's no longer obligatory, but gives good weddings and funerals. He's well liked and I see him occasionally for a sherry. I'll introduce you,' said Calvert.

'And does this charming story bring us to who owns the village?' Jax asked, sipping her ale cautiously.

'Patience. I'm getting there. How's the brew?'

'It's good. Get on with it.'

'Perkins is the grandson of Watkin Perkins who lived in Bigby Manor and owned the village and several thousand acres of farmland and woodland surrounding it.'

'A nobleman?'

'Far from it,' Calvert explained. 'His forebears were peasants. They were among the lucky ones who survived the Black Death in the 14th century, when up to half the country's population was wiped out. There were fewer people to work the land and this meant that agricultural workers could demand higher wages. They were able to acquire land themselves, and the shrewd Perkins clan procured more and more of it over the centuries. Watkin died in a fire that destroyed the manor, and his son Crispin, the parson's father, was killed in the War of the Spanish Succession.'

'So your friend Peter became a wealthy landowner at a young age.'

'But it was the last thing he wanted. His heart was set on life as a simple village parson, and not just any village. It had to be his village. The church isn't always very obliging when it comes to young vicars dictating where they serve the Lord, but he handed them a sizeable chunk of money and got Bigby for life.'

'So he owns the village,' said Jax.

'Nope. He didn't want to be a farmer or landlord, so he gave it in trust to the village on the understanding that it would be managed sympathetically by a council of men and women of good character in the best interests of the village as a whole.'

'And women. Surely, that's almost unheard of at this time, isn't it?'

'Pretty rare, I guess. He also built a new school and pays the teacher's wages.'

'Still loaded then,' said Jax. 'Sounds like this place is pretty idyllic.'

'We're working on it. I like this place, and the people who live here, so I've tried to help make it better for them. The Industrial Revolution is on the horizon and people living tough lives in the countryside will be heading to the towns and cities looking for work.'

'With most of them finding misery and squalor of a different kind,' said Jax. 'So you're trying to make this the sort of rural idyll that people won't want to leave when the machines take over.'

'Not just that. I'm also trying to make Bigby a place that's comfortable for me to live out the rest of my life. Is that selfish?'

Jax downed another mouthful of ale. 'What if you don't have to live the rest of your life here? What if you can get back?'

Calvert stared at her, bread poised on its way to his mouth.

'Impossible,' he said. 'We're trapped here until we're taken out by plague, cholera, typhoid, sepsis, violence or the noose. In fact a hundred things that can't be cured in 1719 - even by Enid

Whipple.'

'I agree,' Jax said with a decisiveness that seemed to bring the conversation to an end. 'The two of us couldn't get back on our own. But perhaps the five of us could.'

Calvert snorted. 'Get the band back together, you mean. Like in the movies. I think the ale has got to you. First of all, how on earth would we find the other three? Jenks, Allstein and Cooper could be anywhere . . . in the world.' His voice was getting quite shrill. 'Just because we've fetched up in 18th century England doesn't mean they have too. They may not even be in the same time as us. They could be in pre-revolutionary America or the Palace of Versailles.'

'But what if they are? If we're both here now, the chances are they are too. Aren't they, John?'

Constable Bartholomew Bartleby was in the Rising Sun, seated at a tacky table near the fire and staring into the top of his tankard. Eli Graves had been studying him for some time from his customary station on the other side of the room. He was concerned. Barty was not known as someone who thought deeply about anything much, but here he was thinking deeply. Eli rose from his settle and walked over to Barty, putting his own tankard down on the table and sitting down opposite the constable. Barty didn't stir.

'Are you expecting a creature to crawl out of your ale, officer?' asked Eli.

'What?' said Barty.

'You are in the midst of a mighty close examination of your ale. I thought perhaps that you were expecting something to poke its head out. Either that or something is troubling you, Barty.'

The constable looked up. 'I have a worrisome theory about Joe Ding's vanishment, Eli. Very worrisome indeed.'

'Surely he's just done a bunk. You know, escaped and run off.'

'No. I was about to let him out. Why would he run off? I think it's something else, but I can't quite fix a word to it. Perhaps coincidence is the word. That is a word ain't it, Eli?'

The carpenter picked up his tankard. 'I believe it is a word, Barty. And how has this coincidence manifested itself? Or should I let fly with a speculation of my own?'

Barty raised his eyebrows in anticipation of his theory being shared by someone else. 'I would be greatly interested to hear if your speculation aligns with my own,' he said. 'But I'd like to take it slowly for fear of my theory appearing foolish.'

'Agreed,' said Eli.

Barty took a large swig of ale. 'Does it involve Joe vanishing at the very moment that young woman arrived in the village.'

'Well, you didn't take that as slowly as I thought you would. But yes, it had occurred to me that the two occurrences did have the faintest whiff of coincidence about them.'

Barty grasped Eli's forearm in gratitude. 'Thank you, master carpenter, thank you. I thought I might be getting a bit obsessed about the whole business. It's a relief to know that someone else has the same inkling, however odd it may seem.'

'So what are you going to do about it?' asked Eli.

'Haven't the foggiest. What would you do?'

'Keep it to myself. For now. There's probably nothing in it and the whole thing just don't make any sense. How can one person turning up make another person disappear. Though, if that is what's happened I've a feeling that Master Calvert might know something about it. But I'm not going to raise the matter with him. He'll just use fancy words and I'd be none the wiser.'

'So, we just wait and see?' asked Barty. 'It's not like anyone's missing Joe. It's kind of peaceful without him . . . and I've never seen his wife happier.'

London – 1719

Professor William Wilberforce Jenks had been so far outside his comfort zone for the past year or so that he would need the James Webb Space Telescope to catch the merest glimpse of it. But here he was in the year of our Lord 1719 at the age of 62, as excited as a ten-year-old schoolboy meeting his football hero. Jenks was sitting nervously on the edge of a sturdy carved-oak chair, pinching his thigh now and again to reassure himself that he wasn't dreaming. He had worked with many great scientists during his career but slouching behind the desk before him was a man who not only possessed the greatest mind of his time but one of the greatest of all time.

Jenks had never considered what Sir Isaac Newton would sound like. Despite reading almost everything there was about the great man, he doesn't recall his voice being described in any of the sources. If he were to define it, he would probably use the word droning. Monotonous even. The man who investigated the refraction of sunlight through a prism, who invented and built the first reflecting telescope, who worked out the fundamentals of calculus, who developed the laws of motion, who taught us about gravity and who introduced concepts of time and space sounded just a bit . . . well, boring. Jenks wasn't bored, of course, because he was meeting his hero. Every scientist's hero.

Here was Newton, lounging in a large chair, hawk-nosed and pink-cheeked at the age of 76. He was not wearing the long wig depicted in so many portraits, and his hair was grey, sparse and unruly, as though he had just flung off the curls. Newton was not talking to Jenks about science but about money. They were seated in the great man's office in the Tower of London, where he was Master of the Royal Mint, charged by the Chancellor of the Exchequer with improving the quality of the country's much-abused coinage and prosecuting counterfeiters, which he did with a ruthless relish. Several went to the gallows.

Jenks was looking wide-eyed around the dim, untidy office, taking in as much as he could while he had the opportunity, when he realised that Newton had stopped talking. He was staring at Jenks with black, piercing eyes. 'I hope I am not boring you, Master . . .' He looked at a piece of paper on his desk. '. . . Jenks.'

'Not at all, Sir Isaac. I could not be more pleased to hear your thoughts on the nation's currency. You've been a great inspiration to me and I know you will inspire many other natural philosophers in the future.' He avoided using the word scientist.

'I believe it is the future about which you speak to me, Master Jenks. The note you presented to the warder at the gate was intriguing, if a little cryptic.' He picked up the paper. 'If time is absolute, how can a human be transported from one time to another? Why do you ask this nonsensical question, man?'

Like the well organised 21st century physicist he was, Jenks had prepared for this. He had managed to get himself in front of Newton and did not want to lose the opportunity of seeking his help by allowing giddy hero-worship to get in the way. 'I am a natural philosopher like yourself, sir, and for many years have been working in a field known as quantum physics, the study of subatomic particles.'

'What nonsense is this? Has that jealous weasel Hooke put you up to this?' asked Newton, leaning forward aggressively in his seat. 'Or Liebniz. I wouldn't put it past that jealous, duplicitous German . . . '

Jenks edged towards the table that separated them. 'As you well know, they are both dead, sir. So please listen,' he said with a forcefulness that halted Newton's outburst. 'What I am about to tell you is important, and will, I know, fascinate you beyond measure. If you will only bear with me for a short while.' Newton relaxed back into his chair.

'Getting to grips with the concept of time is like grasping at mist, but I know that it's something in which you have a genuine curiosity, so please let me start my story from the beginning,' said Jenks, regaining his poise. He settled back in his seat. 'As you know, in the 5th century BC the Greek philosopher Democritus pondered over the idea of cutting something like an apple into smaller and smaller pieces until the last piece was so small that it could no longer be cut.'

'Yes, of course I do. He called this uncuttable, in Greek atomos,' said Newton.

'Indeed. In my time, this final piece is known as an atom. But Democritus' idea was forgotten for centuries until a British natural philosopher named John Dalton conducted experiments that proved that atoms exist.'

'Dalton? I've never heard of him.'

'Of course not, sir. His is a talent that's yet to blossom. He's currently a teenager living in Cumberland, the son of a Quaker weaver, and he has been in domestic service since he was ten years old. There is no reason why you should have heard of him because he is, as yet, an ill-educated country boy. But in decades to come this remarkable man will develop a theory on atoms that will completely change the way we think. And in the centuries that follow, men and women will investigate everything from the very creation of the universe to tiny particles that can exist in two places at once.'

'Your passion for this story is admirable and does indeed intrigue me, but how do I know you are not inventing this tale of future discoveries? In all truthfulness, sir, you appear to be spouting arrant nonsense. And to what purpose, I ask myself,' said Newton.

'I have no motive other than to seek your help and advice, Sir Isaac. I'm not after your money. I am not seeking a position at the Mint. I am not looking for any favours from you. Except one.'

'Aha!' exclaimed Newton. 'I knew it.'

'All I'm seeking is the service of your remarkable mind. That brilliant brain that will change the world. And in return I will offer you a glimpse of the near future that I hope will be of some considerable personal benefit. If you will allow me.'

'Proceed, Master Jenks. It was proving a dull afternoon and you have enlivened it somewhat, I suppose, with your fanciful notions.' It was not the wholehearted enthusiasm that Jenks had hoped for but he had at least earned himself more time in front of Newton.

'I hope you will not think me presumptuous if I offer some advice based on my knowledge of the history of this year,' said Jenks.

'Now you appear to be a fortune teller, sir. But by all means proceed,' said Newton with a dismissive wave of his arm. 'One whiff of chicanery or extortion, however, and I will have the warders here in seconds.'

Jenks was not deterred. 'I am not privy to your financial affairs, Sir Isaac, but I assume that you are a relatively wealthy man, and I know that many men of your station have significant investments in an organisation called the South Sea Company.'

'I have indeed,' said Newton proudly. 'And a most profitable endeavour it is too. My investment has increased tenfold this year alone.'

'It will not last, sir. The South Sea Bubble will burst, and unless you withdraw it you will lose almost everything you have invested in the enterprise,' said Jenks, who had recalled the scandal from his schooldays. 'Trade restrictions imposed by Spain, corruption, bribery and mismanagement will bring the company to its knees.'

Newton looked shocked, but Jenks continued. 'Surely you must see that a business offering such profits while experiencing massive restrictions to its trade cannot be sustained. In September the company will crash.'

Jenks could see Newton's eyes flickering left and right as he considered what he had been told. 'It is obvious,' he shouted. 'Of course it isn't sustainable.' He got up and paced backwards and forwards across his office, waving his arms in the air. 'The whole idea is nonsense but I have been blind to it. Greed has overtaken me,' he said.

'I would add one more thing,' said Jenks. 'The profits of this company have been built on one detestable trade – the transport of enslaved people to the Spanish and Portuguese colonies in the Americas. Men, women and children, sir. Human beings abducted from their homes and transported across the Atlantic in the most inhuman conditions on journeys lasting many weeks. This remains repugnant even in my own time and I would urge you to withdraw your investment not simply for financial reasons but on moral grounds.'

'I have recently seen descriptions and drawings of how people are crammed into these ships,' said Newton. 'And heard rumours of how the sick and unruly are simply thrown overboard at sea. It appals me, and yet I am ashamed to say that I have not uttered a word against this business.'

A religious man, Newton looked genuinely chastened and Jenks felt some guilt at the lecturing tone he had found himself using. 'I regret my words but not the sentiment, Sir Isaac. I hope you will forgive me. In my time, slavery is considered an abomination and still stirs deep emotions.'

'In your time, you say, Master Jenks. Let us assume that I believe you are from the future. How did you arrive here, in my time?'

'By accident, sir. Four colleagues and I were conducting an experiment that went badly wrong. There was a small element of time manipulation but it should not have had such catastrophic results.'

The room was getting dark as afternoon descended and Newton rose to light candles using a taper from the fire. 'Tell me plainly. Is my work forgotten in your time?' asked Newton quietly resuming his seat.

Jenks leaned forwards. 'Quite the opposite, Sir Isaac. Your work is the foundation of so much discovery, and you will be revered by generations to come. Every schoolchild will know of your work on gravity and light, and so much more. I hope I am not being too ghoulish to reveal that you are buried among kings, queens and great poets in Westminster Abbey.'

Newton's head slumped forward as he attempted to absorb what he had been told and Jenks allowed silence to fill the room. 'I have questions,' said Newton, looking Jenks in the eye. 'A great many questions. Following which I will decide whether to believe you, or not. You are a plausible storyteller Master Jenks but I must know more of the future you describe.'

For hours Jenks related key discoveries of scientists over the centuries. Steam power, evolution, electricity, nuclear energy, penicillin, space travel, television, the internet, computing, x-rays, DNA, cloning, Higgs boson, black holes. As the light vanished beyond the grimy windows of his office, Newton asked questions that only a 21st century scientist with an encyclopaedic knowledge of his subject's history could answer. And then Jenks told him about the explosion and waking up in 18th century London, naked, cold, frightened and sickened by the smell that swept over him as he came to. 'My four colleagues may be dead but I must try and find out. I have survived on my wits, taking teaching positions, working in a brewery and even performing conjuring tricks for money in hostelries as I searched for any sign of my fellow scientists.'

Jenks reached down into a leather bag he had brought with him and produced a gleaming metal box from which a multitude of thin coloured wires protruded. He placed it on Newton's table. 'Somehow, this came with me. It is part of the device on which we were conducting our disastrous experiment. An absolutely essential part. If the others also have pieces, we might be able to use them to find a way back to our own time.'

Newton picked up the item and looked at it with moist eyes. 'I feel desperately small,' he said. 'My modest achievements wither in comparison to those of the brilliant minds that are to come but I must take some solace in knowing that I have played a tiny part in this journey of exploration on which mankind has embarked. Thank you, Master Jenks. Thank you.' He placed the device back on the table and dabbed his eyes with a kerchief.

'I cannot tell you, Sir Isaac, what a privilege it has been to talk with you like this.'

'So let me see how I can help you. What is it you wish me to do?'

Jenks took a deep breath, remembering why he was here. 'I would very much like you to think, Sir Isaac. Nobody at this time has an intellect as wonderfully expansive as yours. My hope is that you will be able to offer an idea that will enable me to locate the only people who can work out how this disaster happened, what the consequences were and how we can put things right. How can I find my friends, sir?'

Newton thought for just a few seconds. 'Have you tried advertising?' he said with a smile.

Bigby – 1719

'What sort of thing do you think this might be, Seth?' Enid Whipple asked the blacksmith, standing with her hands on her hips, looking at a metallic object in the gloomy storeroom at the back of the forge. The thing was about the size of a 20th century telephone box, and with its dust cover removed its shiny surface reflected the red glow of Seth's coals in a threatening, slightly hellish manner. A glass display panel contributed to its mysterious allure.

Seth tapped the object with a small hammer and it made a tinny sound that echoed around the store. 'It's not made from a metal I know. Seems rather flimsy, Enid.'

'Should we tell him it's here, do you think?'

Seth shrugged his broad shoulders. 'We could, but he might wonder why we didn't tell him about it straight away. We should probably keep it to ourselves for the time being, what with that woman turning up and Joe Dings disappearing, an' all that. Let's see what transpires, eh?'

Enid walked slowly around the object, wondering what it might be for, and whether it was worth anything. 'You don't think Joe is in there, do you?' she asked casually.

'I don't think it's heavy enough. I could probably push it over quite easily,' the blacksmith said. 'But what's it for, and is it dangerous? That's what we should be asking ourselves. It was hot when we found it beside Master Calvert under that tree, and was trilling like a canary for several minutes. It's a mystery, that's for sure.'

Seth threw the dust sheet back over the box and walked with Enid back through the forge. 'I like Master Calvert. He's done a lot for this village, but I do think we should take care, Seth. See if there's a pattern to all the strangeness that has descended upon us.'

Woodbridge – 1719

Considering his unusual circumstances, Dr Daniel Allstein could not have been more content with life. He had secured a post teaching mathematics to the sons of Suffolk nobles and wealthy landowners at a prestigious boarding school. He had good lodgings, enjoyed walks in the countryside, swam in the River Deben and idled away time reading in the inn just 100 yards from his front door. He had learned to shut out the noise of raucous farmworkers unwinding at the end of the day, sitting in his usual corner of the Wheatsheaf engrossed in Memoirs of a Cavalier, Daniel Defoe's latest novel. He had not been a great reader of fiction in the 21st century but now found it easy to lose himself in the wartime exploits of Shropshire soldier, Colonel Andrew Newport.

Allstein, who was in his late thirties, was as unfussy a dresser in the 18th century as he was in the 21st. In his threequarter-length black jacket, knee-length breeches, boots and brown waistcoat he practically merged into the walls of the smoke-stained inn. He drew the line at wearing one of the fashionable, itchy horsehair wigs and instead grew his thick, dark hair long and tied it behind him. He was happy to blend in. He didn't like drawing attention to himself in case he was asked difficult questions about his past. He sat quietly and turned the pages of his book, a tankard of ale on the table before him.

Anyway, the Wheatsheaf's rustic customers knew better than to bother the teacher. He possessed a coruscating tongue that could shrivel a less educated man's self-regard swifter than sun on ice.

Allstein arrived naked in 1718 in the middle of a cornfield, conveniently close to a scarecrow whose clothes were a reasonable fit for the broad-shouldered scientist, who was to be found in the gym almost as much as the laboratory in his own time. Standing at well over six feet, his physique was another reason the locals didn't tangle with the stranger in their midst.

He had left nothing behind that he was in a rush to get back to. No wife or family. He assumed that the laboratory had been completely destroyed in the explosion and that colleagues in the lab and other parts of the building might even have been killed. He considered his transportation back in time as penance for cocking things up. He deserved to be here, and the only thing he feared was being badly injured or getting ill. Healthcare was basic to say the least and the smallest infection could prove fatal. In the back of his mind was a fact about microscopes being developed in the 1720s but he couldn't be sure and wouldn't know how to get his hands on one. So he boiled his drinking water, and the water he washed in, and, as far as possible, kept a polite distance from other people's breath. Rural 1719 was his prison and, risk of an unpleasant death aside, it wasn't a bad one in his view.

The Wheatsheaf was a well-run coaching inn on the road to London. As a result, it was a hub for news and gossip, and occasionally a few copies of the Daily Courant arrived there. The landlord, Wilson Whiteside, kept one for himself and distributed the rest to those in the inn he knew could read. During the evening he would read aloud to his customers florid reports on foreign wars and natural disasters, often drawing cheers when something unfortunate had happened to the French.

The Courant's arrival always caused something of a stir, and Allstein looked up from his book as the coachmen and their passengers bustled into the bar with their trunks, bags and a bundle of newspapers. Whiteside dealt with his customers promptly, providing food, ale and wine for those that wanted them and rooms for those tired and bruised from their journey along unforgiving highways. Things quickly settled into a gentle hubbub and Whiteside immersed himself in news from London, Naples, Sicily and Paris. As he turned over the crisp, double-sided sheet something caught his eye and he glanced at Allstein, still tucked up quietly in his corner. He wandered over to the teacher and pointed a thick-skinned finger at an advertisement on the back page of the sheet.

'Someone is sending you a message by the look of it, Master Allstein.'

Doctor Jenks is desirous to hear from his colleagues Calvert, Jackson, Allstein and Cooper and would requeft any or all of these fine perfons to dispatch correspondence or, if it pleafe them, to make themselves known in perfon to Sir Isaac Newton at the Royal Mint, Tower of London. Tempus est domum ire.

Allstein casually studied the message and handed the paper back to the landlord with a slight shrug of his shoulders. 'Intriguing but nothing to do with me, Master Whiteside. Allstein is a very common name in some parts.'

'I suppose you could be right, sir. The name just called out to me from the page, that's all. Perhaps a distant relative of yours?'

'Perhaps,' said Allstein, taking a sip of ale and returning to his book as the landlord walked away. But the scientist had memorised every detail of the advertisement and his mind was racing. He had surrendered any hope of seeing his colleagues again but it seemed that Jenks at least had survived and was seeking the rest of the team. It meant that there was a good chance that Cooper, Calvert and Jax too had been propelled back to the 18th century.

He drained the last of his ale, waved a casual farewell to nobody in particular and walked out into the street, striding towards the school library to find paper and ink, the synapses in his brain firing at full throttle for the first time in years. At least one of his friends was alive and contactable. But what the hell had Isaac Newton got to do with it?

Great Yarmouth – 1718

Dr Thomas Cooper had the misfortune to land in the 18th century not once but twice.

Like his colleagues, he was propelled back to 1718 immediately after the laboratory accident, arriving with a considerable splash into the brown waters of the River Yare in the busy port of Great Yarmouth. The tide had just turned and he was being rapidly pulled towards the harbour's mouth and what was then known as the German Sea, where he would certainly have perished.

Luckily for him, a boy who was fishing with his father on the edge of the quay, saw him thrashing about in the water and alerted his dad. The man yelled to a ferryman crossing the river, who rowed into the middle of the Yare and somehow managed to haul Cooper's naked frame aboard his boat. He covered his passenger's pink and shivering body with a rough tarpaulin that reeked of fish. Cooper, dazed and confused, thanked the man through wildly chattering teeth.

'Don't thank me, boy, thank that lad. If he hadn't seen you, you'd be fish food by now,' said the boatman in a languid Norfolk drawl. He rowed against the tide to a ladder fixed to the river wall and, with Cooper's rear in his face and a hint of disgust in his eyes, the ferryman helped the scientist to climb it. The incident had attracted a crowd on the quayside, where two men covered Cooper in a blanket. A group of women pretended to avert their eyes. The men laid him on a narrow hand-drawn troll cart and delivered him swiftly to a tall house overlooking the river.

A woman who had been observing the scene from an upstairs window opened the door with a smile and ushered the group into a parlour warmed by a glowing fire. The two men sat Cooper down, looked at him, shook their heads and left without uttering a word, as if dragging a naked man from the river was all part of a day's work in a seafaring town.

Cooper had never felt so cold. Or so confused. How did he get into the river? Where the hell was he? Through hazy vision he had seen wooden fishing boats, ships with tall masts and flapping canvas sails, people dressed in old-fashioned clothes. Had he crashed onto a film set?

His long hair dripping onto a faded rug beneath his chair, he looked up as the woman handed him a mug of hot sweet cider. He was still shivering. 'Where am I?' he asked her.

'You're in Great Yarmouth, my man. Stay here and warm up, and I'll go and find you some clothes.'

'Thank you, Mrs . . . '

'Mistress Childs, but everyone calls me Aunt Aggie. Anyone who falls in or gets hurt, they get brought here. And your name?'

'I can't seem to recall . . . anything. There was a brilliant flash, and then I was in the river.'

'No mind. It'll come to you,' she said, closing the door behind her to retain the room's warmth. He drained his mug and was lulled into sleep by the fire. When he woke he saw Aggie sitting in a rocking chair, engrossed in a book. Beside her was a pile of men's clothes.

'I've remembered my name but not much else,' he croaked. 'Thomas Cooper, Mistress Childs.'

She folded down the corner of her book and looked at him with a tender smile. 'That's good, Thomas. A start at least. Perhaps the rest will come to you in due course.' She handed him the clothes and said she would leave him to get dressed. They were working men's clothes but seemed barely worn and were a good fit. Even the boots were comfortable. But it all felt like he was wearing a costume for a play or film. He walked unsteadily to the tall bay window that looked out over the port and knew instantly that this was no theatrical set. It was a working port. A port hundreds of years in the past.

Aggie knocked on the door and asked if he was decent. He walked across the room and opened it, thanking his hostess once again. 'I'm still rather befuddled,' he said as they settled into chairs either side of the fire. 'May I ask you what date this is?'

'The ninth day of June.'

'And could you remind me of the year?'

'Why, 1718 of course. My goodness, I hope you didn't swallow any of that water. It can do all sorts of terrible things to body and mind.'

Cooper felt decidedly wobbly. 'Did anyone see me fall into the river?' he asked.

'No. Young Archie just saw you flapping about and summoned help. He and the ferryman saved your life, my man.'

'I'd like to go and thank them. I would reward them but I don't have any money.'

'Don't worry about that now. See them tomorrow, after a good night's sleep. There's a room for you here if you want it.'

'But I can't pay you,' he said, suddenly realising how vulnerable he was in this world. 'I have absolutely nothing. Not even a memory.' He slumped forward with his head in his hands. It was getting dark and Aggie lit two candles, handing one to Cooper and inviting him to follow her to his bedroom.

'You'll feel better after some rest, and might even start to get your memory back. Then we can work out what we're going to do with you,' she said. She led him to a stark room at the top of the house, where there was a comfortable-looking bed, a chest of drawers, a table and chair.

'Settle in here and we'll talk in the morning,' said Aggie. 'I hope you don't mind if I lock the door. Just for my peace of mind, you understand.' He said he didn't, and as the key clicked in the lock he stretched out on the bed and was asleep within minutes.

He had no idea of the time when he woke. His candle had gone out and the room was weakly illuminated by a cloud-streaked moon. His body ached and he rose from his bed, still fully clothed, and walked over to the undraped window. A broad stretch of muddy road separated the house from the river, where old fishing boats were lined up side by side in twos and threes. Near to them were stacks of wicker baskets, wooden barrels and handcarts, presumably for storing and moving fish. Further along the river, closer to the sea, were larger ships, with sails furled and tied against their horizontal spars. A few men milled about the quayside, perhaps keeping watch on the vessels.

Some of his memory had gradually returned during the night. He recalled the experiment, the accident, and the friends who had probably died. Had they been killed in the explosion, or spilled into the river and not been rescued. Why was he in 1718 for goodness sake? And what would happen to him now? Dozens of questions crowded his brain.

Cooper tried the door in case it had been unlocked but it wouldn't open. He laid back on the bed and an early morning light slowly filled the room. He heard footsteps on the stairs, the lock clicked and four men wearing grubby white trousers and dark blue, brass-buttoned jackets burst into the room. Two, with pistols tucked into their belts, grabbed him from the bed. The other two, cudgels in hand, stood by in case Cooper needed subduing. He was bigger than all of them but knew he wouldn't stand a chance if he resisted. As he was pulled to his feet, one of the cudgel bearers pointed at him and bellowed aggressively, 'You've been pressed, Thomas Cooper. Welcome to the Royal Navy.' The sailor turned to the woman, who was standing in the doorway with her arms folded. 'Thank you, Aunt Aggie. Your country thanks you once more for your service.' And as Cooper was hauled down the stairs, the man handed her a few coins.

The port was coming to life as Cooper was marched towards one of the large ships he had seen earlier, his arms pinned behind his back. Still feeling weak, he stumbled several times and was yanked upright by the men who held him. They must have walked him a quarter of a mile or so to their ship, where they pushed him up the narrow gangplank and onto the deck. He fell at the feet of an officer who was wearing shiny black shoes and white stockings. When he looked up, Cooper stared into the sneering face of a weedy, ruddy-cheeked teenager.

'Shouldn't you be in school?' Cooper gasped before being clubbed on the head and passing out.

He woke as he was being dragged to his feet by a small group of scruffy men in civilian clothes. They were being addressed by a sergeant major type man in a dark blue tailcoat, white trousers and bicorn hat. He welcomed the group to HMS Norwich, and said they had the privilege of being aboard a 50-gun ship of the line, recently refitted at Deptford. He introduced himself as Lieutenant Brooks and referred to the men before him as "recruits", but it was clear from the cuts and bruises some of them bore that they had been press-ganged like Cooper. The rest appeared to be experienced seamen looking for the security of Navy pay and adventure. These men were confident in front of the officer and stood up straight, hands behind their backs.

'You, funny man,' said Brooks, looking at Cooper. 'I hope you enjoyed your sleep because you're going to need all your energy when we set sail on tomorrow morning's tide. What seafaring experience do you have?'

'Does being a passenger on a cross-Channel ferry count?' asked Cooper in as subservient a tone as he could muster.

The officer ignored the remark and turned to a burly man on his left. 'Bosun, inform our newcomers of their duties while I talk to our swimmer here. I have yet to decide how he may be deployed.' The men shuffled off and Cooper felt the back of his head where he had been struck. He looked at his hand but there was no blood.

'Clearly, you are no seaman. Your hands are smoother than my sister's pretty face and you are unsteady on your feet even though we are in port. How did you come to be naked in the river? Were you attacked and robbed?'

It seemed as good a story as anything else so Cooper said he believed he had, although he had no recollection of the attack other than finding himself in the churning water. 'I don't even remember my name, but let's settle with Thomas Cooper for now. I've no idea who I am, what work I did or why I am in Yarmouth.'

'So, a mystery man as well as a diver,' said Brooks. 'We will doubtless find out more about you in the months ahead. Who knows, you may turn out to be a useful member of the crew. If you don't die in battle too soon.'

'I know nothing about sailing ships. What good am I going to be?'

'You're a big man,' said Brooks. 'Just what we need for hauling on ropes, swabbing the deck and handling the sails. Just listen to the bosun here and do as you're told. Take him away, Baines.'

He still couldn't believe what was happening to him. Only yesterday, it seemed, his world was one of order and safety. This was the same world but a strange one infused with disorder and violence. He was shoved below deck, where hundreds of grubby hammocks swayed rhythmically in time to the ship's gentle side-to-side movement. About half were occupied, the rest of the men presumably on watch. The smell made him gag. A concoction of unwashed men in sweat-stained clothes, of urine in leaky buckets, of tar and salty ropes. And the stench of despair. Cooper recalled a saying – he couldn't remember who said it – that life on a warship was like being in jail, with the added danger of drowning.

The bosun saw him trying not to vomit and smiled. 'Puke down here and I'll make you lick it up,' he sneered. 'Billings, find our swimmer a uniform and somewhere to kip. And make sure he doesn't try to run off or it'll be 20 lashes for the both of you.'

Billings led Cooper past snoring and farting sailors and showed him a furled hammock. 'You can have this one. It was Blakie's but he died last week.'

'Of what?' asked Cooper.

'Don't worry, it weren't no 'orrible disease or nothin' said Billings. 'Got his throat cut in a bar in Hull, silly sod.'

'Yeh, that was silly of him,' said Cooper quietly. 'Remind me to avoid that particular pub, will you? I've been press-ganged so I'm pretty new to all this. Can I ask you a couple of questions?'

'I suppose so.' Billings' half-closed eyes and dull responses suggested that he had been worn down by an oppressive system that held the 18th century Royal Navy together.

'What's your first name?' asked Cooper. 'Mine's Tom.'

'Nobody's ever asked me that before. I've been on the Norfolk two years and that's the first time. Dick,' he said, a glimmer of light in his eyes. 'My name's Dick. Welcome to hell, Tom.' He shook Cooper's hand.

'Pleased to meet you, Dick.'

Cooper found out that HMS Norwich was a three-masted, fourth-rate ship of the line with 50 guns. Dick told him that it was a full-rigged ship, which meant nothing to Cooper, and had a crew of more than 300 men. This last fact took him aback. How the hell could this cramped, two-deck vessel accommodate so many people? By cramming them in like sardines alongside the cannons was the answer.

Dick put a consoling arm on Cooper's shoulder. 'The first few months are going to be pretty tough. Follow orders or you'll get the lash. Don't skive or you'll get the lash. Don't get drunk or you'll get the lash. Don't kill anyone or you'll get hanged. Oh . . . and you're probably going to feel very very seasick.'

'Any advice you can offer on that?' asked Cooper.

'Don't be sick on the captain. I'll get your uniform.'

And with that, Cooper was in the Royal Navy. He learned the ropes, made friends and enemies among the crew, discovered he didn't suffer from seasickness, ate rank salt beef and rock hard biscuits, chased Spanish ships but never caught them and visited European ports, where the crew enjoyed boisterous nights ashore. Cooper joined them but was careful what he drank. He had seen sozzled shipmates clubbed, stabbed and robbed on port visits. He didn't want any injuries that might require him to put his trust in a ship's surgeon who would probably cut your leg off to cure your chilblains. The crew appreciated his propensity for self-preservation, found it amusing almost, but they knew that they could rely on their sober shipmate to wade in and help if things got a bit feisty in a dockside tavern.

Indeed, pub brawls were the most action Cooper saw in his months as a Navy man. Until the Norfolk, HMS Advice and HMS Dover encountered a squadron of three Spanish vessels off Cape Vincent, Portugal, and the dull boom of a single cannon shot broke through the swirling air. It landed just feet from the Dover, which turned sharply to aim its guns at the closest of the Spanish ships. More enemy fire followed before the first of the

British ships could discharge their guns.

Then hell was unleashed. Cannonballs burst through the sides of the ship, sending deadly shards of timber crashing through the gun deck. Musket balls fizzed around his ears, splintering the masts and shredding the sails. Brave men barked insults at the enemy. Men with tattered flesh and shattered bones screamed in agony. Cooper, manning a deck gun, fired and kept his head low. He was ordered below to the gun deck, which sported jagged holes where none should be. These were above the waterline but the sea splashed in. He had taken part in gun drills but never under fire, and never on a sea-slick floor.

His team had fired twice when the gun-captain yelled for more powder. 'Where's that damned powder monkey?' he screamed, before turning to see the boy's lifeless body sloshing crazily in the swirling water.

'I'll go,' said Cooper, who sped off to the cargo hold to fetch more gunpowder. He made his unsteady way down the stairs and saw dozens of floating powder kegs crashing into one another. Not wishing to be there longer than necessary, he grabbed one and headed for the stairs. As he reached the gun deck he heard an almighty boom erupt behind him. The keg fell from his grasp and he flew as if in slow motion towards the base of the main mast. A crackle of brilliant energy filled the air and he braced himself, waiting for the impact that he knew would probably kill him. He was wrong.

Bigby – 1719

'Ahh, the mysterious newcomer. Come in, come in,' said Parson Perkins, answering the door to the vicarage with a napkin tucked into the white Geneva band at his throat.

Calvert and Jax followed him into the flagstone-floored entrance hall and through a door on the right leading to a dining room. A plate of ham, cheese and pickle was on the table and beside it lay a copy of Jonathan Swift's satirical pamphlet An Argument Against Abolishing Christianity. The clergyman noticed them looking at it. 'Have you read it? It's very funny,' he said. 'I would very much like to meet Master Swift. He has a mischievous wit. But you're not here to discuss radical literature, John. I take it you wish to present the young lady who has become the talk of the village.'

'Indeed I am. Peter, may I present Esmerelda Fortescue-Jackson. Jax to her friends and anyone who values their shin bones. Jax, it's my pleasure to introduce you to Parson Perkins.'

'Please call me Peter. It's a delight to meet you, Jax. Please sit.'

They declined his offer of lunch and apologised for disturbing him. 'Well, if you don't mind watching me chew I am happy to listen while you talk. You should know that Enid has been to see me, so I am prepared for a narrative that is full of holes and intriguing detail in equal measure. Miss Whipple may try to poison us all with her wicked brews but she has a mind like a weasel trap and sees it as her mission to get to the bottom of a mystery.'

'Like Miss Marple,' said Jax without thinking. Calvert nudged her.

'I do not know the lady but I am sure they are kindred spirits when it comes to tackling a conundrum,' said Perkins.

'Indeed they are,' said Calvert.

Perkins dabbed his mouth and lay his napkin on the large mahogany dining table. 'The rest can wait. My appetite now is for conversation, my friends. Let's settle ourselves somewhere more comfortable so that you can relate your tale. Either the one you told Enid, or another one, if you wish.'

They settled into a group of mismatched and ancient looking armchairs by a window overlooking a ragged garden. Sunlight struggled through the glass and glinted on the dust motes that danced around their heads. Calvert thought most of the furniture in the room probably dated from the 1600s and may have been rescued from the manor house fire in which the parson's grandfather perished. Nearly everything made of wood in the room was almost black with age, from the creaking wide-boarded floor to two intricately-carved cupboards. Jax felt she was in a museum display.

She decided to take the lead. 'We did not intend to mislead anyone, Peter. The story we told Enid was a poor attempt at easing her curiosity, and by extension the curiosity of everyone else in the village.'

'She made it pretty clear that she didn't believe a word of it as we walked away from her cottage,' said Calvert. 'But the truth sounds so far-fetched, even to us when we say it out loud, that nobody would believe it and we would probably have been turned out of Bigby.'

'That's the last thing we need at the moment,' said Jax.

'So, we thought we would try out the truth on you and see how you take it.'

The parson shifted in his chair and rested his hands in his lap, and the merest hint of a smile crept across his generous mouth. He was clearly looking forward to this. 'Proceed, my friends. I love a good yarn.'

Over the next hour or so Calvert and Jax batted back and forth their tale. From their studies in quantum physics to the experiment that resulted in the explosion and their inexplicable arrival in the summer of 1718. Their narrative had eradicated the smile from the clergyman's face. And as they told him of their frustration at having no means of contacting their colleagues he reached over to a small side table and picked up a folded copy of the Daily Courant which he placed on his lap.

'What are the names of your colleagues?' he asked. They told him. 'Then I believe your colleague, Dr Jenks, may have already made contact,' he said.

They looked at the tiny advertisement, crammed in among ads for goods and services that would have their promoters in court in the 21st century. 'Jenks is alive,' said Calvert quietly. 'Why the hell didn't we think of doing this? It's ingenious.'

'Will is a genius,' said Jax, taking the Courant from him. 'I hope to goodness the others have seen this.'

The clergyman smiled. 'Tell me more about the future,' he said calmly. 'Does the church still thrive? Are people kinder to one another? Is our country well run?'

'Then you believe us?' asked Jax. 'Please say you do. It would be such a relief.'

The parson rose and picked up a chunk of cheese from his plate. 'We have already established that you are such terrible storytellers that even an ill-educated village healer could see through your original tale like sunlight through lace,' he said.

'However, the story you have just related to me might well have sent poor Enid to the madhouse. But I have to say that it has a greater veracity than the one you told her. There is the scent of truth about it, and I believe that you are truthful people. I would, of course, like to know a great deal more about the years to come, but what is more important now is the immediate future. We must take a walk, I think.'

He led them purposefully from the parsonage and directly to the forge, where Seth was shaping bucket handles for Eli. 'Good afternoon, parson, Master Calvert, Miss Jax,' said Seth, dipping a hissing curve of metal into a tub of water. 'How can I help you fine people?'

'I've just had an interesting conversation with my friends here and I would like to show them the item you have tucked away in your store, Seth.'

'Are you sure that's wise, parson? Enid and I felt it better kept under wraps for the time being. Until we know more about . . . you know.' And he nodded towards Jax.

'I'm intrigued, Seth. What is it you have tucked away?' asked Calvert.

'I'm not sure about this, parson. Really I'm not.' By the time he had finished his sentence Parker had led them through the forge and into Seth's store, where he tugged the dust cover from the tall metal box.

'It's the Wells chamber,' exclaimed Calvert. 'It's the bloody Wells chamber.' He walked around it with a look of utter astonishment on his face.

'It must have arrived with you,' Jax said. 'Why on earth didn't you tell him it was here, Seth?' She sounded cross and reached into the leather bag slung across her shoulder, pulling out three small silver-coloured boxes packed with electronics. 'It goes with these,' she said, holding the devices towards the parson and the blacksmith. Calvert looked at her open-mouthed.

'And when were you going to tell me you had these?' he asked her sharply. 'Good grief, does anyone else have anything to share with me? Or should I just wait for Enid to surprise me with a particle accelerator she's been hiding up her apron?'

Jax laughed. 'I'm sorry, that's just a very weird image to put into someone's head. But it means that more of this equipment probably travelled back with us, which is interesting, eh Doctor Calvert?'

'Doctor?' Seth and the Parson blurted out together.

'Never mind that,' he said, grabbing Jax excitedly by the arms. 'We need to get the band together. We have a letter to write – to Sir Isaac flippin' Newton.'

'And what do we tell the villagers?' asked the Parson.

'Everything,' said Calvert.

London – 1719

Jenks woke early. He had slept fitfully on a creaking wooden cot and lumpy mattress, his mind fizzing with the thoughts he and Newton had shared the day before. It was barely light outside and all he could hear was the rough caw of ravens and the scratching of a pen nib through the open door to Sir Isaac Newton's office. He was astonished that Sir Isaac had believed him so readily. But perhaps it demonstrated the free-ranging mind that had enabled Newton to investigate so many facets of the natural world.

He lay still for a while, taking in the starkness of the stone-walled room and its sparse furnishings. He wondered if this was where the ageing scientist took a nap during the day. He had invited Jenks to stay the night rather than risk returning on foot through unsafe streets to his lodgings in Aldgate. 'It would be a pity to lose you when I have so much to learn,' Newton had said, resting a friendly hand on his guest's shoulder.

Jenks rose and found Newton hunched over his desk, spectacles perched on his hawk-like nose, writing furiously on coarse paper. 'Have you been here all night, Sir Isaac? What are you doing that is so urgent, sir?'

'I have to capture it. Everything you told me. Wondrous things.' He looked up, an intensity etched on his face. 'I trust that is acceptable, Master Jenks. I have no intention of stealing your ideas, I simply wish to write these things down so that I may remember them when you have gone. Underground travel, flying machines, computers . . . television,' he exclaimed, returning to his scribbling.

'Do you believe that my colleagues and I will be able to find a way back?' Jenks asked him.

Newton placed his pen on its rest. 'I must be truthful and say that I feel that it is unlikely, my friend. A great many barriers stand in your way, the most monumental of which is the intense power you would require to operate your fantastical equipment. It is not to be found in our time.

'In addition - and please correct me if I have misunderstood the concept - but the notion of time travel, if it is to be at all practical, would appear to be the ability to move between one age and another in a precise manner. It occurs to me that you and your friends were deposited here by means of a freak accident and had no control over where and when you would arrive. You were tossed here by time, and I fear that you are as marooned as a sailor on a soulless island.'

Lincolnshire – 1719

Dr Thomas Cooper landed on his feet the second time he arrived. But not literally, alas.

His arrival point after being blasted from the gun deck of the warship was the formal gardens of Muckleborough Hall, a few miles from Lincoln. There was lush grass in the garden, plus some nice soft box hedging and colourful beds of foxgloves and Canterbury bells, all of which would have been more pleasant to land on than the rose bushes in which he awoke. He was discovered by an elderly gardener, who called for assistance from other gardeners, who donned leather gauntlets before wading into the bed to extract their profusely-bleeding and sweary intruder. They laid him gently on the lawn and as the lady of the house rushed out to see what the commotion was all about the youngest of the gardeners removed his brown canvas apron and laid it over Cooper to spare her ladyship's blushes. Her ladyship, fortyish, recently widowed and a force of nature in a voluminous black gown and veil, was not prone to blushes and prodded Cooper in the side with a pointy shoe.

'Who the devil are you?' she asked, looming over the wincing scientist.

'Not sure,' he croaked, looking up. 'Is it fancy dress? Nobody told me.'

'Clearly not,' said her ladyship with a smirk that Cooper

missed because he had passed out. 'Take him to the billiard room and remove his pricks.'

'All of them, my lady?' asked the cheekiest of the gardeners.

'Just the ones he doesn't need,' she said over her shoulder as she made her elegant way back to the house. 'And find him some clothes. His late lordship's should fit.'

Cooper came to lying face down on the slate-hard bed of a billiard table. A middle-aged woman wearing a long black mourning dress, grey apron and mop cap that was failing to contain straggly wisps of grey hair, was picking rose thorns from his buttocks with tweezers. 'Hold still, I've nearly finished,' she said, sensing his awakening. 'I've done yer front. That was the worst.'

'It's very sore,' he groaned.

'What is, my man?'

'I'll give you three guesses.'

'Oh that. Well it did look rather like a pin cushion, so I'm not surprised.'

Cooper lifted his face from the table and looked around him, and then at his nurse. 'Why is everyone dressed like this? Did I get drunk at a party that I can't remember? I'm a bit confused. Sorry, what's your name?'

'Nettie, sir, a kitchen maid. I tends to get asked to do this sort of thing. Well not this sort of thing exactly. Usually is cuts and bruises and the like. I can't say I've ever had to remove thorns in such profusion from a gentleman's . . . parts. There, that's you done. No longer a hedgepig. I'll avert my eyes while you get up, sir. Just take it slow, like. There's clothes at the baulk end of the table.'

Every movement was agonising, but after half an hour or so Cooper was dressed. He slumped forward on an elegant chair and hoped he wasn't bleeding on the fine material. He was sweating and his head was pounding. He glanced up and Nettie was regarding him with a sympathetic look. 'What should I call you then?' she asked. 'You look very much the gentleman in his lordship's fine clothes. But what are you, exactly?'

'That's a very good question, Nettie. I believe my name is Cooper, but I couldn't be absolutely sure. Things are a bit hazy. Possibly Thomas Cooper? Where am I exactly? I have no recollection of coming here, or indeed where I've come from.'

Before she could respond, a tall man wearing a long velvet coat, knee-length breeches and a stern face topped by a short white wig slid into the room and coughed genteelly, just in case nobody had noticed him. 'Her ladyship has asked to see you, master . . .'

'. . . Cooper, I think. Not too sure but let's go with that for the time being.'

'Follow me, please.'

'What's your name?' asked Cooper as they processed in a stately fashion through sumptuous galleries and corridors.

'Fellowes, sir. Senior footman.'

'I didn't know footmen still existed, apart from in places like Buckingham Palace, of course. But the wig and everything, you don't wear that all the time, surely.'

'Not when I'm in bed sir, no,' replied Fellowes dryly.

'You must excuse my idiotic questions. I'm still a bit befuddled. Where are we? I have the smell of the sea in my nostrils. Are we near the coast?'

'No, sir. This is Muckleborough Hall. The home of Lady

Muckleborough and his late lordship, who passed away just two months ago, may God rest his soul.'

'Ahh, that explains your black armband. I'm sorry but I don't recall reading about his death. Her ladyship must be devastated.'

'Mmmmm, quite,' was Fellowes' response as they approached a tall set of double doors, which he opened to reveal an opulent drawing room occupied by Lady Muckleborough and another woman, also smartly dressed in black who retired briskly to a seat in the corner of the room. Her ladyship put down the book she was reading and rose from her silk-covered sofa, walking towards Cooper with a confident extended arm. She shook his hand.

'Welcome, mysterious man. Please be seated,' she said, indicating the sofa opposite hers.

'Do you mind if I stand, Lady Muckleborough? I'm still a little tender in the . . .' He was struggling to find a polite term to use in the company of this weirdly-dressed pair.

'Derrière?' her ladyship offered, sitting down and examining him with an intensity he found unnerving. He couldn't work out how to stand appropriately in the clothes he had been given and after hopping from foot to foot for a while decided to risk taking a seat. He grimaced.

'Nettie tells me that your name is Thomas Cooper.'

'I think so. It was certainly the name that came into my head when she asked me.'

'Are you dangerous?'

'I damn well hope not.' He saw the lady in the corner stiffen at the d-word. 'Sorry, I mean I don't believe so. But I have only a vague recollection of a blinding flash and then waking up entangled in some shrubbery that wouldn't let go of me. May I ask you a question?' Her ladyship nodded her handsome head. Where exactly is Muckleborough Hall? I'm afraid I've never heard of it.' The companion stiffened again.

'You've probably just forgotten it, sir,' her ladyship said kindly. 'It is one of England's finest houses, but an hour's carriage ride from Lincoln.'

'Carriage ride?' exclaimed Cooper, thinking that this was taking the whole dressing up thing a bit too far. 'So, no car then?'

'Car?'

'You know, automobile, nice Rolls-Royce or Bentley?'

Lady Muckleborough looked over shoulder at her companion who shrugged and offered a don't-ask-me face.

'It all sounds rather new. Perhaps His Majesty, King George, will arrive in an automobile when he comes to pay his respects next week.' The companion nodded, this time adopting a that-would-be-nice face.

Cooper felt a little wobbly. 'King George the . . .'

'There has been only one, sir, so King George the First. I don't know how we are going to manage when he comes as I understand he speaks very little English and my German is quite rudimentary.'

Cooper felt the warm room go all swimmy as certain facts crept up on him. He had been in the Navy, on a warship, in a battle. A child floating lifeless on the sloshing deck. An explosion.

Lady Muckleborough stood, concern etched on her face. 'You don't look well, Master Cooper. Quite peaky, in fact.' She called for Fellowes and asked him to find their guest a bed in the servants' quarters, and to send for Dr Goodnight.

When he woke a couple of hours later Cooper found himself lying in a windowless room with his left sleeve rolled up and six glistening leeches helping themselves to his blood. Earnestly taking in the pulsing action from a stool beside the bed was a sallow-faced doctor admiring his charges through small, round, metal-rimmed spectacles. Nettie stood behind him, holding a jar containing more leeches.

'Remove them,' said a suddenly-alert Cooper, looking at Dr Goodnight with menace.

'But they have not completed their work, sir. Give them a little more time.'

'Remove them now. Please. Or I will be forced to draw blood in a different way.'

The doctor got the message. 'Of course, good sir. As I observe from your abrupt and much to be welcomed wakefulness my work here has been successfully completed.' Affecting a smile, he slid a long, grubby fingernail under each of the creatures' mouthpieces to detach them, and plopped them into the jar Nettie was holding. He took the receptacle from her, placed it in a capacious leather medical bag and made a quick exit.

'You look better,' said Nettie. 'First time I've seen them little buggers do any good. Memory come back?'

'I think it's getting there, Nettie,' said Cooper, sitting up on the bed. 'Just one thing I'm not sure about. What year is this?'

'What year? My word, it's clear that some confusion remains in that poor noggin of yours, Thomas. Why it's 1719, of course. September.' He felt wobbly again. The time was the same but he had somehow been plucked from the bowels of a sailing ship off Portugal and deposited in the gardens of a magnificent stately home. His life had initially been spared from an explosion that had probably killed his colleagues and destroyed their lab. And now he had survived another blast that surely should have killed him. His mind was racing. Was fate keeping him alive for a special purpose? Was he indestructible, like Superman? Did he have any supernatural powers that he had not yet discovered?

And then he came to his senses, promising himself that he would never, ever, say these things out loud. To anybody.

'I think I'll take a walk in the grounds, if that's permitted. Clear my head a bit. I might even do a bit of shouting when I'm far enough away from the house. Apologies in advance if you catch any bad language. And please don't worry, this shouldn't take long. 1719, you say. And you're absolutely sure about that?'

'Oh yes. I'll be 40 this year.'

'You're 39, Nettie! Good grief, you look much . . . younger.' He caught himself just in time. 'I would have said no more than 30.'

Nettie blushed brilliantly and tucked a straggle of hair under her cap. 'Get away with you, you terrible man,' she said, grinning and escaping from the room before she caught fire.

Cooper made his way out through the servants' door, gradually becoming steadier on his feet the nearer he got to the huge lake that dominated the view at the front of the house. Beyond it were trees and natural looking countryside that could well have been sculpted by human hand for all he knew. It seemed that he had somehow been deposited in the 18th century for a second time. How was that possible? He was a scientist. Look for the evidence. Well, to start with everyone was wearing the right period clothes. Tick. He looked at the sky and could see no aircraft contrails. Tick. The house had no visible TV aerials or dishes, and certainly didn't have electrical sockets or radiators in any of the rooms he had seen. Tick. Nettie seemed like a pleasant woman and appeared to have no reason to lie to him. Tick. He had seen at least six gardeners during his extraction from the rose bed and lots of maids, footmen and other servants inside the house. More than any modern manor house that hadn't been turned into a hotel could possibly afford. Tick. It was all adding up to just one conclusion. It was 1719.

'Aaaaaargggghhhh,' he shouted at length across the lake, again and again, sending shrieking water birds dripping into the air. He was a 21st century man. He needed computers, machines, his favourite beer and wine, his friends, transport that didn't rely on horses, clothes that didn't itch. His science. His projects. Why hadn't the blast sent him back to his own time? His own comforts.

Cooper sat on a hump beside the lake and put his head in his hands. He was not a man who wept easily, and yet here he was in this English Heritage world, weeping copiously. And remembering.

He remembered the lab, almost drowning in the Yare, being violently press-ganged, his smelly shipmates, the horrible food, the back-bending work, and the bloody battle in which he waited for death. But didn't die. Instead, transported once more, into a bed of roses, of all things. Was this to be his existence now? To be flung about at the whim of time each time his life was about to be snuffed out.

'Aaaaaargggghhhh,' he cried again to the ducks and geese.

'Master Cooper, please stop making that din and join me in my study,' said Lady Muckleborough, who had arrived in silence behind him. Hers was an imperious command that brooked no dissent. 'And please wipe that . . . slime from your face, man. It's most unappealing.' She turned and walked smartly away.

Cooper did as he was ordered. He washed off the tears and snot in the lake and trudged dejectedly back to the three-storey Jacobean pile, its red-brick façade and golden mullion windows glowing in the low, evening sunlight. He entered through the servants' door, where he was greeted by the smell of meat roasting on a spit. He asked a young kitchen maid how to get to her ladyship's study and set his senses on high alert for any sign of the 21st century. What he wouldn't give for a glimpse of a stray fire alarm or framed photograph to prove that this was all an elaborate charade.

A passing footman helped him find the right door. He knocked and entered. He was expecting to see the lady of the house sipping tea from a China cup or reading a book, but he found her sitting at a large desk, papers spread about her and quill pen in hand. Her widow's veil had been discarded and lay on the floor beside her. Her long auburn hair was artfully arranged and held in place by a tortoiseshell comb.

'There you are,' she said, rising from the desk with ink-stained fingers and settling into an elegant chair. She pointed at its twin and Cooper sat, feeling as though he was about to be interviewed. He waited for her to speak but she simply looked at him, inspecting him for several minutes, like a butterfly specimen.

'So, Master Cooper, tell me all,' she said with such a piercing, dark-eyed gaze that he felt sweat begin to trickle down his back.

Bigby – 1719

Calvert and Jax hadn't a clue how their explanation to the villagers would go down. It was agreed that the meeting should take place in the 14th century parish church, which was the only building big enough to hold everyone. The parson had agreed to conduct the meeting and had set up three seats at the front for himself and the two scientists. It was noisy and the Rev Perkins had to shout to bring down the level to a gentle murmur. Village meetings in the church didn't happen very often so there was a mixture of nervous anticipation and excitement among the people.

'My good friends,' Perkins boomed. 'I think you will all agree that Master Calvert has been a welcome addition to our community since his arrival. Helping us to make our homes more comfortable, and our village cleaner and more productive. Life is undoubtedly better in Bigby thanks to his ideas and inventiveness, and I know many of you have sought his sound advice on numerous matters. Some mystery surrounds his sudden appearance here, and indeed that of Miss Jax. Also, the worrying disappearance of Joe Dings. Please hear them out, and be prepared to have receptive minds. What they are about to tell you will greatly challenge what you think you know about our world.'

The congregation muttered as Perkins took his seat. Calvert rose and stood at the end of the nave. Coloured light streamed in through ancient windows and danced on weathered, attentive faces. There was a respectful silence.

'This is a difficult story to tell, and you will have questions even when Jax and I have told it.' He paused and looked around.

'I know all of you here. You are good people and Bigby is a wonderful place to call home. What I am about to relate will take some believing. But it will be the truth.' Calvert paused to gather his thoughts. Edith sat in the front pew and gave him an encouraging nod.

'Jax and I, along with three friends, were caught up in a violent explosion that should have killed us. We know that one of our friends also survived as he has placed an advertisement in a newspaper attempting to contact us. We don't know about the other two.' There was shuffling and some burbling among the villagers.

'Instead of sending us to our graves, the explosion appears to have transported us to different places in England. I arrived here, Jax woke up in London, where one of our friends also appears to be with Sir Isaac Newton.' The great man's name caused a ripple of chatter.

'My colleagues and I were working together on an experiment in a little understood area of science - what you know better as natural philosophy - and Jax and I believe that an error on our part was responsible for our inexplicable transportation.'

Before he could go any further a squat man in a ragged hat shot up in the middle of the church. He was red-faced and looked angry and agitated. 'A punishment from God is what it was, sir. I knew that your coming to Bigby was unnatural. You have been meddling in things you should not have meddled with,' he shouted. 'It is unnatural, an abomination, and it sounds very much like . . .'

'Do not utter that word, Craven Dinsdale.' It was Edith, standing on the pew and turning to glare at him. We do not use the w-word in Bigby, and you of all people should know why.'

She looked around at her neighbours, defying them to support Dinsdale's outburst. 'I was but a child when I witnessed poor Miss Paine dangle from that tree. She was odd and quite unfriendly sometimes, but that was all she was. This village was caught in a sort of fever. We are not those people any more, so sit down Craven before I come over there and knock your ruddy block off. Pardon me for the ruddy, parson, but the stupid man got my dander up.' She sat down, arms folded and looking like she would be cross for a while.

Jax got up and Calvert sat. 'I'm sorry, Edith, but I am going to use the w-word. More than 500 people – nearly all of them women – were executed in England for being witches. Most of them were poor and elderly. As recently as four or five years ago, Mary Hicks and her nine-year-old daughter were hanged in Huntingdon for being witches. The charge - taking off their stockings to cause a rainstorm.' Jax was visibly upset. She had read widely on the persecution and murder of women on charges of witchcraft. 'For centuries women were killed for being different and for the most ridiculous reasons.' She looked at Dinsdale. 'There is no such thing as witchcraft, you silly man,' she bellowed. 'It's an excuse to kill people in horrible ways for nonsensical beliefs.'

Dinsdale sat down heavily and muttered something to his neighbour.

Edith jiggled in her pew and beamed a smile at Jax, who resumed her seat. Calvert put a gentle hand on her shoulder as he made his way back to the end of the nave and waited for the hubbub to subside.

'I am speaking truthfully when I say that I do not know how we all survived the explosion and how we came to land in different parts of the country. The answer may lie in the equipment that arrived with us. But I have yet to impart the piece of information that may shock you the most.' He looked across at Jax and the parson with a nervous expression and then returned his gaze to the villagers, who were now silent in anticipation.

'The experiment we conducted and that went so disastrously wrong was not a year or so ago when I first arrived in Bigby. It was 300 years in the future. In the year 2030.'

He was expecting uproar but what he got was near silence. Twigs and branches scratched at the outside of the stained-glass windows. Dead leaves crackled in the porch. A baby sneezed wetly in a far corner of the church. But no one spoke, until the Rising Sun's landlady Magnolia Drake rose impressively in the middle of the congregation. 'Let me get this straight, Master Calvert. Are you saying that you and this woman, and some of your pals were exploded here from hundreds of years in the future, arriving in one piece like, no bits missing?'

Calvert looked her in the eye. 'That's exactly what happened, Mistress Drake, and unbelievable though it sounds, it's the truth. And Jax and I don't understand it any more than you good folks.'

Silence loitered in the church for a few more seconds as Magnolia looked at the people around her. And then she laughed. And laughed. And laughed, doubling up and collapsing on the pew next to her husband, who looked as though he had never heard such sounds emitted by her. And then he laughed and his neighbours laughed, until it sounded like comedy night at the Hackney Empire. Calvert thought it would never stop. Parson Perkins wondered if this ancient building had heard anything like it. Jax sat there smiling, eventually rising and indicating that

Calvert should resume his seat and let her speak. She held up her hands, palms facing the villagers and eventually calm triumphed over cacophony.

'Believe me,' she said loudly to overcome the last remaining guffaws, 'we know how ridiculous this sounds. We tried making up a more plausible story to tell Edith but she saw through it immediately, wise woman that she is.' Edith blushed at the compliment. 'So we decided to tell the Rev Perkins the truth, incredible though it seemed, and he believed us.' The parson nodded.

Calvert got up and stood beside Jax and held up the Daily Courant. 'What helped to convince him was a small advertisement in this newspaper. He asked us the names of the three people who had been with us when the explosion happened and who may also have been propelled back in time. We told him that their names were Jenks, Allstein and Cooper. The parson then showed us the advertisement, which I will read to you.'

Doctor Jenks is desirous to hear from his colleagues Calvert, Jackson, Allstein and Cooper and would requeft any or all of these fine perfons to dispatch correspondence or, if it pleafe them, to make themselves known in perfon to Sir Isaac Newton at the Royal Mint, Tower of London. Tempus est domum ire.

'It seems that our friend Dr Jenks is alive and has somehow found himself in the company of one of the greatest minds of all time,' said Calvert. 'If he has managed to convince Sir Isaac Newton of our predicament, then I hope that Jax and I can earn your belief in our story.'

A woman wearing what was clearly her Sunday best bonnet raised her hand and Calvert nodded to her. 'Is Sir Isaac the one with the apple what invented gravy?' she asked in a serious attempt at displaying her knowledge.

'Indeed,' he said. 'The apple that fell from the tree helped him establish his theory of gravity, which is the natural force that keeps us all from floating away into space.'

'Gravity,' the woman said to her neighbour. 'I meant to say gravity. Gravy was invented years ago but I don't think Newton had anything to do with it.'

A boy of about 12 years old stood up behind Edith. 'What does tempus whatsit mean?' he asked, licking away a tiny rivulet of snot.

The parson answered him. 'Time to go home, Roddy. Dr Jenks is telling his friends here that it is time to go home.'

The blacksmith Seth stood up and strode to the front of the church with a determined look on his face. Calvert wasn't sure what the huge man's intentions were and he glanced nervously at Jax and the parson. Seth motioned for the scientist to sit before facing the villagers.

'I believe these people,' he said simply. 'Master Calvert arrived in our village in a strange way, that's for sure. But it was not by magic or witchcraft or any other such nonsense. It was by what he and Miss Jax call science. Great people like Sir Isaac are making amazing discoveries about our world every day. Just think what people will be capable of in 300 years' time.

'I am a simple beater of metal. In my store is a box that arrived with master Calvert, made of materials that I have never seen before and constructed in ways that boggle my brain. And Miss Jax too has devices of such complexity that they are clearly not of our time. I say that we must trust them and, if we can, help them to tempus whatsit.'

Parson Perkins stood as the blacksmith returned to his seat. 'I know that some of you will never be fully convinced of the tale you have heard today but I hope that most will. Master Calvert and Miss Jax have agreed to remain in the church for as long as necessary to answer any questions you might have. As the villagers filed out of the building, chatting animatedly, young Roddy walked towards the scientists. 'I believe you too, mister,' he said to Calvert. 'Can I stay and listen to what people ask? I'd like to be a sytist one day.'

'That's brilliant, Roddy. Stay as long as you like,' said Calvert as a group of curious villagers began to assemble in front of him and Jax.

Lincolnshire – 1719

Dr Thomas Cooper held a small glass of sweetish wine, which had been delivered to him on a silver tray by a servant in full flunkery. It smelled funny and he sipped it reluctantly while Lady Muckleborough continued to study him as if he were skewered in a display case. He had worked with a lot of very serious women scientists but none that intimidated him as much as this woman in black. She appeared to be waiting for him to say something, but he couldn't think of anything to say that would make sense to her. Or indeed to him.

'Thank you so much for your kindness and hospitality, Lady Muckleborough,' he eventually offered, looking for somewhere to place his glass but finding no table within reach. He knocked back his drink to get it over with and tried not to pull a face.

'Never mind all that claptrap, man. What are you, and what the devil are you doing here?' She settled back on her sofa. 'I won't say I'm not intrigued by your somewhat bizarre arrival. I'm sure you didn't fling yourself willingly into my rose bushes so please attempt an explanation that will forgo the need for me to contact the magistrate, a cousin who is very much in love with me . . . and my fortune.'

Cooper quickly decided against telling the truth but wasn't sure he could come up with a story that this formidable and intelligent woman would swallow. But he would give it a go.

'My mind is still a little foggy after everything I have endured but I will do my best to assemble the facts as they return to me,' he said. Not a bad start, he thought. Try and keep it simple.

'I am a scientist, a natural philosopher, whose specialism is . . . he recalled the smell of the sea . . . the behaviour of fish.' You genius, he thought. He was a keen angler so knew a bit about fish, and he was sure their behaviour hadn't changed much in 300 years.

'Indeed? That's most interesting,' said her ladyship, although Cooper had already detected a note of scepticism in her voice and had barely formed the story in his head. 'Please continue,' she said, rising from her seat and gliding towards a wall full of leather-bound books tooled in gold lettering. She clearly knew her library inside out because she went straight to one tome and plucked it from the shelf before walking gracefully back to her seat and placing it in her lap. She looked at Cooper, indicating that he should get on with it.

'What's that?' he asked, his mouth suddenly dry.

'It's a signed copy of The Compleat Angler. Do you know of it?'

'I do indeed,' said Cooper. 'By Izaak Walton.' Of course he knew it. Well, knew of it. Every angler had heard of it but he didn't think many people in the 21st century had actually read the thing. He hadn't.

'He was a very good friend of my grandfather,' said Lady Muckleborough. 'He came here often and they would cast their rods in the lake to see who could catch the largest salmon.'

Her Craftiness is trying to catch me out, he thought. 'I fear they would have been there for some time, madam. I have not had the opportunity of studying the lake in any detail yet but I feel sure that carp or pike would have been their quarry, salmon being a river or sea fish. As I'm sure you well know, Lady Muckleborough.'

She directed a cold smile at him. 'A simple test and not one that yet convinces me that you are who you say you are. Fish seems an odd field of study, particularly when Master Walton has clearly covered it so extensively. And it's surely not an area that would generate much in the way of income. How do you support yourself, sir? I know all the great families of England so please avoid any fabrication, if you would.'

Hell's bells, she takes no prisoners, he thought. 'Would it be possible to have another glass of that delicious wine?' he asked, playing for time.

'No. It's foul stuff and you did all but hold your nose to get it down. Get on with it or I'll have Fellowes strip you of those clothes and throw you out into the wilds of Lincolnshire. I will admit I am a little absorbed by your arrival but as the servants will tell you, my patience is limited.'

OK, I think I've got this now. Here goes, he thought. And then he fainted.

When he woke an hour or so later he was back on the cot in the windowless room. Nettie was sitting on a stool, knitting. The clicking stopped when he opened his eyes. 'What happened?' he asked, turning towards the maid and holding his head. 'You passed out in front of her ladyship and banged your noggin on the arm of the chair. She thought you was fakin' it and gave you quite a kick in the ribs to check, but you was out cold. It can happen when the leeches take too much blood. Makes you woozy.'

Cooper rose to sit on the edge of the bed. He could feel a lump on his forehead, and his ribs hurt.

'She says you can stay here the night but she wants the full guff tomorrow or you're out on your arse.'

'She used those words?'

'Of course not, she's a lady, but that's the gist of it,' said Nettie, gathering together her needles and wool and shutting the door behind her. He heard the key turn in the lock.

He spent a restless night but was awake when the door opened and Fellowes entered with a tray of bread, ham and ale. He placed it on the stool and stood looking at Cooper while he stirred. 'I'll come and collect you in half an hour, Master Cooper,' he said. 'Regarding your story. Make it a good one, sir. I detest throwing people off the estate.'

'Good advice. Thank you Fellowes. The fish thing, worth expanding on, do you think?' he asked while tucking into the food.

'It's worth a go, sir, but you should be aware that I will have six gardeners on standby should her ladyship request that you leave.'

'Understood, Fellowes. I think my ducks are now fully aligned.'

'I very much hope so, Master Cooper. The gardeners can be quite . . . brusque.'

Cooper felt fully alert and on top of his game when the footman came back to escort him to Lady Muckleborough's study. She was at her desk sorting through papers when Cooper was ushered in, and she invited him to sit in the chair he had fallen from the previous day.

'You look much brighter today, sir. I trust I will get more sense out of you than I did yesterday. All that nonsense about fish.'

'Oh, I am indeed researching the behaviour of fish, Lady Muckleborough. In particular the migration of herring along the coast of the North Sea . . . sorry, I mean the German Sea.' He hoped his visit to Great Yarmouth's Time and Tide Museum one rainy summer's day was going to pay off.

'Herring!' shrieked her ladyship.

'It is a truly abundant fish and I believe will one day prove to be of huge economic significance to our country.'

'Herring?'

'Indeed, madam. In the autumn the shoals migrate from Scotland and down the east coast of our country. The fishing fleets follow them and catch the silver darlings, as they are called, in their millions. It is already a significant enterprise but one I believe will become of national importance in the decades ahead.'

'And what is your role in this, Master Cooper? You do not look and sound like a sea fisherman.'

'In recent years I have travelled with the boats, recording the extent of their catches, the size of the fish being caught, the facilities in the port where they are landed and improvements that can be made to our boats so that we can overtake those of the villainous Dutch, who are stealing fish from our waters.' Heck, this was good. Thank you Time and Tide.

'And to whom do you report your findings?

Uh-oh.

'To the master of the Scottish fleet.'

'Who is?'

'Sir Andrew . . . Murray.' Ridiculous, but not bad on the spur of the moment.

'And do you have Scottish roots yourself, Master Cooper?'

This could go very wrong at any moment, he thought.

'Very slender ones, I must admit. Indeed I owe a great deal to a very, very distant uncle who died without issue and left me a small but welcome legacy in his will.'

'And his name?'

What's a common Scottish name that would be difficult to track down, he thought. 'Angus MacTavish,' he plumped for. 'Do you know him at all, Lady Muckleborough?'

'Of course not. I'll have nothing to do with the Scotch. This whole Act of Union, Great Britain nonsense will end in tears, you mark my words. So, where is your home?'

Uh-oh, again.

'My research makes me something of a wanderer, I'm afraid. Lodgings here and there along the coast. I was brought up in Cambridge and went to university there.' The first true thing he had uttered all morning. And probably the last. 'I was riding from Grimsby to Lincoln to visit an ailing aunt when I was waylaid by thugs who took my horse, my clothes and all my belongings. I must have wandered in a daze onto your estate and collapsed into your roses.'

'Hmmmm. An interesting story, most of which would, of course, be difficult to verify, sir. If I choose to believe you it seems you have endured something of an ordeal, and plainly you did not dive into my roses of your own volition. You are educated, you appear to have some arcane knowledge of the herring, for goodness sake, and have so far not attempted to steal anything. So, you are welcome to stay for a few days to fully recover from your injuries, following which I will provide you with some clothes and a little money, and bid you farewell.' With that, she rose and returned to her desk, indicating that the interview had ended. Cooper left the room and found Fellowes standing stiffly in the corridor. 'This way if you please, Master Cooper,' he said, leading the way towards the broad, curving staircase in the grand entrance hall.

'Where are we going?' asked Cooper.

'Her Ladyship has allocated a room for you, sir. You should find everything you need there.'

They walked up the stairs at Fellowes' customary dignified pace and along corridors lined with portraits of Lord Muckleborough's ancestors, stern judges and haughty military men, all of them looking down on Cooper with disdain. Fellowes opened a door into a fine room with a large bed and two tall windows overlooking the formal gardens and lake. 'I trust this will suffice, Master Cooper.'

'Erm, yes . . . thank you. This is . . . quite acceptable,' said Cooper, taken aback by his promotion from a rickety cot in an airless room to five-star country house luxury. He took in the view from the window and when he turned back Fellowes had slid from the room and silently shut the door. 'Bloody hell, I've landed on my feet here,' he said to himself.

Bigby – 1719

Calvert and Jax returned to his cottage after the meeting in the church and wrote a letter to Sir Isaac Newton. They had tossed a coin to decide who would pick up the quill to do it because both wanted to experience the thrill of writing to one of the founding fathers of modern science. They felt that the letter would stand a better chance of reaching Jenks if it was addressed to the Master of the Royal Mint at the Tower of London. They wrote:

Sir Isaac.
Please inform Professor Jenks that his friends Dr Esmerelda Fortescue-Jackson and Dr John Calvert are alive and well. They have the Wells chamber and other items, which they will transport to London in the hope that he is in possession of equally important objects that may facilitate their return.

And they both signed it with undisguised glee before folding the letter and sealing it with red wax. Eli the carpenter had agreed to take it to the Crown coaching inn on his next visit to Crassacre and arrange for it to be sent to London on the next available stage. If they were lucky the message would get to Jenks in a few days.

The meeting had been a success, thanks mainly to the intervention of Seth, whose strength and size was wrapped in a modest demeanour and quiet eloquence. He told the two scientists that about a quarter of the village would never believe the story but that he would continue to work on them. 'You have done enough for this village, Dr Calvert, to be awarded our gratitude, and our belief in what you have said,' he had told them as people left the church and gathered noisily in the graveyard. 'We have nothing to lose in placing our trust in you, and everything to gain from learning so much about what the future holds.'

Enid joined them and a look of surprise spread across her face when Jax leapt forward and engulfed her in a hug. 'You marvellous, magnificent, wonderful woman,' said Jax.

'Careful, my girl,' said a grinning Edith. 'You'll crumble up my second best apron.' She stepped back and gripped Jax's arms. 'My grandmother told me of the terrible things done to women accused of you-know-what. She lived through it, a time of madness and ignorance she called it, and curse anyone who tries to revive such horror. Well, not curse maybe,' she said looking around in case anyone heard her. 'But shame on them, anyhow. I won't let it happen.'

'And neither will I,' said Jax.

Woodbridge – 1719

Dr Daniel Allstein smoothed out the square of paper laid out before him on the gnarled oak table in the school library. Lessons had long since finished and he was enveloped by a restful darkness pierced only by a candle flame dancing in the faintest of draughts. He had been staring at the paper for some time, unsure of what to write, or even whether to write at all. Was there any point? Even if he did contact Jenks, what then? Their chances of getting back to the 21st century were almost non-existent, and to find out what Jenks had in mind he would have to give up his comfortable life in the country for an uncertain one in dangerous, disease-ridden London. It was well past midnight when he took up his goose feather quill, dipped it in the inkwell and wrote his resignation to the headmaster.

It was another two days before the next stagecoach was due at the inn. He spent the time gathering up his possessions, settling payment for his lodgings and selling his horse. He had considered riding the near 100 miles to the capital but the risk from highwaymen was very real and he knew he would be safer travelling on a coach with an armed man sitting beside the driver. The journey would take two days, with stops every ten to 12 miles to change the horses, and an overnight stay at an inn in Colchester. He feared it would be a cramped and uncomfortable journey and that he would be lucky to get a seat inside the coach, but when it arrived at the Wheatsheaf the next morning it was carrying just five passengers, two young men choosing to sit, wrapped up, in the cheaper outside seats. Allstein tossed his leather bag up to the guard for it to be stowed on the roof and then ensconced himself in a front-facing corner of the coach. His companions were a well-dressed man in his fifties wearing a short grey wig, who peered intently at a newspaper through gold-rimmed spectacles, and two warmly garbed women who could have been mother and daughter or governess and charge. None of them took much notice of him as he settled into his seat, for which he was grateful. He disliked idle conversation. He extracted his half-read copy of Memoirs of a Cavalier from his coat pocket and hoped to lose himself in Colonel Newport's adventures.

The coach did not linger at the inn. Just time enough to rest, feed and water the four-horse team. They were just on the outskirts of the town when his worst fears materialised.

'Are you going all the way to London, sir?' asked the young woman, who was probably about 16, Allstein thought. He looked up briefly from his book. 'I am, miss,' he said, hoping that his curt reply would stop the conversation there.

'As are we,' she said with a smile. 'I'm going to a ball.' He saw the older woman give her a slight tug of the arm.

'I hope you enjoy it,' he said, returning his gaze to his book.

'I hope to find a husband,' she said.

'Abigail! That's enough,' her companion said quietly but forcefully. 'Let the gentleman read his book.'

'I'm sorry, Miss Gray, but it's exciting. My apologies for disturbing you, good sir. I will not utter another word.' Allstein suddenly felt guilty for being so churlish, put his finger in the page he had reached and looked at the two women. They were fashionably dressed and wore expensive-looking woollen cloaks. He had grown used to dealing with boys at the school but had little experience of communicating with young women. He had no family and no girlfriend at the time of the explosion. He forced a smile at the two. The older woman could not have been much more than 20 and bore an impassive expression that probably reflected a sense of protective responsibility towards her charge, and a caution of strangers, particularly men.

'Where is the ball being held?' he asked. Abigail leaned forward, pleased at having started a conversation that could enliven the journey. 'Pimlico Hall, the London home of Lord and

Lady Banham. Do you know them, Master . . .?'

'Allstein, miss. Daniel Allstein.'

'I am Abigail Totness, and this is my governess Miss Viola Gray.'

'Dora Gray. How do you do, sir?' said the older woman, seeming to relax a little. 'May I ask what you are reading?'

'It is Daniel Defoe's latest work.'

'Ah yes, Memoirs of a Cavalier. Quite a masculine book I'm given to understand,' said Miss Gray.

'Indeed. Lots of derring-do. Is there an author you like, Miss Gray?'

'I know he is a controversial figure, but I am an admirer of Jonathan Swift.'

'Oh, Gulliver's Travels?'

She looked puzzled. 'I do not know it, sir. Is it new? I must look for it in London.'

Oops, thought Allstein. It may not have been published yet. The trouble is, he didn't know the title of any other of Swift's books. 'I may be getting him confused with another writer,' he said. 'I must confess that I have never been a great reader of novels but am trying to make up for lost time. Mathematics is more my field.'

'Mine too,' interjected Abigail, realising that she was being left out of the conversation she had initiated. 'Books bore me, but numbers are a great fascination. Although women are generally discouraged from such interests.'

'Not by me,' said her governess, turning to her ward.

'No, indeed, Dora. I could not wish for more enlightened instruction. May I ask what takes you to our capital city, Master Allstein?'

'I am going to meet a friend I have not seen for a long time, and I'm also hoping to make the acquaintance of a man of great intellect that I much admire.' The man in the corner who had been engrossed in his newspaper lowered it and regarded Allstein over his glasses. Keen to keep out of talk of parties and books, the man had hidden himself behind the paper, but now that the potential for some gossip had arisen he was suddenly alert.

'Intriguing, sir,' he said in high-pitched voice. 'I am a London man myself. I might know the gentleman. May I ask who it is you aspire to meet?'

'Yes, do please tell us, Master Allstein. Is he famous? Is he royalty? Please don't tell us that it is King George? That would be just too much,' she twittered.

Her governess tutted. 'This is none of our concern, sir,' she said to Allstein. 'It is probably a personal or confidential matter for which you are making this dreadful journey and is no one's business but your own. Please feel free to keep this gentleman's name to yourself,' she added as one of the coach's wheels lurched over an object in the road. 'Unless, of course, you wish to tell us,' she added, looking Allstein square in the eye.

The scientist carefully considered what he was going to say. It was going to be a long journey, and he supposed they had to talk about something. He would keep it vague.

'Very well,' he said. 'I suppose it will do no harm for you to know.' His companions smiled. 'I am travelling to meet a fellow mathematician I have not seen for well over a year. You will not have heard of him but you will know the gentleman whose acquaintance he has recently made and to whom he is going to introduce me.' His audience shuffled forward on their seats. 'He is one of the greatest men of our age. Sir Isaac

Newton.'

The two women were wide-eyed. 'My goodness, I would not know what to say to a man in possession of such knowledge,' said Dora. 'It would be intimidating beyond words.'

'Pah!' said the man sitting beside her. He leaned forward again, angrily this time. 'Newton. A thief and as thin-skinned as an overripe peach. Robert Hooke was a great friend of mine and he was twice the man that Newton is. He took all the credit for Hooke's ground-breaking work on gravity and calculus. He even abused his position as Royal Society president to anonymously write a report claiming that he had invented calculus. The man is a disgrace, sir. I will hear no more of him.' And with that he hid behind his newspaper once more.

The women looked at one another and then at Allstein. He knew about the intense rivalry between the two men, and the factions that arose in support of each side, but he was alarmed at meeting such a vociferous Hooke proponent at the start of what could be a long and awkward journey. The prospect of spending two days in the company of the man was not a pleasant one.

'What do you think of our king?' he asked the women, plucking a subject from thin air and hoping that would offer a lighter subject for conversation. The man rustled his paper testily but said nothing.

Cambridge – 2030

Angela Hawkins, late thirties wearing jeans, trainers and a Motorhead sweatshirt, was sitting on a plastic garden chair on the edge of a car park, looking at the space where a laboratory used to be. It's something she did from time to time, hoping that an answer to the puzzle about the disappearance of the building, its contents and its five people might pop into her head. Joel Williamson, an astrophysicist working on another part of the 150-acre Science Park, walked over to her balancing two take-away coffees and a paper bag containing pre-packed sandwiches. He handed her one of the coffees and she dipped into the bag and retrieved a tuna sandwich. Like Angela, Joel was in his thirties, and was married only to his work, and the supposedly humorous line, "It's not rocket science", whenever strangers asked him about his job.

'One minute it was there, a nanosecond later it wasn't,' she said. It was a phrase she had used a hundred times, because that's exactly what she had witnessed – the disappearance of a building and people before her very eyes as she walked across the car park more than a year ago with the keys to her classic 1975 Ford Cortina in her hand. A blink of the eye and the whole lot was gone. No blast, no bang. She was the only person to see it happen. The laboratory simply disappeared as if it were a magic trick, the big finish to a Las Vegas illusionist's act. She had stood open-mouthed on this very spot, looking around her to see if anyone else had seen it. There was no one around. Every time she returned, Joel came over to bring her lunch and to share in her bafflement. But mainly because he fancied her.

They didn't speak much. She thanked him for the coffee and sandwich. He said it was OK. And then they stared in silence at the scene. Bravely breaking with this tradition Joel said, 'You'd think with all the brainpower there is in this place that someone would have come up with an answer.'

'Hmmm,' she said, biting into her sandwich without

removing her gaze from the empty site. 'Someone suggested aliens,' she added quietly.

'The Americans, wasn't it. I wouldn't be surprised if the CIA weren't involved.'

'They promised us they weren't,' said Angela.

'Case closed then.'

'Hmmm.'

'Is anyone still looking into it, do you know?' asked Joel.

'There's a committee, I think, but the steam has gone out of it. They planted that tree on the anniversary,' she said, nodding towards a twiggy amelanchier that was shorter than she was.

'Yes, I was there. No one really knew what to say, did they? If I'm honest it was all a bit embarrassing. Like the guys hadn't died, but just sort of left without telling anyone.'

'That's a nice thought, Joel. I quite fancied Tom Cooper.'

'Oh,' said Joel. He gathered up the empty coffee cups and sandwich wrappers, put them in the paper bag and trudged off dejectedly towards his office. 'Then I hope he is dead,' he muttered to himself.

About half an hour later Angela rang Joel's mobile. He was still annoyed at her for fancying Cooper so he let it ring a few times before answering. 'Hi, Ange.'

'Joel, has anyone tried repeating the experiment they were working on? I know it was sort of off the books but it must have had something to do with their disappearance. Unless it was aliens, of course.'

'All their notes, records and computer files went with them, didn't they? The police, the accident investigation people, and the weird bunch who came from that government department no one has heard of, found nothing. They even searched their homes and gym lockers and what have you. There was nothing, not even in the Cloud.'

'That's always seemed strange to me,' said Angela. 'Whatever they were doing in such secrecy must have been important to them all. You'd have thought they would have stuff backed up away from the lab in case of a fire or something ordinary like that. It's common sense, standard practice.'

'The authorities spent six months looking into all that and there was nothing, Ange.' Joel was getting tired of the conversation, which they had gone over a dozen times or more. 'Why don't you just let it drop, eh?'

'I suppose it's more difficult for me because I was there. I don't think I'll ever be able to forget it . . . escape it.'

He thought he would take a punt. 'Let me take your mind off things. Come over to mine tonight and I'll open a nice bottle of wine and cook something. How does lobster thermidor sound?'

'Oh my god, brilliant,' said Angela.

'Yes, it sounds pretty good to me too, but you'll be getting spag bol and be grateful,' said Joel with a smile in his voice.

'That would also be lovely. Thanks Joel.'

Angela had changed into a dress topped with a bolero-style cardigan when she arrived at the door of Joel's flat that evening. In her hand was a bottle of Morrison's Finest Montepulciano d'Abruzzo that she had collected on her way over. In the couple of years that he had known her this was the first time that Angela had agreed to meet after work. But when he came to think about it, it was the first time he had plucked up the courage to ask her. She stood on tiptoes and pecked him on the cheek.

'Thanks for doing this, Joel. I got really stewed up about the whole disappearing lab thing today. More than usual, I think.'

Joel went to the fridge and took out a bottle of chenin blanc. 'OK if we start with this? It makes a nice aperitif. Then we can open yours.'

'Blimey, a two-bottle night. I haven't had one of those since I was at uni,' she said while browsing his huge collection of vinyl records. 'Your taste seems to extend from Procul Harum to Val Doonican. What's that all about?'

'On the surface that is a bit embarrassing, but in my defence I have to tell you that the selection of Doonican, Des O'Connor, Max Bygraves and Harry Secombe LPs were my mother's. I hadn't the heart to part with them when she died.'

'Oh Joel, I believe you,' she said teasingly. 'Thousands wouldn't.'

'Thank you. I look forward to tearing your music collection to shreds one day,' he said, handing her a chilled glass. 'Cheers! Here's to science.'

'Here's to the mysteries that science solves,' she said, clinking glasses.

As promised, Joel had prepared spaghetti Bolognese, which he carried over to his small, round dining table in a double-handled pot and dished up into white Ikea bowls. She helped herself to a generous amount of Parmesan cheese and tucked in. They were now on the Italian red and Angela felt relaxed enough to raise a subject that she knew could spoil the mood.

'Do you mind if I try out a theory on you? I won't if it'll make you cross.'

It was a tricky moment to answer. Joel looked at her with a mouthful of pasta, thin tails of spaghetti dangling from his mouth. He chewed them off and they fell into his bowl. It would normally make him tetchy but he had got her here, they were having a good time and he felt that something, he wasn't quite sure what, was blossoming between them.

'OK, let's hear your theory. After we've eaten. It had better be good.'

'Agreed.'

After dinner, Angela sat in a large, comfy chair with her knees bent under her. A half-full glass of wine was on the coffee table. Joel sprawled on a sofa, wishing that she was on it too. He sipped his wine. 'Go on then. I'm all ears.'

She stretched for her glass, wondering how to start. 'Do you think they tried the post office?' she asked, knowing that it sounded somewhat feeble.

'Who?'

'The people who investigated all this. The police, the university, the guys from spook central. They looked in the Cloud and went through all their stuff searching for clues, information on what they were doing, research notes, but found absolutely bugger all. Isn't that a bit strange? I know they were working . . . what's the word?'

'Clandestinely?' offered Joel.

'Good one. I'm glad you can still say that after all this plonk. I mean, if I was doing something what-you-said I'd want to make sure I had everything backed up if something went tits up.'

'And what do you think their back-up plan might have been?'

'If it was me, I'd keep it simple.' She sipped her wine. 'Like maybe post a hard drive with some serious encryption to a friend every week?' She turned it into a question in case it sounded so daft that Joel laughed at the idea and she could back out of the thought by saying it was just a theory, forget it, it's daft.

But Joel didn't laugh. He sat up and put his glass down, a serious expression on his face. 'Bloody hell, that's just the sort of thing John Calvert would come up with. He once told me he didn't trust the Cloud. And they would never just back up sensitive research on a computer, in the lab or at home. Much too risky. But isn't putting something in the mail just as dicey?'

'But it's such a boring, everyday thing to do, pop down to the post office with a small package. I agree that it's not the most secure method but it would enable them to keep an off-site record of what they were doing.'

'But where were they sending their parcels from, and who were they sending them to? Should we be sharing this idea with the police?'

'Not yet, I think. They would probably just laugh at the idea. Let's see if we can find something concrete to hold up my theory. Any more wine?'

'Would Chateau Petrus be acceptable?'

'You haven't got any of that, have you?' she said, knowing the answer.

'Of course not. It costs more than we earn in a month. You'll have Chianti Classico . . '

'. . . and like it,' she said with a grin.

Lincolnshire – 1719

After a couple of weeks, Dr Thomas Cooper had found himself promoted – from the cramped and noisy servants' dining room off the kitchen to the silver and crystal bedecked table of Lady Muckleborough and her companion. Fellowes had beckoned to him as he was about to settle into his usual place in the staff room and led him upstairs. 'Where are we going?' Cooper asked the footman. 'Am I being chucked out? I'm really quite hungry. Perhaps I can eat first and then you can chuck me out.'

'Her Ladyship has requested the pleasure of your company at dinner, sir. I am simply escorting you to the formal dining room and have received no instructions regarding your removal from the hall.'

'Phew, that's a relief. Are there guests? Will I have to be on my best behaviour, Fellowes? Make sure I use the right fork, don't guzzle the wine, that sort of thing?'

The footman stopped and Cooper nearly bumped into him. 'If I may be so bold as to make a suggestion, sir.' Cooper nodded. 'Please try and sound a little less . . . frivolous in the presence of Her Ladyship and her companion, the Honourable Cecilia Creighton. It will stand you in good stead.'

'Thanks Fellowes, much appreciated,' said Cooper, patting the footman on the back and causing the man's entire body to stiffen. 'So the young woman who retreats to the corner every time I enter the room is Miss Creighton is she? I can't say I've ever heard her speak. What's her story, Fellowes?'

'I beg your pardon, sir?'

'I mean, tell me a little about her. Why is she here? It can't be for her scintillating conversation.'

They had arrived at the dining room door. 'It is not for me to say, sir. Enjoy your dinner, and try to . . . '

' . . . behave?'

'Precisely, sir,' said Fellowes, opening the door.

The two ladies were already seated at the massive dining table, in the centre of which was an elaborate silver confection depicting a pack of hounds tearing into an alarmed-looking fox. Lady Muckleborough was at the head of the table with Miss Creighton immediately to her right. A place was set on Her Ladyship's left and Cooper walked towards it, wondering whether he was required to bow before taking his seat. He didn't.

'Master Cooper, please come and join us.' Lady Muckleborough nodded to a young footman who was holding a decanter. He stepped forward and filled their glasses with a pale gold liquid, which Cooper looked at with concern.

'Please don't worry. It's not that foul stuff I gave you when you arrived.' He sipped it. It was delicious. 'Thank you for inviting me to join you at dinner, Your Ladyship. I must admit I was somewhat surprised at your invitation.'

'Oh, it wasn't my idea, my dear fellow. Miss Creighton thought it would be an opportunity to get to know you a little better. Did you not, Cecilia?'

'I did, Constance.' They were the first words he had heard her utter. 'Miss Creighton is an astute observer of people, Master Cooper, and she has some observations that she would like us to air over what I am sure will be a most entertaining repast.' Cooper's senses clicked on high alert. He said bugger to himself several times and put down his wine glass in preparation for a stern defence, at which point the first course arrived – a lukewarm and over-salty soup made from indeterminable ingredients.

'For example,' said Miss Crichton, pausing with her spoon in mid-air. 'Your speech patterns and use of language are most odd for a man of your obvious intelligence and education. Have you, by any chance, spent some time in the Americas, where I understand the spoken word has developed a somewhat lax disposition?'

'I have, miss, and my time there must have instilled in me an unfortunate negligence in the manner in which I express myself. I hope that my slovenly use of language has not caused me to overstep the boundaries of propriety in any way.'

The two women looked at one another and smiled in a way that disconcerted Cooper. They all finished their soup and the staff cleared away the dishes. Cooper's empty glass was refilled and he made a mental note to take it easy just in case a trap was being laid.

'Another thing that has concerned me is your arrival, er . . . unclothed,' said Miss Crichton delicately. 'We are a little off the beaten track here and robberies of the sort you described are very rare indeed, and on the few occasions they have happened the victims have had their valuables taken and occasionally their boots but never their entire clothing. It is most odd.'

'Indeed it is,' added Lady Muckleborough, barely concealing an unladylike smirk behind her wine glass.

'If you were attacked so brutally on the road, as you say you were, how on earth did you manage to stagger the length of Muckleborough Hall's extensive gravel drive, barefoot. It is a feat of considerable strength and endurance, would you not agree Constance.'

'Remarkable beyond belief, Cecilia,' she agreed theatrically.

Cooper set down his glass and was about to speak when Miss Crichton raised her palm towards him before he could utter a sound. 'I have not yet finished Master Cooper. I also have some concerns regarding your injuries, which were indeed terrible to witness. All over your poor body, you unfortunate man.'

'You saw them?' he asked. 'All over? Everywhere?'

'Oh yes. I must confess I have never seen . . . anything quite like it. It was an alarming sight to be sure, sir.' Neither her face nor her voice indicated that she had been alarmed in the slightest, thought Cooper. They were both enjoying all this. Once again he tried to speak but she stopped him.

'There were indeed dreadful injuries from all those horrid thorns, but not one sign of a bruise or abrasion from your beating, sir.' Cooper drained his glass and it was immediately refilled.

'And just one more thing concerns me. You said you had fallen into the rose bed but you were found in the very middle of it, and the gardeners had to wade in to retrieve your poor . . . naked . . . body.'

Lady Muckleborough could contain herself no longer and exploded with laughter. Miss Crichton, like an 18th century Poirot, merely smiled, raised her eyebrows questioningly and fixed her gaze at Cooper.

Lady Muckleborough dabbed her mouth delicately with a napkin and brought her amusement under control. 'What my friend is saying Master Cooper is that your story contains more holes than a pauper's bucket and you appear to have a great deal to hide from us. This either means that you are a felon, and possibly dangerous, or fear that we will not believe the true reason you came to be found among our roses.'

The fish course arrived. 'It's not herring, I'm afraid, Master Cooper, although perhaps your story was a red herring of some kind,' said Her Ladyship, raising to her lips a forkful of white fish plastered in a thick, gooey sauce.

'Red herring . . . very good, Constance,' smiled Miss Crichton, also tucking in. Cooper sat with his hands in his lap, having suddenly lost his appetite. He stared at his plate. What the hell was he going to tell them? He had enjoyed his couple of weeks at Muckleborough Hall. His injuries had healed nicely, he had been well fed, he had enjoyed walking the grounds, and he got on well with the staff. If he was going to be marooned like Ben Gunn in the 18th century, this was a whole lot better than a desert island. He had perhaps become complacent.

He looked at the women in turn and their faces had become serious. But he knew they would not believe the truth of his arrival. 'I have truly enjoyed my time here, and you have been the most magnanimous hosts it is possible to imagine,' he said. 'But I cannot tell you the truth because you would not believe me, and would probably have me taken to an asylum, where I would spend the rest of my life. Indeed, I myself find it difficult to understand how I came to be here. One moment I was going about my work, the next I was lying in agony in the grounds of your estate, Lady Muckleborough. My poor explanation of the robbery and my background in fishing research was all I could conjure up when asked to explain my presence, and I knew it was a story as thin as air.'

The women watched him patiently and in silence, waiting for the truth. Cooper pushed his chair back from the table and stood. 'I regret, Lady Muckleborough, Miss Crichton, that the facts of my arrival are so utterly bizarre that it would be better for me to remove myself from this quite wonderful place. I serve no purpose here and will always be viewed with suspicion by yourselves and the staff. Rest assured, I am no criminal. I possess only the things you have so kindly given me and will depart in the meanest of rags tomorrow morning.'

He was halfway to the door when Miss Crichton spoke. 'Well, Constance, that has to be the most pathetic speech I have ever heard.'

'I agree, my dear. Master Cooper, straighten your shoulders and remove that hangdog expression from your face. You are not getting out of this room so lightly. Meanest of rags indeed. You're not on the stage, you know? Although you probably could be. Don't you think, Cecilia? '

He stopped, trying to decide whether to continue his flight or to return to the table and think of another, more plausible, tale. Or try the truth.

He returned and sat down. The fish course had been silently removed and replaced by large plates of a fine pink beef. 'If I tell you the truth will you promise not to lock me up, however fantastic it may sound?'

They looked at one another. 'I think we can agree to that,' said Miss Crichton. 'But if we don't believe you, you will leave Muckleborough Hall – in rags.'

'Indeed he will, Cecilia. Though are there any rags at the hall? Perhaps I'll ask Fellowes to seek some out, just in case we need them.' They tittered unnervingly.

Cambridge – 2030

Joel liked being a passenger in Angela's musty smelling Cortina. He could look at her while she concentrated on the road. He liked the way her long, dark brown hair always seemed to be held perfectly in place by a pair of specs, either her reading glasses or sunglasses. And how her face could be transformed in a moment from a look of steely determination to one of relaxed amusement. Everyone seemed to like her. She had the ability to make people feel at ease, even though she was nearly always the smartest person in the lab.

Joel knew that his anonymous looks – untameable brown hair, patchy beard, lightweight stature, denim everything – and inherent shyness deterred colleagues from forging anything other than a working relationship with him. He was outstanding at his job but knew he could be hard work to talk to. 'What's the plan then?' he asked as Angela confidently reverse-parked into a space outside a village convenience store that doubled as a Post Office. It was the nearest one to the science park, and the first on their list.

'I've got a picture of Cooper on my phone.'

'Of course you have,' he said tartly.

'Which I'm going to show to the person behind the counter to see if they recognise him. I thought it might be a good starting point, unless you have a better idea.'

'No, no, it's a good idea,' said Joel. 'Where did you get the picture?'

'I took it at a funder's reception when he wasn't looking. Don't look at me like that. I took it . . . for a friend. She'd heard about him.'

'From you.'

'Yes. Look, shut up and let's give this a go. It's the first one we've tried. If it doesn't work we'll have to think of something else.'

The bell on the shop door clanged, 1950s style, and they walked towards the Post Office counter at the rear. A large man of about 40 who was leaning on the shop counter reading a gardening magazine folded down the corner of the page he had reached and walked round to the Post Office section. 'How can I help you?' he asked with an expressionless face that said he couldn't be bothered if he helped or not.

'We're worried about a colleague who disappeared rather suddenly. We think he might have been a customer here, dropping off parcels. Do you recognise him?' She held up her phone. The man didn't look at it immediately, his face seeming to struggle to take in what he was being asked. His stony gaze moved ponderously from Angela's face to her phone, which she pressed against the security glass. The man studied the picture. Joel suspected that nothing got done very speedily when this man was on duty.

'He does look a bit familiar. Is his name doctor something?'

'Yes it is,' said Angela looking excitedly at Joel. 'Dr Thomas Cooper. We work with him at the Science Park.'

'Haven't seen him for a while. Came in from time to time, maybe once a month, to post a padded envelope or something.'

'Any reason in particular that you remember him?' asked Joel.

The man moved his eyes slowly from the phone to Joel's face. 'The women who work here fancy him,' he said drearily. 'He's handsome, apparently.'

'He really is, isn't he? But we're extremely worried about him,' said Angela. 'I don't suppose you can tell us who he sent the parcels to. We'd like to contact them to find out if they know where he is.'

'That's not allowed. Do you want any stamps or anything?' His voice was a dull monotone.

'Yes, let's buy some stamps, Joel,' said Angela breezily, fearing that the man was trying to end the conversation. 'I'll have a dozen first class please. Pay the nice man, Joel.'

Joel huffed and tugged his wallet from the back pocket of his jeans.

'I know you can't give us an address but how about a postcode. That will at least narrow it down for us and we can take it from there,' said Angela, putting on her most winning smile and slipping Joel's £20 note under the glass partition. 'We don't really need the stamps.' She winked at him.

The man's stare was unmoving. 'How about a date?' he said.

'What? No. That's a bit . . . I'm seeing someone,' Angela lied.

'Not you. Him,' said the man, turning his eyes to Joel.

'Let's go, Ange. Now, please.' And Joel fled, the shop bell reverberating behind him. Angela waited for him to get into the car. 'If I can get him to change his mind, will you help me? Get me an address?' she asked.

'I'll think about it. And I'm keeping the twenty.'

'Of course. I'll be back, Mr . . . '

'Clapper. Colin. He's alright, your friend. Not too handsome.'

'Right. I'll let him know, Colin.'

Angela walked out of the shop and opened the passenger seat of her car. Joel was staring straight ahead with his arms folded. 'There's the Red Lion across the road,' she said. 'Let's go and have a quick drink and move on to the next place.'

'I'm not going on a date with that man. He's weird. It's outrageous.'

'Come on, I'll buy you a pint and we can discuss tactics.' She virtually dragged him out of her car and gripped his arm tightly to make sure he didn't try to escape. The pub was quiet and they sat in two large comfy chairs beside a window. Halfway through his pint of bitter Joel seemed to relax a little. Angela leaned forwards and patted his knee. 'Feeling a bit better now?' she asked.

'The cheek of the man,' said Joel, savouring the pat on the knee and taking a swig of his ale.

'I know, but ignoring that, we have made some progress, haven't we? Our theory was right, it seems. They are posting back-ups, though using the nearest one to the Science Park was a bit lax. But if we can find out where they're going it would be another step towards finding out what happened to them. All of them, not just Tom. He's not my type, anyway.'

'Really?' said Joel. 'I thought you fancied him.'

'No, he's got a bit of a reputation. Thinks he's God's gift, and all that. I prefer a more down to earth man.' She hoped she had sounded convincing.

'Another drink, Ange?' asked Joel, taking his glass to the bar and getting her a second tomato juice.

'Look, I know Colin called it a date . . .'

'Colin! He's called Colin? Well that makes all the difference. Let me at him,' said Joel.

' . . . but what if he'd asked you for a drink? That would be alright wouldn't it? Just two blokes having a friendly drink. You want to know what happened to our colleagues as much as I do. I would have gone for a drink with him if he'd asked me.'

'Don't give me that. You thought he'd asked you, and you got all flustered.'

'Fair point, Joel. How about this? You agree to go for a drink with him, I'll drive you and wait in the car in case you need to make a quick getaway. Then, when we have the information we need, we'll have a night out. A nice restaurant, my treat.'

Bugger, thought Joel. She's played her trump card. 'Damn it, Ange. That's not fair.'

'I know. But you agree?'

'Bloody hell, yes, but you've got to provide me with an escape route.'

'Agreed. Stay here I'll go and tell him.' She gulped down her drink in one and sped out of the pub and across the road to the shop. A woman in her sixties was just ahead of her and she stood in front of Colin with a stern look on her face. 'Are you reading my gardening magazine again, Colin Clapper? I wouldn't mind but half the corners are turned down.'

'Sorry, Mrs Davies. There's a good bit on compost heaps on page 23,' he said, handing over the publication. The woman stuffed it into her shopping bag and stomped off.

Angela replaced her at the counter and smiled at Colin. 'He's agreed to go for a drink with you. Do me a favour and don't call it a date. Tonight at 8? The place across the road?'

'OK. What's his name?'

'Joel. I'll call in tomorrow and you can help me with that postcode.'

'Agreed.' Colin smiled. It didn't suit his face.

That night, Angela drove a nervous Joel to the Red Lion and parked her car down the street so that she could watch the door. Colin arrived a few minutes later, having emerged from a doorway beside the shop and crossed the road to the pub. He must live in the flat above it, she thought. She was half expecting

Joel to emerge a few minutes later but it was nearly 11 when the two men walked out and shook hands, Colin crossing back to his home and Joel walking towards Angela's car and getting in.

'Well?' she asked. She was expecting a full-volume ear-bashing.

'Nice chap,' he offered. 'We had a couple of pints, played darts, couple of games of pool. It's a good pub. I'll probably come back.'

'Well . . . that's nice,' said Angela, failing to keep the surprise from her voice. 'You had a good time then.'

'He apologised for calling it a date. Said it was a slip of the tongue. He doesn't have any mates, apparently, and just fancied a blokes night out. I'll probably give him a bell some time.'

'Heck, I wasn't expecting that. Thought you'd shoot out of that door like the hounds of hell were after you. Well done, Joel, I'm so proud of you. I'll pop back here tomorrow and see if he'll part with some info.'

Joel, who had been staring fixedly out of the front windscreen, turned and handed her a piece of paper on which was written a postcode. 'No need. He gave me this. And told me a number . . . 42.'

'The meaning of life, the universe and everything?' asked the Douglas Adams fanatic.

Joel smiled. 'I think it's more likely to be a house number, Ange.' She couldn't help herself. She kissed him on the lips. 'Dinner's on me then, you clever old astrophysicist.'

Bigby – 1719

Calvert estimated that the journey from Bigby to London would take them five or six days. He and Jax had hired a sturdy cart from farmer Dick Cobbitt, who had also offered them one of his horses, Solomon, on condition that they looked after him and told him what a good boy he was at the end of each day. Jax started to laugh but Calvert stopped her with a subtle nudge. 'We certainly will, Dick. Thank you for helping us.'

Seth had insisted on traveling with them, partly to provide them with a degree of security on the journey but also to help should the cart be damaged on the treacherous roads. Calvert offered to pay him but the blacksmith said his reward would be the opportunity to meet Sir Isaac Newton. The two scientists were relieved that they would not be making the trip on their own.

It took six people to carefully remove the Wells chamber from the back of Seth's forge, and the sight of the gleaming metal box emerging into the pale afternoon light caused much excitement among the 50 or so villagers who had gathered to see it loaded onto the cart.

'It is a mighty strange device and no mistake,' said Enid. 'It looks like silver, but my instincts tell me it is a great deal more valuable to you than even that precious metal,' she said, hooking her arm through Jax's. 'I would ask you what it does but I doubt if I would be any the wiser after you'd told me.' She stopped and looked at Jax square on. 'I do hope you have a safe journey, my dear. Please accept this bottle of plum brandy to warm your insides on the cold nights that lie ahead. Don't worry, it's the good one,' she added.

They were planning to leave at dawn the next morning and Dick said Solomon should be able to cover about 20 miles a day if he was properly fed and watered, and was spoken to nicely from time to time.

That night, there was a leaving party. A huge bonfire was lit in the centre of Bigby, trestle tables were set up, villagers brought out bread, cheese, pies and ale, and two fiddle players worked their way through a medley of jaunty tunes that all sounded remarkably similar to Calvert's ears. Dancing quickly broke out and the scientists, mugs of ale in their hands, moved slowly backwards into the shadow of the forge, fearful of being dragged into the mayhem. But they weren't quick enough. Enid spotted them and grabbed each by the arm. 'Come on, it's Whiffler's Knob, one of my favourites,' she shrieked. 'Don't worry, you don't have to know the steps 'cos there aren't any. Just throw yourself about a bit and try and keep in time. You'll love it.'

Enid was right. The mayhem embraced them. Jax was swept up by farmworkers, thatchers, drovers and even the parson. Calvert found himself jigging with wives, widows and the landlady of the Rising Sun, who had supped more ale than was wise, mainly because it had been provided by others and was therefore free.

The party died down along with the bonfire at about 10 o'clock but Calvert and Jax had stopped drinking well before then, aware of the long journey that lay ahead of them the next day. Seth had spent most of the night heaving his giant frame around the fire, occasionally in time to the music. As the party subsided villagers approached Calvert and shook his hand, wishing him a good journey, thanking him for what he had done for Bigby and urging him to be careful in that London. Young

Roddy asked them to say hello to Sir Isaac and handed him a drawing of a man lying unconscious beneath a tree with an apple beside his head. 'Please give this to Sir Newton and tell him that I will become a sytist as soon as I can read.'

After everyone had returned to their homes, Calvert and Jax sat on the seat outside his cottage and gazed at a cloudless sky liberally sprinkled with more stars than they had ever seen before. 'I love this place,' said Jax quietly. 'Especially the people. I hope the Industrial Revolution doesn't spoil this life for them. It's pretty nearly idyllic, isn't it?'

'If there wasn't this slim chance of us getting home I would probably be happy to spend the rest of my days in Bigby.'

'And it is a mighty slim chance indeed,' she agreed. 'But we have to try, don't we? It's who we are.'

It was still dark when they woke the next morning to the sound of Solomon's hooves clopping in the direction of the cart outside Seth's forge. Each had packed as many of their belongings as they could into large leather bags, which they placed on the cart beside Seth's much smaller cloth bag. Then everything was covered in bales of straw to deter prying eyes as they passed through towns and villages on the way to the city. The blacksmith had also stowed a bag of tools, a musket and a lethal looking double-edged sword beneath the seat of the cart.

As they were setting off, a few villagers came out to wave them on their way, including a young, newly married couple to whom Calvert had given his cottage and furniture. They hugged one another, smiled and waved as the cart passed them. A tearful Enid dashed out of her cottage with a basket of food, and at the edge of the village Parson Perkins stood at the side of the lane and shouted, 'God speed, good people'. He opened his Bible and started quietly reading a prayer as they passed, making their way to the edge of the forest and the winding path to the north-south road.

It was a cool overcast day and Solomon had made light work of the heavy load he was hauling by the time they reached the junction. 'Good boy, Solomon,' said Seth as they turned south on the highway. 'I know this horse as well as any man or woman in the village,' he said to his passengers. 'I've shod him for years and he's the most decent, hard-working beast in Bigby. We are lucky to have this fine creature and we must look after him.'

Constable Bartholomew Bartleby was enjoying a dream about an enormous meat pie when he was woken by a hammering on his cottage door. He rose groggily and pulled a blanket around his shoulders before opening the door a couple of inches to witness Enid's face in full emergency mode. 'You'd better come, Barty. Quick as you like. There's a banging,' she said with urgency. 'And get some clothes on. That blanket ain't long enough to cover . . . everything.'

'But where is this banging taking place, Enid,' he bellowed to her back as she scuttled off.

She didn't look back. 'The lock-up. Bring the key,' she shouted.

A crowd had gathered outside the tiny gaol by the time the constable arrived, looking flustered and hoping this wasn't going to involve any paperwork. He unhooked the iron key from his sturdy leather belt. 'What's going on? Who's making all that racket in there?'

Enid looked at him with her arms folded across her chest. 'I don't think we're going to have to call on Sir Isaac to answer that question, are we now, Barty?'

'It's me . . . Joe,' said a voice from behind the door. 'Stop mucking about, Barty, and let me out. I'm thirsty.'

'Joe Dings, is that you?' enquired the constable, knowing the answer but stalling because he realised that all sorts of questions were going to be asked once that door was unlocked, most notably by Joe himself. It had been nearly six weeks since he had been locked up for the night. It was no wonder he was thirsty.

Joe's wife Peg had pushed her way to the front of the crowd. Enid put her arm round her. 'Can't we just leave him in there, Barty? I've really enjoyed having the house to myself, and not getting thumped when he's had a bucketful of ale. Give me that key and I'll chuck it in the pond so no one finds it.

'Come on, it stinks in here.' Joe hammered on the door and the villagers, as one, took a step back.

'We've got to let him out, Peg,' said Barty. 'But goodness knows what we're going to tell him.'

'You leave it to me,' said Enid. 'I'll have a little word with him.' The constable unlocked the door and pulled it open. Joe emerged, blinking at the daylight and wondering why his exit from the gaol had attracted a crowd. It hadn't before. 'What's going on? Why are you all looking at me like that?'

Enid stepped forward and put a hand on his brawny shoulder as Parson Perkins arrived on the scene, Bible in hand. 'Is it OK if the three of us go to the church for a little talk?' she asked the clergyman. 'I'd rather go to the inn,' said Joe, but Enid was already steering him in the direction of St Martin's, with Perkins close behind. A few paces further back was most of the rest of the village, also walking in the direction of the church. When they got there, the parson closed the door, leaving the villagers milling about in the graveyard.

Enid and Joe sat on a pew at the front of the nave while the parson perched on the steps leading to the altar. He began. 'What we are about to tell you will sound far-fetched, although the village has become used to strange ideas in recent weeks. You will recall, Joe, that Constable Bartleby locked you up for the night for being drunk.'

'And disorderly,' chipped in Enid.

'Of course I remember. I wasn't that far gone,' said Joe.

'But that was nearly six weeks ago. When he came to let you out the morning after he arrested you, the gaol was empty,' said Perkins.

'You'd vanished. Totally not there. Barty was beside himself, poor man,' Edith added.

Perkins told Joe that his disappearance had coincided with the arrival in the village of a friend of Master Calvert, and when the two of them left this morning he had reappeared in the gaol. Joe slowly released a smile. 'Come off it,' he said. 'I was in the Rising Sun last night, had a few and tripped over my breeches. If I hadn't had anything to eat for six weeks I'd be dead, wouldn't I? This is the village playing a joke on poor old Joe, ain't it? It's a good one, mind.'

'I swear on this book that it is not a joke,' said the parson, tapping his Bible.

'It's not, Joe. You've been gone from us,' Edith said, putting a friendly hand on his knee and then quickly removing it and wiping it on her apron. 'It's a mystery, and even Master Calvert with his clever brain could not provide us with an answer.'

'Did Peg miss me?'

'She did not, Joe,' said Enid with a bluntness that surprised even the parson. 'Would you mind leaving us reverend, so that I can offer Joe some frankness. I think I need to take this opportunity to explain a few things to him.' The parson seemed more than happy to comply, rising quickly from his step and exiting the church. The sound of animated chattering filtered into the building as the door opened and closed. Joe remained seated with his head in his hands, trying to absorb what he had been told.

'I'm going to be blunt, Joe. I've never seen your unfortunate wife happier these past few weeks. No cuts and bruises, she's had a spring in her step and a smile on her face. She thought – hoped – you had gone for good. That you had died, even. You have tormented that poor woman for long enough, so I am going to give you a warning.'

'What sort of warning.' A belligerence had returned to Joe's demeanour but it quickly subsided when he looked into Enid's eyes.

'If you lay another hand on Peg, if you cause trouble in the inn, if you steal from anyone, if you hurt anyone, we will drive you out of Bigby so that we can enjoy the peace that we had while you were gone. We will tolerate you no longer, Joe Dings. Change or be gone.'

Enid rose and walked slowly out of the church, trying to control her breathing so as not to show how scared she had been delivering her lecture. Joe remained where he was for two hours and when he left the church the villagers had dispersed. He trudged home and knocked gently on the door. Peg opened it silently and stood back to let him in.

They stopped every few miles to give Solomon a rest and some water, and as dusk fell Seth turned the cart into the entrance of a ramshackle farm. 'Don't let the appearance of this place fool you,' he told the scientists. 'These are good people who make a decent living here. The untidy nature of their buildings is deliberate, to deter unsavoury types who may wish to take what they've worked so hard for.'

'Are they expecting us?' asked Jax.

'They are not,' replied Seth, 'as you can see.'

When they looked towards the wonky-roofed farmhouse a wiry, angry-looking man was standing defiantly, pointing a musket at them. Another gun lay ready for use on a nearby barrel. Beside him was a woman they assumed was his wife, tall with a muscular physique, grasping a sword in one hand and a long dagger in the other. A pirate would have looked less menacing.

Seth pulled Solomon to a stop about 50 yards from them. 'Good evening, Joshua. Good evening, Maria. It's me, Seth the blacksmith from Bigby. May I approach you please?'

They saw the man and woman talking to one another. 'Who did you say it was?' barked the woman. Seth got down from the cart and raised his hands. It was getting dark so he walked a few paces towards them. 'Seth the blacksmith from Bigby,' he repeated. 'I have come to ask permission to spend the night at your farm. We require no food or accommodation, just your consent to rest in a field for the night.'

'Is that you, Seth?' shouted the woman. 'And is that Solomon? Come closer.'

Seth gestured Calvert and Jax to remain on the cart and walked towards the farmers, keeping his hands raised to show that he was unarmed. 'Put your hands down, big man. You and your companions are welcome here,' said Joshua, lowering his weapon. 'Let's put Solomon in the stables with some grub, and provide sustenance for you good folks.'

Seth beckoned for the others to join him and Calvert took hold of Solomon's reins and led him forward. Maria put her fingers to her lips and produced a piercing whistle that caused a strong-looking teenage boy to sprint from the house and take charge of the horse without a word being spoken. 'Thank you Edmund,' said Seth before introducing the scientists to the farmer and his wife. He explained that he was accompanying them to the Tower of London for an appointment with the renowned natural philosopher, Sir Isaac Newton.

'They're not criminals are they, Seth?' asked Maria. 'Only he has caused a lot of people to be hanged since the king put him in charge of our money . . . rogues like clippers and counterfeiters who make coins worthless to hard-working folk. Good on him, I say.'

'They are good honest people,' Seth told them. 'Master Calvert here has done much for Bigby and we felt it was our duty to help him and Miss Jax in their mission to seek the assistance of Sir Isaac on a matter of great importance to them.'

Maria ushered them all into the warmth of the farmhouse, where a fire crackled brightly in the grate and the smell of stew drifted from a simmering pot. The main room could not have been more different from the tatty, but carefully staged, exterior of the building. It was well furnished with abundant cushioned chairs, a large table, a home-made dresser, and window and door drapes. Smooth flagstones covered the floor.

Jax took it all in and said, 'You have a beautiful home, Maria. Thank you for your kind welcome.'

'Yes, indeed,' said Calvert. 'However, we don't wish to inconvenience you. We will let you get on with your supper and, with your permission, will go and join Solomon in his stable for a night's rest. We have food with us.' Seth smiled at Maria, knowing that he and his travelling companions would be invited to join them at their table.

'I'll forgive you for saying that, Master Calvert, because you don't know us. You are most welcome to join us in our mutton stew and then make your bed in our hay store, which is warm and dry and home to very few mice.'

'Thank goodness,' said Jax. 'The smell from your cooking pot set my mouth watering the moment we walked through the door.'

Edmund, who was about 14 but had the build of a well-fed grown man, walked through the door, having settled Solomon into his stall. Seth introduced him to the scientists and told him who they were going to meet. Edmund asked Calvert to tell him about the great man.

As Maria ladled chunks of meat, chopped carrots and parsnips into wooden bowls, her husband brought two loaves to the table and invited their guests to tear into it, which they did with enthusiasm. 'So, who is he, this Newton chap?' asked Edmund, dipping bread into the thick gravy in his bowl.

Calvert spooned a piece of meat into his mouth while he considered where to start and Jax jumped in to set the ball rolling. 'I think the best way of explaining why this man is so important is to describe him as a solver of mysteries,' she said. 'For example, have you ever considered why an apple falls from a tree to the ground?'

'Because its stem breaks when it's ripe, of course. Or when

the wind blows strong. It's obvious,' said Edmund.

'But why doesn't it rise upwards when its stem breaks.'

'Because it's heavy?'

'But a feather is light, and that still falls downwards, even when there is not a breath of wind in the air,' said Jax.

'Well, that'll be gravity then,' said Edmund with a cheeky smile. 'Sir Isaac described it in his Principia some three decades ago. Have you heard of it?'

Joshua and Maria smiled at one another. 'The boy is clever,' said the farmer. 'He gets it from his mother, who is a great reader of books. Me, I just think it's all squiggles.'

Jax had put down her spoon and sat there with her mouth open. 'The Principia is in Latin, is it not? I don't believe there is an English version.'

'Ma and I both read Latin,' the boy said nonchalantly. 'And Greek also, but I like that less.'

'That's truly amazing, Edmund,' said Calvert. Jax and I were in full-time education until we were well into our twenties and neither of us can read much Latin. You're a remarkable young man.'

Maria explained. 'My father was a classics scholar at Cambridge and poured knowledge into his only child at every opportunity. And I have done the same with our son. We have many books here but keep them from inquisitive eyes. We are, after all, humble farmers scratching a living from the land,' she said knowingly. 'There are few opportunities for women to educate themselves fully and when I met Joshua at the Cambridge fair many years ago I fell in love with this great, stringy lump and moved here to be with him on his family's farm,' she said, grasping Joshua's arm affectionately.

'I hope to go to university when I am a little older, and Ma is preparing me for that,' said the boy. 'May I ask what it is you need from Sir Isaac?' His mother said it was none of their business. 'But, Ma, we are sitting with people who are about to discuss something with one of the greatest men of our age. Are you not curious?'

'Of course I am, but it's not polite to be nosy.'

Calvert glanced at Jax and told Edmund that they wished to discuss an experiment with Newton and their colleague. That they were natural philosophers like him, and that others would be gathering at the Tower to assist. Edmund leaned forward eagerly with his elbows on the table. 'What is the nature of this experiment? If it is secret we promise not to tell anyone. We are good at keeping secrets, aren't we Pa?'

'Keep me out of this. My snout isn't as long as yours, Ed.'

Jax looked at Calvert, who nodded to her. 'We are interested in the theory of time travel. Whether it is possible to find a way to travel between one age and another. Sir Isaac's remarkable mind and insatiable curiosity enables him to explore all manner of phenomena, and we would like to see if he can help us to develop our theories.'

'Is that why you have that shiny box on your cart? Is it part of your experiment?'

Maria reacted strongly and told Edmund to cease.

'You're a bright young man,' said Calvert slowly. 'We are taking to London some equipment that we have created and that we believe might be of interest to Newton.'

'The metal is most unusual. Did you help to make this, Seth?' said the boy, continuing what Calvert and Jax were now starting to believe was an inquisition. The blacksmith looked surprised to suddenly be included in the conversation. 'Well, erm, let me just say that my forge and workshop were at Master Calvert's disposal.'

Edmund sat back and looked sceptically at the three visitors in turn. 'Very well, I am sorry if I have pressed this matter too far but I have never before considered that travelling from one time to another might be possible. For what it's worth, I think the whole idea is nuts. If it was possible, then why have we not already been visited by people from the future?' And with that, the boy tucked into his meal.

Suffolk & Essex – 1719

Allstein and his fellow passengers ran out of conversation after only a few miles and he settled into reading his book while Hooke's supporter snored and the two women tittered and gossiped, mainly about potential husbands. The road was rutted for long stretches and he welcomed the opportunity to exercise his muscles and joints whenever they stopped to feed or change the horses at an inn. He made sure he was first off the coach when they reached Colchester for their overnight stop, keen to make sure he had a bed. The landlord told him that the only room available was for two people and that he would have to share. He reluctantly agreed in the hope that nobody else would require the other bed. He was unlucky. His room-mate that night was Hooke's irascible and free-snoring friend. The two women shared the only other available room, which they had reserved in advance.

Allstein was in the bar eating a dinner comprising a large

pork chop and boiled vegetables. As the landlord brought him a tankard of ale his grumpy room-mate slumped down into the seat opposite him and asked for the same. He held out a hand across the table. Allstein put down his knife and fork and shook it. 'I wish to apologise Master . . .'

'Allstein . . . Doctor Allstein. Apologise for what, Master . . .'

'Podger, sir. Crispin Podger. For my disgraceful behaviour at the start of our journey today. By way of explanation, but not excuse, for my outburst was inexcusable, I would just say that I am a poor traveller, loathing long journeys and constantly in fear of what perils we might encounter on our lawless roads.'

He looked at Allstein's food, eagerly anticipating the arrival of his own. 'Please continue with your food, sir. I have no wish to come between you and that delicious-looking repast.' Allstein took a swig of his ale and cut off another chunk of meat. 'There's no need for an apology Master Podger. I too detest long journeys and I regret my mention of Newton's name before such a fervent advocate of the esteemed polymath Robert Hooke.' He forked the meat into his mouth. 'I am no friend of Sir Isaac, sir, but as a natural philosopher myself I felt I could not pass up the opportunity to accept the invitation of my former colleague to meet the gentleman. I knew that Newton, Hooke and Leibnitz were bitter rivals and had I been invited to meet either of these other great men I would have done so with eagerness.' Podger's meal and ale arrived and he polished off both with noisy enthusiasm well before Allstein had cleared his plate. He waved at the landlord, who refilled his tankard from a large earthenware jug.

'I knew Hooke most of my adult life and he was a decent,

hard-working and honest man with an astounding intellect,' he said after Allstein had finished eating. 'After Hooke died in 1703, Newton went to great pains to pour scorn on much of his work and it is said that he was responsible for the destruction of the man's only portrait. It demonstrated a considerable jealousy and, indeed, meanness of spirit that does not seem to have tainted Newton to any great extent. Mere mention of his name brings about a fury in me, and I apologise once more for my outburst.'

Allstein realised that he knew very little about the background to Newton's animosity towards Hooke. He could think of no comparisons in 21st century science, which he considered a generally collaborative affair, with scientists from different countries often sharing knowledge. Well, up to a point. Nobody wanted their potential Nobel award being shared too thinly, which was perhaps why he and his colleagues had taken a cloak and dagger approach to their particular experiment.

The passengers gathered early the next morning to begin the second leg of their journey to London. They were joined inside the coach by two more people, a Mr and Mrs Quince. It was dark, cold and misty as they set off, the coach-and-four rattling through the streets of Colchester before arriving at the main road that would hopefully see them in the capital by nightfall. They were 20 minutes or so into their journey, and just concluding formal introductions, when the coach slewed to a sudden halt on a narrow section of road lined on each side by thick hedges.

Allstein heard shouting and lowered the window to see what was happening. Two mounted figures, masked and dressed in dusty black cloaks and tricorn hats, had appeared in the road. They aimed pistols at the driver and his assistant, who had been too slow to raise the musket that lay across his lap. The men ordered the passengers out of the coach. Allstein alighted first and helped the three women down. Podger was gripped by fear and remained glued to his seat. 'Come, sir, if we do as these gentlemen ask no harm will come to us,' Allstein said to him in as calm a voice as he could muster. The two outside passengers and five from the inside of the coach had made their exit, Abigail Totness and Dora Gray looking more concerned about getting their fine shoes dirty on the muddy road than they were about being robbed. 'This is disgusting,' shouted Miss Totness defiantly. 'They're completely ruined.'

'Get the fat one out or I'll start shooting the horses,' one of the robbers said. Allstein took him to be the leader. Beneath his cloak he wore a scarlet military tunic with yellow edging and brass buttons, some of which were missing. He looked to be in good control of his horse considering he was holding a flintlock pistol in each hand. The man was stout and may have been in his fifties, Allstein thought. The other rider was slimmer and younger, and his horse more skittish, turning this way and that in the road. He too sported a pair of pistols, which meant that they had four shots between them. Allstein knew that flintlocks were not particularly accurate over ten metres, while muskets like the coachman's had a decent level of accuracy over 20 metres. He was trying to calculate the odds of their survival.

Allstein looked into the door of the coach and offered a hand to Podger. 'You must get down, sir, or someone could be badly hurt.' The frightened man looked at the scientist, took his hand and rose from his seat, joining his fellow passengers in the road.

'Let's get on with this,' barked the leading rider. Take this bag and fill it with your jewellery and cash. If I suspect that anyone is holding anything back, one of you will be sorry.' Allstein stepped forward to take the canvas tote, seeing it as a potential opportunity to drag the man from his horse. 'Not you,' said the rider, 'the pretty one.' Miss Totness stomped forward and grabbed the bag. 'I hope you hang for this. These shoes cost a small fortune.'

'Did they indeed? I'll have those too then. Put 'em in the bag.'

Miss Totness looked distraught. 'But my stockings!' she shrieked.

'Want me to take those too?' asked the rider with a sneer. The girl awkwardly removed her shoes, holding on to the arm of her companion, and put them in the bag, which she passed to Podger. He emptied his pockets nervously and whimpered softly to himself. While all this was going on Allstein noticed that one of the men who had been riding on the outside of the coach had disappeared. He was presumably in cahoots with the robbers. But as each of the passengers removed their valuables and placed them in the bag the missing man emerged from the bushes behind the second rider and plunged a knife deep into his thigh. His horse reared, both pistols exploded into the air and he fell to the ground, screaming in pain.

The lead robber looked round and aimed a gun at his partner's assailant but before he could fire Allstein flew across the muddy road and was upon him, dragging him from his saddle and down to the ground. He punched the man twice about the head and the flintlocks fell from his hand. The driver and his assistant dropped down from their seats and helped to subdue the robbers. Miss Totness marched across the mud and kicked the leader hard in the face. 'You do not steal a lady's shoes,' she bellowed.

Allstein gathered up the men's weapons and put them by his seat in the coach. He didn't want to be caught out if they were stopped again. He thanked and shook the hand of the man who attacked the smaller of the two robbers. Their saviour identified himself as Nicholas Drake and said he and his brother Simeon were on their way to London to join the army. Allstein said the country was in safe hands with such brave men. 'So brave,' gushed Abigail Totness thrusting herself at the young man and planting a lustful kiss on his lips.

The coach driver and his assistant trussed up the robbers and tied them to the rear-facing seat at the back of the coach where the army recruits had sat. The other passengers insisted that the two young men should join them inside for the rest of the journey. The highwaymen's horses were tied to the back of the coach, which moved off smartly with everyone feeling they had had a lucky escape.

The attempted robbery and disarming of the culprits had taken less than half an hour, and not a coach, cart or individual had passed them in that time. Miss Gray surrendered a woollen scarf to bind the wound of the stabbed man, who was pale and clearly in a great deal of pain. When they reached Witham, 15 miles away, the robbers were hauled down from their seat and handed over to the local constable. They were immediately thrown into the town's gaol, the Witham cage, to await a visit from a justice of the peace. Once he was untied, the older man scrambled to the side of his companion, who had lost a lot of blood and was close to passing out. 'Get some help for my boy,' he growled. 'He is but 16. He will die without assistance.'

The gaoler looked at him without a morsel of compassion

and said, 'He'll die anyway. The justice will see to that.' Allstein knew that both would be hanged.

They left the robbers' horses at the local coaching inn and clattered on their way, the mist still curling about them and silence swamping the passengers, who passed around the bag so that they could retrieve their items. They all realised that it had been a close shave, and that their journey was not yet done.

'They were a father and son, it seems. I wonder what desperation drove them to such measures,' said Miss Gray, attempting to slip her feet back into her mud-encrusted shoes.

'Not desperation. Greed,' said Podger. 'These are lawless times and travellers offer rich pickings for men who are prepared to risk the noose for their brazen actions'. He pointed at the brothers. 'These young men deserve our undying gratitude, as do you Dr Allstein, for your calmness and swiftness of thought. We are in your debt, sirs.'

The passengers, driver and guard were on edge for the rest of the journey, chatting nervously and alert for any sudden threat. But as the gloomy day turned to a chilly dusk they entered the capital, making their way along Whitechapel and their first stop at Aldgate, part of London's medieval wall, where Allstein was to exit. His fellow passengers, who were getting off the coach elsewhere in the city, bade him a heartfelt farewell. Podger leaned forward and shook his hand vigorously. 'Whatever my feelings regarding Newton, I hope your meeting with him is everything you hope it to be, my good friend. It has been a pleasure to travel with you,' he said.

The driver tossed Allstein's bag down from the roof of the coach and expressed his appreciation with a nod and a smile. Allstein paused as the coach pulled away, mentally steeling himself for a brief but potentially hazardous walk through one of the world's smelliest, noisiest and most dangerous cities. Every aspect of the place attacked his senses. Emaciated people slumped in alleys like bundles of discarded rags appeared invisible to those walking past them clad in colourful silks, velvet and fine woollen cloth. The rattle of coaches and carts competed with the shrill cries of street vendors, assailing ears more accustomed to the gentle clopping of farm horses and the calling of birds in his country idyll.

Allstein walked through the Aldgate arch and attempted to locate where he would be in the London he would recognise. He guessed it would be between Boots and the Nationwide Building Society on the corner of Jewry Street, which led down to the River Thames. But he couldn't miss the most prominent landmark of them all. Looking south, there was the thrilling sight of the keep of the Tower of London, the 11th century White Tower. He headed towards it, and the meeting with Sir Isaac Newton and Professor William Wilberforce Jenks that could get him home.

Lincolnshire – 1719

Thomas Cooper was cold. Nettie had found him some clothes that had belonged to a gardener who had died a few months back, comprising boots, breeches, shirt, waistcoat and a thin woollen overjacket.

The two women hadn't believed a word of his story about explosions and quantum physics and had risen from the dining table, their looks of amusement replaced by ones of fury. 'First you insult our intelligence with nonsense about herring and now you expect us to believe this frankly deranged tale about coming from the future,' said Lady Muckleborough.

'But . . .' he said, but got no further.

'FELLOWES!' she bellowed. 'FELLOWES! Throw this man out of my house now and give him a kick up the pants for his insolence.' The footman entered in his usual calm manner and simply nodded to Cooper while holding open the door. He knew then that his luck had run out. He got up, thanked Her Ladyship for her hospitality, and followed Fellowes out of the room. Nettie rummaged in a cupboard to find clothes for him to change into and rustled up bread, cheese and a leather flask of wine, all wrapped in a muslin cloth bag tied up with string. All he needed now, he thought, was a pole to hang the bag on and a black cat to accompany him on his trek to wherever he was going. The clothes felt itchy after the fine apparel he had been used to, and he hoped that this was due to the roughness of the material rather than an infestation of some sort. He tried not to think about it.

Fellowes and a couple of gardeners accompanied him to the gates of the estate and instead of giving him a kick up the pants as instructed the footman shook his hand and discreetly gave him a pouch of coins. 'From Miss Creighton, sir. She bids you a safe journey.'

'Thank you, Fellowes, and thank Miss Creighton when the opportunity arises. It's been good to know you,' said Cooper, suddenly feeling uncertain about his future. This was England, but not as he knew it.

'You're welcome, sir. Meeting you has been . . . an education.'

The road beyond the gates was little more than a lane that

might just allow two coaches to pass. The surface was compressed mud.

'Lincoln is that way, Master Cooper,' said Fellowes pointing to the right. 'Good luck on the next stage of your adventures.' He and the gardeners didn't pause to wave him off. When Cooper looked over his shoulder a few paces down the road, they were already making their way along the drive to the hall.

The day was overcast and chilly, and Cooper fastened up his jacket. The bag of provisions was bulky and difficult to carry, so he scoured the hedgerow to find a branch suitable for balancing the bag on his shoulder in the way that Dick Whittington did in all the illustrations he had ever seen of London's most famous Lord Mayor. He needed to get a move on. Fellowes had told him it would take about three hours to walk to Lincoln and he wanted to get there in good time to find somewhere to stay.

As he walked he inspected the copper and silver coins the footman had handed him. Some were quite heavy and the denomination of each was difficult to determine. And he had no idea how much anything cost.

He had travelled about a mile when he heard the trundling of wheels behind him. He stopped and turned to see a small cart pulled slowly by a single horse. Holding the reins was an elderly man, bundled up in layers of warm-looking clothing and wearing a rough cloth hat. He appeared to see Cooper but didn't stop. The scientist trotted beside him. 'Are you going to Lincoln?' he asked.

'I am. Hop on the back if you want a ride. I'm not stopping,' said the man without taking his rheumy eyes from the road.

Cooper thanked him and tossed his bag and pole on the back of the cart before jumping on and finding himself in the company of two large dead pigs, each with a vivid gash across its throat. He touched the bristly skin of one of them. It was still warm. Suppressing his 21st century revulsion, he snuggled up between them to try and take the chill from his body. A few minutes later a blanket was flung at him by the driver. 'Your teeth are a clattering. It's annoying,' the man said. Cooper thanked him and wrapped it around his body.

'I'm a stranger here,' shouted Cooper over the noise of the wheels. 'Where would I find cheap accommodation in Lincoln, my friend?' There was no reply. 'Did you hear me, sir?'

'I'm thinking.' It went on for several minutes. 'Mrs Crust has a lodging house off Steep Hill. That'll be the cheapest. Or there's the Ram in Bailgate.'

'How much might a bed for the night cost me?' Cooper asked through still-chattering teeth. There was no reply.

'Are you thinking?' he asked.

'Yes,' said the driver, before eventually offering, 'Perhaps thruppence at Mrs Crust's, though she don't change the sheets much, or double at the inn, which will be cleaner. But not much.'

Cooper looked in the pouch again to see if he could tell how much each coin was worth. It looked like Miss Crichton had been quite generous, perhaps feeling guilty that her interrogation had resulted in his expulsion from Muckleborough Hall. Then again, she didn't look like the type to feel much guilt for anyone. He guessed that the big, brown, chunky coins that looked like cartwheels were pennies and the smaller brown ones were probably halfpennies or farthings. There were also some silver coins in the pouch but he had no idea how much it all added up to as there appeared to be no denominations surrounding the chubby-cheeked portrait of King George. He didn't think it would be wise to ask the cart driver in case he decided to bash in the head of his freeloading passenger. Cooper tucked the purse into the deep pocket of his jacket and snuggled down into his blanket.

After a few miles of silence he asked the driver if there was a market in Lincoln. He waited patiently for a reply. 'If there ain't, I've killed them pigs for nothing,' he said. 'I'm late. That's why I'm hurryin',' he added some time later. Cooper hated to think what speed they would be doing if he was taking it easy. 'What time will we get there?'

Sparrows conversed raucously in the hedgerows. The wind coaxed a crisp rustling from the trees. The cartwheels clunked over cold mud and stone. 'Mid-morning,' said the driver.

Cooper judged that it was at about that time that they reached the outskirts of Lincoln, although the twin towers of the city's magnificent cathedral had already dominated the skyline for an hour or more. Cooper perched on one of the pigs, blanket draped around his shoulders, to get a better view as they made their way past homes and shops that appeared more prosperous than he had been expecting. Lincoln looked like a well-to-do place in 1719.

As they reached the market square, Cooper got down from the cart and handed the blanket back to the driver, who looked at him for the first time. 'You have an aura of disappointment about you, my friend. If you can afford it, settle yourself at the Ram tonight,' he said. Cooper dipped into his purse and offered the man what he believed was a penny. 'Keep it. I've a feeling you'll need it.'

As they spoke two hefty men in aprons were hauling the pigs from the cart and carrying them to a covered stall at the edge of the noisy market. Within minutes one of them was butchering one of the carcasses on a sturdy wooden trestle, with customers milling around him. The other approached the driver and handed over a bag which Cooper assumed contained money. 'You're late, Jacob. I've lost custom.'

The driver took the purse and picked up his reins without looking at the butcher. 'My apologies, Jonah, but my wife died this morning. Please excuse me if I don't take an ale with you today.' With an almost imperceptible movement of the reins he turned his cart around and slowly left the market. Cooper and the butcher looked blankly at one another. 'I'm sorry, Jacob. I'm so sorry,' shouted Jonah across the hubbub. He returned to his stall and spoke quietly to the other butcher, who briefly paused his hacking and sawing to look in the direction of the departing cart.

Cooper was rooted to the spot, dumbstruck, for several seconds until he was nudged in the back by a young man rushing past with a basket full of loaves on his head. 'Excuse me but which way is Bailgate?' he asked him before he could get too far away. The man flung out an arm in the direction of a road between two shops and shouted, 'Up Steep Hill'.

The town was so busy that Cooper's presence, with his stick and parcel over his shoulder, attracted no attention whatsoever. There was no missing Steep Hill, which lived up to its name and left him gasping for breath as he reached the top and came across the Ram Inn.

The place was crowded and fuggy from the smoke of clay pipes clamped in the jaws of half the customers. He suddenly felt grateful that he had not been thrown out of Muckleborough Hall in the good clothes he had been wearing. The old gardener's clothes he had been given allowed him to blend in with the various shades of brown, black and grey working wear that filled the bar. He had determined to make a confident entrance, and as he stepped through the door not an eyebrow was raised. One or two men even nodded as though they recognised him.

There was no bar, just a long table on which stood large jugs, pewter tankards and rough pottery cups. A pretty young woman stood by it, looking hawk-like for empty containers to fill and money to take. She had seen Cooper walk in. She waved an empty tankard at him and he nodded. As she walked towards him with his ale, he tucked himself into a corner and perched by a shelf which ran along one of the wood-panelled walls. The woman handed over his tankard with a broad smile. 'Well, you're a good looking one, and no mistake,' she said in a manner that his mother would have described as saucy. 'Where have you sprung from?'

He took a gulp of ale. 'Muckleborough Hall. I was a . . . gardener there for a while.'

'Ooh. Bet you've got strong hands,' she said, moving in closely and keeping her eyes locked on his.

'Maud! Get back to work,' bellowed a voice, presumably belonging to the landlord.

'Shut it, you old goat, I'm being nice to a new customer,' she rifled back. 'He just happens to be bloody gorgeous,' she added quietly.

Cooper threw back some more ale and said it had been a while since he had been to Lincoln. Could she tell him how much the ale was and did the inn have a room for the night? Her eyes lit up when he asked about the room.

'Maud!'

'Ha'penny for the ale and fourpence for the room. I'll come and tuck you in,' she said with a broad grin as she turned to resume her duties. Cooper wondered if it was too late to try and find Mrs Crust's. Maud refilled his tankard a couple of times, and as market day wound down the bar slowly cleared. Cooper sat at an empty table and began to wonder what the future might hold for him. He realised he had enjoyed a cloistered life in his short time at the hall but once again he was alone in a world he didn't understand. He didn't know how much money he had. He didn't even know whether inns like the Ram had toilets, which he now needed quite urgently.

Eagle-eyed Maud saw him fidgeting. 'The privy's out the back, handsome man,' she shouted, nodding towards a door. His nose directed him to a small shed, where he found a heavily-stained wooden seat resting on a bucket - and thought it was the most welcome sight he had every clapped eyes on.

The bar was almost empty when he returned to his table, and Maud was perched on a stool beside it. He sat down on a pine bench against the wall. 'You're no gardener,' she said. 'You've got the hands of a priest, and not one of the naughty ones we get in here, whose hands always seem to go where they shouldn't. What's your story, mister?'

Cooper looked at his hands, which had grown creamy smooth during his time at Muckleborough Hall and agreed that he had never lifted a trowel in his life. 'I got lost after arriving in Lincolnshire and arrived at Muckleborough Hall injured and in a confused state. Her Ladyship kindly took me in, got staff to tend to my wounds, fed me, and when I was better she sent me on my way with a little money and these clothes,' he said. He had been considering what to say to Maud throughout the afternoon.

'The truth is,' he lied, 'I was attacked and as a result I've lost my memory. I can remember nothing of my past. Everything I see and hear is unfamiliar, and a little frightening. I don't even know the value of the coins in my purse.'

She grasped his hand across the table with a look of genuine concern on her face. 'You poor devil. I have heard tell of such a thing and it must be truly terrifying to have no recollection of your history. Do you know your name?'

'I think it might be Tom,' he said meekly, warming to the role of amnesiac, which in hindsight might have been a better ploy at the hall.

Maud manoeuvred herself to block any nosy customers' view of the table and asked him to show her his coins, which he did cautiously, one by one. She identified each one and told him what he could buy with them. 'You have nearly five pounds in that pouch of yours. A fortune. Don't go out tonight. People have been murdered for a good deal less than that.' Her manner had changed from jokingly flirtatious to seriously concerned.ey

She showed him to his attic room, which contained two narrow beds, each with a lumpy mattress and a grey woollen blanket. Wide wooden boards creaked beneath their feet and a small rug, a token attempt to brighten up the room, sat at an odd angle, not quite in the middle of the floor. 'Don't lift that,' Maud said, pointing at it and heading for the door. 'Seriously, I mean it.'

Alone, Cooper sat heavily on one of the beds, and wondered what the hell was to become of him.

Cambridge – 2030

The postcode they had been given took Angela and Joel to a tidy but unremarkable street in King's Lynn, where most of the houses, including the detached one at number 42, looked to have been built in the 1950s. It had a neat front garden with a square of lawn and narrow borders of roses and other plants that neither of them could identify. They sat in Angela's Cortina observing the house for about an hour but there wasn't even the twitch of a curtain to interest them.

'Balls to this,' said Angela suddenly. 'They might be on holiday. They might be dead. Let's ring the bell.' She got out of the car and Joel followed her to the double-glazed front door. Angela nodded to the bell and Joel pressed the button. 'What are we going to say?' he asked.

'No idea, we'll wing it.'

Joel had been expecting to see someone techie. Someone a bit geeky, like himself. A gamer, perhaps, with indoor pallor and twitching thumbs. What he saw was a slender woman in her sixties dressed in fitness lycra and trainers. She was putting on a light jacket and had a rolled-up exercise mat at her feet. She looked at them, waiting for them to explain who they were and what they wanted. 'Well, come on then. I have a class to get to.'

Angela was flustered. Joel jumped in. 'We're so sorry to bother you but do you know Tom Cooper?' he asked as the woman stepped outside and closed the door behind her. 'The comedian?' she said. 'Well, I know of him, of course.' She had her car keys in her hand now and was heading for the navy blue Audi TT convertible in her drive. She tossed the exercise mat onto the back seat and got behind the steering wheel, winding down the window. 'Look, if you want to save my soul or sign me up to something, you can bugger off. If it's important, I'll be back in an hour or so and I'll make you a cup of coffee.' She wound up the window, reversed out of the drive and drove away.

'You were quiet, Ange,' Joel said. But she hadn't heard. She was trying to see through the Venetian blinds in the bay window. 'You can't do that. There might be someone else in the house. Husband, kids. It looks dodgy.'

She ignored him. 'Try that gate. We might be able to get round the back.'

'No. Anyway, it's probably locked. Let's go and come back in an hour. We might even get a piece of cake.'

Angela tried the gate herself and then kicked it. 'I'm not leaving. She might come back sooner and I don't want to miss her,' she said. 'We know that parcels have been sent to this address, so we'll wait in the car.'

After an hour and a half Joel's stomach started rumbling. He looked in the glove compartment and found a tin of boiled sweets which looked like it had never been opened. The multi-coloured contents were stuck together and it took him ten minutes to prize a couple of them loose with his front door key. He offered Angela one and when she declined with a look of disgust, he popped them both into his mouth.

'Here she comes,' said Angela, looking in the rear view mirror. She waited until the woman had parked and hurried up to her as she got to her door. If she tried to shut it, Angela had decided that she would put her foot in it.

'Sorry I'm late,' said the woman breezily. 'Got chatting to the girls afterwards. Coffee? I think I've got some scones, if you're interested. Come in. The lounge is in there, make yourselves at home.'

The large, comfortable room was expensively furnished with two modern sofas and a pair of easy chairs. It wasn't a matching suite, everything was different but in complementary styles that Angela felt reflected exquisite taste. A Scandinavian-style display unit bore a collection of oriental pottery and carvings that would not have looked out of place in a gallery or museum. Joel picked up a piece of blue-grey porcelain that was as light as air.

'That's 350 years old, so please don't break it,' said the woman calmly, entering with a tray bearing a cafetiere, three mugs and a heap of fruit scones. Joel replaced it carefully and joined Angela on one of the sofas. The woman placed the tray on a low glass-topped table and poured the coffee. She settled back in one of the chairs. 'So, Angela and Joel, what can I do for you?' she said.

'How . . . ?' asked Angela.

' . . . do I know who you are?' said the woman. 'Do you know who I am?'

'No, we don't,' admitted Joel.

'You could have looked me up in the electoral register. It's not hard. You found this address.'

'Damn. We didn't think of that. But how do you know us?' he asked, reaching for his coffee.

'Work it out. You're both smart. Milk?'

Angela looked closely at her for the first time. She had shoulder length auburn hair which made her look younger than the 60-something she probably was. Good cheekbones on an intelligent face, and a confidence that showed she was used to being in charge. 'You got my name from the numberplate on my car,' said Angela. 'I'm assuming you have the resources to do that. And you probably got Joel's from Colin at the Post Office or from colleagues at the science park.'

'Easier than that, I'm afraid. It's on the lanyard round his neck.'

Angela and Joel looked sheepishly at one another. 'We're rubbish at this, aren't we, Ange?'

'We've got this far, which is more than the police or the spooks did, so not rubbish at all. Are you going to introduce yourself, or are you going to make us look you up in the electoral register?' she said.

'Mrs Carter,' she said, sipping her coffee. 'I'm afraid you're wrong about the authorities. They have been here, and they have taken away a great many of the external disc drives you're interested in.'

Angela leaned forward. 'A great many . . . but not all of them?'

'Who am I talking to here?' asked Mrs Carter. 'Colleagues trying to find out what happened to their friends or scientists looking for data that will enable them to replicate what they did? The two aren't necessarily the same. If it's the latter, you could just be trying to capitalise on years of work by a dedicated team of people, but without the catastrophic end result.'

Angela looked cross. 'I saw that building, with those five people inside it, just disappear. I want to know why and I want to know what happened to them. I didn't know any of them particularly well.'

'Although you do have a picture of Tom Cooper on your phone,' said Joel.

'But the authorities, as you call them, have never seemed

interested in the people who were involved in this,' said Angela. They just want to know what they were working on and what they did wrong. For them it seems like it's just a health and safety matter. These five scientists died and no one seems to care about them.'

'But did they die?' asked Mrs Carter, placing her mug on the table and resting her hands in her lap. 'How do we know they died?'

'What!' shouted Joel and Angela in unison. They looked at one another in amazement and then looked at this strange, assured woman sporting a Mona Lisa-style smile. 'What do you mean, but did they die?' asked Joel. 'If they're not dead, where the hell are they?'

Mrs Carter stopped smiling and said, 'Perhaps the question we should be asking is when are they?'

'Oh, for crying out loud, this is doing my head in. I'm just a simple astrophysicist. What on earth is going on,' Joel said, putting his head in his hands.

'Let's start by asking ourselves what they were working on,' said Mrs Cooper. 'A secretive little experiment in the field of quantum physics regarding wave-particle duality.'

'What?' exclaimed Joel yet again.

Angela looked at him. 'It has been theorised for a while that quite large molecules, we're talking a few thousand atoms, can exist in two places at once in what physicists call quantum superposition. It's based on the idea that groups of particles – from bacteria to stars – are also waves occupying two places at the same time.'

'Hang on,' said Joel. 'Hang flippin' on. Even a humble star man is familiar with this. Between bacteria and stars you have people. Are you suggesting that people can occupy two places at the same time?'

'In theory,' said Angela. 'But what are you suggesting, Mrs Carter?'

'That they may not be dead. That's all,' said the woman. 'Let's say, for example, that their experiment somehow resulted in the particle wave they were working on being split.'

'Well, the experiment would just fail,' said Angela.

'Unless the energy source was somehow unbalanced, and the particles – the scientists, the equipment, the building – disappeared at one end of the wave . . .'

' . . . and not at the other,' said Joel, slowly. 'In which case they could be somewhere else?'

'Not exactly,' said Mrs Carter. 'I think they could be somewhen else, most likely the past.'

Angela sat bolt upright. 'Oh my god, you're Felicity Carter. You wrote about this stuff 20 years ago in the New Scientist. A piece called Time Sling. You speculated that some unexplained disappearances could be the result of people being propelled back in time through power surges like explosions and solar anomalies.' She turned to Joel. 'Felicity Carter inspired me to become a physicist.'

'Nobody took the notion seriously. It was just an idea I wanted to get off my chest at the time, and I thought little about it until I bumped into Bill Jenks at a conference and he told me that he and some colleagues were working on an experiment to take wave-particle duality to the next level. To show a recognisable object in two places within a laboratory, and to shift one of them backwards or forwards a few nanoseconds in time. The idea excited me and I agreed to secretly store their backup files. Apparently my codename was Cloud 9, which I rather liked.'

Angela and Joel settled back on the sofa to digest the information and Mrs Carter sipped her coffee and nibbled at half a buttered scone. Brushing crumbs from her top, she rose from her chair and walked over to a large bookcase containing volumes in a range of science subjects. Joel noticed a thin, leather-bound volume of H. G. Wells' The Time Machine among them.

'The back-up drives were a centimetre or so thick and about the size of a playing card, so they didn't take up much space. There were 135 in all, stored behind these books.'

'And you had to hand them over.'

'I'm afraid so.' Mrs Carter left the room and returned with a plastic box full of techno junk. Cables, USB drives, keyboards, wireless mice - and an old-fashioned, chunky, black external hard drive, which she pulled from the bottom of the box. 'But they didn't seem to notice this old boy,' she added, holding aloft the unassuming box. 'I backed everything up onto this.'

'What use is it?' asked Angela.

'I'm not exactly sure. But if they are still alive and if they haven't been trampled on by dinosaurs or killed in the Wars of the Roses we might be able to help them get back. I have half an idea. Well, more like a quarter of an idea.'

The Road to London – 1719

After one night at Joshua and Maria's farm and two more sleeping on or under the cart, Calvert, Jax and Seth were making untroubled progress towards London. They had been rationing the provisions they had with them, including some pickle and bread given to them by the farmers, and as light was fading on the fourth day they arrived at a village. This was the furthest from Bigby that Seth had travelled and he shouted to a man carrying a sack of flower, asking him the name of the place. The man told him it was Bow.

'We're nearly there,' said Calvert. 'By midday tomorrow we should be knocking on the door of the Tower of London.'

Jax nodded. 'It's hard to believe that in 300 years' time these windmills, fields and marshes will have been forgotten, buried beneath mile upon mile of brick, concrete and tarmac.'

Seth pulled gently on Solomon's reins and brought him to a stop beside a farm entrance. 'You two sound sad. I thought you would be pleased to be so near to our destination,' he said.

'Oh we are, Seth,' said Jax, grasping the blacksmith's arm. 'And we could not be more grateful to you for getting us here. It's just that this lovely village by the river will be swallowed up by London, and little but its name will be remembered.'

Solomon chewed contentedly at the grass beside the road while Seth walked to the farmhouse to ask permission to spend the night in the field. He returned a few minutes later carrying a small sack of cheese and apples. 'The place is run by a widow and two young sons. I said we would help her repair her barn in return for a little food and an overnight stop, if that's acceptable to you. An hour this evening before it gets properly dark, and then a couple of hours at first light.'

They said they would be pleased to help. Seth climbed into his seat and steered Solomon through the gate and onto a neglected field. After giving the horse water and some oats, and freeing him from his harness, the blacksmith pulled his bag of tools from beneath his seat and led the way to the woman's barn.

'Bloody hell,' said Jax slowly. 'That's seen better days.' Seth said it wasn't as bad as it looked. The roof was in reasonable order but clapboards had come loose or fallen off on two of the most exposed sides of the building. One of the sons, a sickly lad with a worrying cough, emerged from the farmhouse with hammer and nails and told Seth where he could find ladders and more tools.

'These boards overlap, so we'll start at the bottom and work our way up until we start hitting our thumbs in the dark,' said the blacksmith. They had secured about two-thirds of one side when they called it a day, and the woman came out to inspect their work. She invited them in to eat soup and bread with her and her sons. 'I'm sorry it's not much but it's a struggle since my husband died and Jamie here took ill,' she said. 'Young Arthur is a good boy, and willing, but he's just ten and isn't strong enough yet to do all that needs doing. I don't think we're going to be able to hang on much longer.'

The farmer, who could not have been more than 30, looked worn out, and her downcast manner was reflected in the interior of the single-storey farmhouse. It had an earth floor and comprised a dark, shabby room with a stove, a table and some battered chairs. A poorly-made door led to what Jax thought was probably a communal sleeping area. The place smelled damp. Jax could not help comparing it with the farm at which they had stayed three nights earlier.

Seth and the scientists introduced themselves and the farmer told them her name was Beth. She looked close to tears as she spooned a warm, thin vegetable soup into bowls and sat down heavily, apologising for the lack of meat or bread to accompany it. Seth got up from the table and left the room, returning a few minutes later with the cheese and apples Beth had given him earlier, plus the bag of food Maria had provided. He unpacked it and placed the contents on the table. The boys looked at the blacksmith, who simply nodded to invite them to tuck in. Their mother told them to go easy as their guests would need some food for their journey, but Seth said they were welcome to it. He would source more in the morning.

The woman leant forward, placed an elbow on the table and wept into her hand. Arthur, half-eaten apple in his fist, got up and rested an arm around her neck. Then he cried too. She gathered him up onto her lap and calmed herself, looking at her visitors with wet eyes. 'This isn't right,' she said. 'You are my guests. I should be providing for you. But the fight has gone out of me, as you can see by this place. It was different when John was alive – hard work but we had a good farm and a tidy home.'

Jax had finished her soup. 'How did John die? Do you mind me asking?'

'The cart rolled on him a few months ago. Crushed his back. Died the following day.'

'How much land do you have here, Beth?' asked Calvert.

'Almost 30 acres, but the three of us can't cope with it. I thought we could but the work is too much. We managed to get the wheat in but it was a poor harvest and we made little money. I can't afford to pay anyone to help, so we have two choices - we struggle on or we sell up to Jack Parkin next door. He's keen on the land but we would lose our home and I would have to find work for me and the boys.'

Tears streaked her face once more. 'It's more than I can

bear. I am beaten.'

Seth looked at his companions and asked how urgent it was for them to reach London. Could they spare a couple of days to help Beth with some of the chores that needed doing. The scientists readily agreed to help. Seth said if they were prepared to continue repairing the barn in the morning, he would walk into the village and buy some more provisions. They spent the night in the barn with Solomon.

Jax and Calvert were hammering in the last board when Seth returned mid-morning with a sack of food. With him was a small man wearing a leather apron. Despite being a good foot shorter than Seth, the man had a powerful physique and muscular arms. He walked with a rolling gait. 'This is Giles, the village blacksmith,' he announced. 'He's come to talk to Beth.'

Seth escorted the man inside and emerged a few minutes later. He handed them some bread and cheese, and the three of them perched on the back of their cart to eat. 'It turns out that Beth's husband was not a popular man. Surly and spiteful, and not one to readily help out a neighbour, as is the custom in all farming communities.'

'That explains a lot,' said Jax. 'So when he died they weren't too sympathetic towards Beth and her family.'

'The fire of resentment was stoked by her neighbour, Master Parkin, who covets this land. But I managed to persuade the blacksmith here to come and witness this family's distress for himself. Bow seems like a reasonably well-to-do village and I hope they will rally round to help this poor woman to get back on her feet. In the meantime, we too have some fences to mend if we are to stop those pigs from escaping.'

Jax couldn't help herself. She hugged the big blacksmith.

The three spent the day carrying out repairs to outbuildings. They patched the roof of the farmhouse and sealed window frames and doors to keep out draughts. Ditches were cleared to improve drainage from the fields. Fallen timber was gathered, cut and stacked for firewood. And at the end of the day they sat at the table with Beth and her boys and ate well.

'Giles is going to talk to people in the village. He says he thinks they will help us get back on our feet,' Beth said. 'I don't know where you have come from, but you were sent to help us. My boys and I will be forever grateful,' she said between tears and smiles. The warmth from the stove filled the room and Beth invited her visitors to spend the night in the farmhouse.

As dawn broke, Seth, Jax and Calvert gathered their belongings and loaded them on the cart. Solomon was already harnessed, standing patiently between the shafts. Beth, Jamie and Arthur stood by the farm door and waved as the three set off. As the cart trundled down the track it passed half a dozen villagers walking towards the farmhouse carrying forks, shovels, axes, saws and other implements that would help restore Beth's farm, and draw her and her family back into the Bow community.

London beckoned the scientists and the Bigby blacksmith as they crossed the bow-packed bridge from which the village got its name, but it was some time before anyone spoke. 'Is anyone else nervous about what lies ahead?' asked Jax. 'I'd forgotten about it while we were helping Beth but now we're approaching the city I suddenly feel a bit . . . apprehensive.'

London – 1719

There was a fine drizzle, and the city reeked. After walking through the Aldgate arch penetrating the old London wall, the smell was so fierce that it made Allstein gag and his eyes stream. He pulled his neck scarf across his nose and mouth but to little effect. From his knowledge of modern London, he knew he had to turn left towards the river and along Jewry Street, which had retained its name more than 300 years into the future. He had already seen the top of the White Tower but he kept his eyes fixed on the path ahead of him, which was slick with refuse and a liquid that had long since ceased to be water. It gurgled along an open gulley in the middle of the footway and ran slowly down the slope until it reached the soggy body of a long-dead cat. Here it flowed into the path of jostling pedestrians, whose dark, dirty clothing, grimy skin and haggard faces made them appear as noxious as their environment. He wanted to take all this in, to be a witness to life in 18th century London but feared standing out, appearing like a stranger, a tourist. So he walked purposefully, head held high, like a Londoner on a mission. He passed pubs and a brewery, a medieval church, fly-plagued food stalls whose produce would kill a 21st century customer. He thought the nearer he got to the Thames, the fresher the air would smell. It didn't. The river was a sewer, and if you fell into it, that would probably kill you too.

After about 20 minutes he found himself at Tower Hill and by the walls of William the Conqueror's great fortress. But first he wanted to take in the view of the Thames that stretched out before him like a computer-generated scene from a big-budget movie. The swirling, rushing river was crammed with wooden ships, some partly in sail, making their way towards Tilbury and the open sea, others moored and discharging their cargoes at the wharf. Dozens of rowing boats ferried men and women between the two banks, making a wide arc as they battled the strong current. He was mesmerised. 'If only I had a camera,' he said to himself.

'I beg your pardon,' said a man who was also taking in the scene. He was tall, lean and well dressed, and held the bowl of a long churchwarden pipe that appeared to have gone out. 'Were you addressing me, sir?' he said without looking at Allstein.

'Apologies, sir, I didn't see you there. No, I was just muttering to myself. There is such energy in the enterprise taking place before us. I'm a visitor here and was simply marvelling at it. Do you live in London?'

The man's eyes remained on the river. 'It depends on what you mean by London. There are actually three Londons – the City and the Court, with all those fine brick buildings that replaced those destroyed in the Great Fire and, across the river, Southwark, which was untouched by the flames. My home is in the City. And you, sir, what brings you here?'

'I have come to visit a friend in the Tower.'

'Oh dear,' he said, turning to Allstein and attempting to suck his pipe back into life. 'What is he doing there?' he asked gloomily.

'Time,' replied Allstein, walking away, looking pleased with himself for coming up with a line that would have suited a character in his CGI movie.

The first thing he noticed about the Tower was the stench from the water in the moat. He remembered from a school visit that the Duke of Wellington had it drained in Victorian times because of the awful smell. He also recalled that the Tower was not just a prison and a mint at this time, it was also a menagerie. Even so, as he walked towards the two scarlet-suited Beefeaters manning the turreted entrance, he was startled to hear the roar of lions from beyond the fortress wall.

'Your business here,' bellowed the older of the two yeoman warders, whose uniforms bore the GR cypher of King George. Both were armed with long pikes that looked more threatening and less ceremonial than they did in his time.

Allstein paused. 'I am here to see Sir Isaac Newton and Dr Jenks.'

'Your name, sir?' This man had just the one volume.

'Daniel Allstein. I am expected.'

'Ah. Indeed you are, sir. Walk with me.' The man had the voice of a sergeant major and a bearing to match as he led the way through the double-gated entrance, turning left along a cobbled street. The squeal of monkeys and the booming of other beasts filled the air as they made their way through a Tower complex less pristine than its modern, tourism-focused version. The animal noises were gradually supplanted by the sounds and smells of industry. People shouted, machinery clanged and a sulphurous odour drifted on the breeze. They were approaching Sir Isaac's domain, the Royal Mint.

The yeoman warder led him through a wide, arched entrance and into a workshop in which men and women were operating cast iron presses turning blank disks into coins. Allstein's first thought was that there didn't seem to be enough of them to manufacture coinage for an entire country. The warder opened a large door. 'Your other guest has arrived, Sir Isaac.'

Two men stood as Allstein entered the office of the Warden

of the Mint. The great scientist himself, and Jenks, who rushed at him and engulfed him in a bear hug that made Allstein grin. 'I've never known you do demonstrative, Bill. You must be pleased to see me.'

'You are most welcome, Dr Allstein,' said Newton, who walked towards him with an outstretched hand.

Jenks' emotions had indeed got the better of him and he wiped tears from his face with his neckerchief. 'Pack it in, Bill. You'll have us all at it,' said Allstein, putting down his bag and shaking Newton's hand. 'It is a great honour to meet you, Dr Allstein,' said Sir Isaac.

'You must be joking, Sir Isaac. Never in my wildest dreams did I think that I would shake the hand of the man who has inspired so many people over the centuries. I take it my friend has told you our story. Do you think we will be able to get back?' asked Allstein, getting straight down to business.

Newton looked at him squarely with an old man's red-rimmed eyes. 'Of course not,' he said. 'But I know that will not prevent you from trying.'

Allstein asked Jenks if he had heard from any of their colleagues. He told him he had received a letter from Calvert and Jax saying that they would make preparations to travel to London. 'Most interestingly of all, however, they seem to be bringing with them the Wells chamber, which might increase our chances of returning home by a small degree at least.' Allstein leapt to his feet and reached into his travel bag, hauling out some electronic items, a black box and two aluminium tubes attached to dials, all slightly dented but otherwise in good condition. He put them on Newton's table. Jenks disappeared from the room and returned with the items that had travelled back with him, which he placed next to Allstein's.

'Well, it's a start,' said Allstein. 'I wonder if Tom Cooper has anything. Have you heard from him, by the way?'

Lincoln – 1719

Cooper shivered in his bed. There was no heat in the room and wind sliced through gaps in the window. He was fully clothed but the cold he had experienced during his journey was deep inside him, and the blanket provided by the inn was threadbare. He wondered if the oddly-placed rug would provide some extra warmth but remembered the warning Maud had given him about touching it. Why shouldn't he use it? What could it be hiding that he shouldn't know about? Rotten floorboards, perhaps? Some filthy graffiti? A bloodstain hinting at a gruesome murder?

After about half an hour of tossing and turning he was so desperately cold that he decided he would risk Maud's wrath and got up and grabbed the rug. He flung it over the bed before looking back to see what was beneath it. It was hardly noticeable at first. There was something there but he struggled to tell what it was in the dim light of his single candle. He moved closer.

It was a hole in the floor about an inch across. He knelt down and put his eye to it. In bed in the room below was Maud. Lying on her back, blankets chastely pulled up to her neck, she looked straight at him with a broad grin and waved a you-naughty-boy finger at him. 'I knew you couldn't resist taking a peek,' she said, turning onto her side and snuggling down. 'Goodnight, Tom.'

Red-faced with embarrassment, he grabbed one of his boots

and placed it over the hole before diving into bed and pulling the rug over him.

When he came down to the bar the following morning Maud was already at work, sweeping and cleaning. He sat at a table and she brought him some bread and ale, accompanied by a smile and a wink, and asked him how he would be spending the day. He admitted that he had not thought that far ahead and had spent the night trying to keep warm and worrying about keeping his money safe. She sat beside him and advised him to keep a few pennies in his coat pocket and to tie the pouch containing the rest inside his breeches. Then if someone tried to rob him he might get away with only having to part with a few pence.

'I'm sorry for looking through that hole last night,' he said, tucking into his bread. 'I wasn't being nosy. I just needed the rug to put over the bed.'

'It's of no matter. I'm constantly asking Amos the landlord to fix it but he says he keeps forgetting, the dirty old goat. I usually hang a cloth on a nail just beneath it to block the view. But I must have forgotten last night for some reason.'

'In that case, I'm not sure who was the naughtiest, young Maud.'

'Oh, definitely you, Master Tom,' she said, getting up and fetching ale for customers who had just piled in through the door, blowing warmth into their hands.

Cooper finished his breakfast and wondered not just how he was going to spend the day, but what he would do with the rest of his life. Although he hadn't been there long, he had grown used to the comforts of Muckleborough Hall and had perhaps taken things for granted there. If he had to remain in 1719, it would not have been a bad place to spend it. But he had messed things up by not concocting a credible story. The two women were too clever to believe his rather hurriedly fabricated herring tale and understandably thought his time travel explanation an affront to their intelligence.

He sat back in his seat to think. He had studied at Cambridge University and worked in the city. It's only about 80 miles away. Perhaps he should attempt to get there and try and seek a post at the university. He had no paper credentials to present but he might be able to talk his way into a job. It would be a good idea to remind himself of what natural philosophers were studying at this time. Were there any scientific thinkers in Lincoln? If there were, where would he find them?

He caught Maud's eye and asked her where he would find a library. She wiped his table down and picked up his tankard when he declined her offer of more ale. 'Two minutes from here is one of the finest libraries in the country, so I'm told. Built by that famous architect bloke, Sir something-or-other. Him what did the big church in London after it burned down.'

'Sir Christopher Wren?'

'That's him.'

'So where will I find this library?'

She stood looking at him, hands on her broad hips, like he was an idiot. 'You see that enormous building, just out the back there. The one with the towers and twiddly bits,' she said. 'It'll be in there somewhere, although I haven't seen it myself, being just a woman and therefore not important enough to teach how to read. Anyway, I wouldn't have thought you'd got time for books. Shouldn't you be looking for a job . . . or a wife,' she added, looking over her shoulder mischievously as she departed.

Cooper felt like an idiot. The Wren Library was famous. But would he be allowed to examine the books there? He hadn't had a library card for years. He thanked Maud, stepped out of the Ram and looked up. The city's 11th century Gothic masterpiece loomed gigantically above him like a sheer cliff face, prompting a stirring of optimism in his 21st century heart. Books were the key to learning in this century, and he had a lot to learn.

There were three doors in the broad west facade of the cathedral, and people seemed to be coming and going not through the impressive entrance in the middle but through a smaller open door to the right. The building was enormous, monumental. Cooper couldn't imagine how awesome - in the truest meaning of the word – it would have appeared to peasants in medieval times.

There was no ticket office. He walked straight into the heart of the building and stood at the end of the light-infused nave, the ribbed ceiling supported by slender pillars. He didn't possess the architectural language to do the building justice, but the complexity of the construction, the artistry of the carvings, the blazing colour of the rose windows stopped him in his tracks. He wished there was a pew to sit on to take it all in but the interior was one large open space, with not a chair in sight.

He spotted a young man dressed in black scurrying along the aisle to his right, his arms full of scruffy books. He was heading for a narrow door and Cooper had to move quickly to intercept him. 'Excuse me,' he shouted as the man reached the door. 'Sorry, but where might I find the library?'

'Could you get that for me please?' asked the man, nodding at the door. 'I'll put these away and show you. It's above the cloisters but the staircase can be tricky to find.' Cooper helped the man to place the books in two neat piles on a large table. The room seemed to be a storage space but there was nothing valuable to be seen, just shabby tomes, old vestments and wooden boxes containing bottles. The place looked in need of a good clean.

The man introduced himself as Father Paul and said he was new to the cathedral and still finding his way around. He asked Cooper if he wanted to see any particular books.

'Not really,' said Cooper after telling the clergyman his name. 'I've seen Wren's library at Cambridge University, where I studied, and was keen to see his building here.' This was a lie. Although he had studied at Trinity College he had never visited its Wren Library and hoped he wouldn't be called upon to compare the two. 'It's my first time in Lincoln and I thought it would be a sin not to visit this wonderful cathedral and its famous library.'

They arrived at the cloisters on the northern side of the church and climbed a narrow staircase to a dimly-lit room crammed with books of great age. 'This is the medieval library,' said Father Paul. 'Also known as the chained library because books were very valuable in medieval times and it was felt that the best way to ensure they weren't stolen was to chain them up like criminals. I think it is sad to witness them like this. But it is perhaps better than watching them disappear one by one. Through here is our Wren Library.' He called to a wiry, sad-faced man in his forties who was engrossed in an atlas spread across a high table.

'Master Potter, you have a visitor. May I introduce Dr Thomas Cooper, who is a man of science. He wishes to admire your library.' Potter reluctantly tore his gaze away from the map and limply shook Cooper's hand.

Wren's library could not have provided more of a contrast from the medieval collection next door. It was a long, tall room, well illuminated by natural light. Thousands of leather-bound, unshackled books filled the floor-to-ceiling shelves that lined one side of the white-painted room. Along the other wall was an array of large, symmetrical windows overlooking the cloisters.

Father Paul said he would leave the two men to chat. Potter didn't seem too pleased at the prospect. He didn't look like a chatterer. Cooper would have to find a way in.

'I'll leave you to look around,' said Potter glumly. 'I don't expect you'll have any questions, but if you do . . .' He left the sentence hanging in the air and returned to his atlas.

Cooper walked up and down the wall of books and reached up to pluck out one at random. 'Please don't touch them,' said Potter, without looking up. Cooper lowered his hand and scoured the titles on the broad spines of the volumes in front of him. A look of concern crossed his face. He inspected more titles, and realisation dawned. All the books appeared to be in Latin. He couldn't read Latin. He needed the librarian's help.

'Master Potter,' he said. 'May I look at the map that so engrosses you?

'No, you may not,' he shouted. 'What the devil do you want?'

'Intelligent conversation, sir, that's all,' said Cooper, walking towards the librarian. Flattery. It was worth a go. 'I've been in Lincoln only a short time but have yet to meet anyone with an ounce of wit, and I felt sure that I would encounter a modicum of it here in this wondrous place.'

Potter raised his head from his book and slowly removed

his spectacles. He looked at Cooper properly for the first time. 'A trait, sir, which I abhor more than any other is sycophancy. If you need to look it up I can find a book which defines it for you. Would you like that?'

Cooper remained calm. 'May I offer in return a human characteristic that exasperates me even more, good sir. Condescension. Shall I explain what it means? It might be quicker than looking it up.'

Potter folded his spectacles and slipped them into a pocket. He walked slowly towards Cooper with what was either the beginnings of a smile, or a sneer. Cooper thought there was probably little difference.

'I would counter your condescension with superciliousness, but will spare you the embarrassment of looking for its spelling in a dictionary. Just know that it is a word.'

My god, he's flirting with me, thought Cooper. 'I am fully aware of the word, Master Potter. I was born with such a haughty sneer on my face that my parents landed me with the middle name of Supercilious. It's something of which I have grown to become enormously proud.'

'Ha! Excellent. Supercilious indeed. What a first rate exchange,' exclaimed the librarian, extending his right hand. Cooper grasped it and found it firmer and more welcoming than earlier. 'My apologies, Dr Cooper. I haven't enjoyed a verbal sparring like that for many a month. People come here to gawp at the building, hum tunelessly with their hands clasped behind their backs in what they think is a regal manner and ask me how many books there are. It is tedious Dr Cooper. I tell them I'm not sure and ask if they could help me by counting them. They can't wait to leave. Scarcely one in a hundred exhibits any learning, and less than one in a thousand any wit.'

'It must be most frustrating for a learned man such as yourself,' said Cooper.

'You may stop now, doctor. You have earned my attention.'

He had broken the ice but the trickiest part was yet to come. How was he going to get Potter to help him? Indeed, exactly what sort of help did he need? If he was going to land a job at Cambridge University, he needed to know what was going on in the world of science in 1719. He couldn't read the books so he would have to rely on what information he could obtain from the librarian. Was he a man of words or numbers?

'I am travelling the country talking to educated men of all backgrounds about the latest thinking and practical developments in the field of natural philosophy.' He felt this was a decent enough opening gambit. Suitably vague but perhaps enough to get a conversation going.

'To what end are you taking on this task?' asked Potter.

Cooper looked around him and found inspiration on the shelves. 'A book,' he said louder than he had intended. 'Perhaps initially a paper to present to the Royal Society that draws together the diverse thinking and experimentation of the best minds our country has nurtured, not all of them well known or even acknowledged in their areas of expertise.'

'A bold endeavour and a worthy one, I would add. There must be many brilliant minds working in arcane fields whose work is practically unknown,' said Potter.

Cooper wondered if the librarian was genuinely as excited as he sounded or if he was mocking him.

Potter started pacing the room, looking deep in thought. 'It is well known,' he said, 'that Sir Isaac Newton was engaged in a great many endeavours for years before he published a word, fearful that his ideas would be stolen before he was able to prove them. You are seeking other Newtons, Master Cooper. It is ingenious.'

Now the librarian was explaining it back to him, it did seem like a good idea. He knew that the Royal Society was a relatively new organisation, established to encourage scientific advancements. But its leading lights were the famous men of the age, not the unknown enthusiasts thinking, studying and experimenting quietly in their towns and villages. He was getting excited about the idea. But reality quickly beat him over the head and told him to stick to the plan, which was not about trudging round the country and writing a book that probably wouldn't earn him a penny. He knew he had no chance of getting back to his own time so what he needed was a nice cushy job teaching something he was familiar with, like mathematics. And maybe using his 21st century knowledge to make some "discoveries" of his own.

He asked Potter what he knew of the latest advancements in natural philosophy. He disliked that term and wondered if he could introduce the word scientist, which he knew wasn't widely used until the 19th century. It could be his first invention.

'You will, of course, be aware of the work of Sir Isaac. But what do you know of Lincoln's own Robert Grosseteste?' asked the librarian.

'I've never heard of him, but tell me more.'

'He used experiments to replicate and confirm his observations of the natural world, and wrote about optics, the tides, mathematics, astronomy and the nature of light. He attempted to establish a set of physical laws to understand the cosmos and even had thoughts about the nature of the universe. It might be heresy to say this in a house of God but he also suggested that the universe might have been created by an immense explosion that resulted in the stars and planets we see in the sky today.'

'What!' exclaimed Cooper. 'Why haven't I heard of this man? Where can I find him?'

'Come with me Dr Cooper. I will introduce you,' said Potter with a smile. They walked in silence down to the ground floor of the cathedral and into the south transept where the librarian stopped at the foot of an impressive tomb bearing the inscription:

Robert Grosseteste
Bishop of Lincoln
1235 – 1253

'Ah,' said Cooper. 'He's not going to be very talkative, is he? What a mind he must have had to have explored such ideas nearly 500 years ago. He was the Newton of his day, was he not?'

'Indeed, Dr Cooper. And I believe that it is to Sir Isaac you must turn if you are to make progress in your endeavours. May I be impertinent and ask how you might finance your work in researching the book you wish to compile? It sounds a costly enterprise that will incur expenses in travel, sustenance and accommodation. Are you perhaps a man of independent means?'

'Alas I am not, Master Potter. I have a little money but it is my intention to seek a teaching position at a university, perhaps my old Cambridge college, Trinity.'

'Where Newton was a Fellow,' added Potter. 'You are an intriguing man, sir, and, I have no doubt, an ambitious one. I would be pleased to write a letter of introduction to a friend at Sidney Sussex College if you feel that would be helpful. He might know someone of influence you could meet.'

Cooper was taken aback at the librarian's generous offer. He had only known Potter an hour or so and here he was offering his help. Was there a catch? A quid pro quo – one of the few Latin phrases he knew? There was.

'In return,' said the librarian, 'might I ask a favour of you?'

'Please ask. I will help if I can.'

'There is a book I wish to acquire for my library and all attempts to secure it have failed. The Trinity library has a wonderful edition of The Romance of Alexander dating from the 13th century. I wish you to steal it for me.'

'What! How do you expect me to do that?' asked Cooper.

'Very easily, doctor. I will help you to secure a position at Trinity. You will use their Wren Library for research, and at the first opportunity you will smuggle the Romance from the building. I will travel to Cambridge to collect it from you. Nothing could be simpler.'

'But you're a man of God and you are asking me to commit a mortal sin for you.'

'I am not a man of God,' he exclaimed, 'I am a man of words, and I will have the Trinity Romance for my collection, or you will have no job.'

'What on earth is so special about this book that it's worth the risk of prison, or even worse, execution?'

Potter said, 'It is the history of Alexander the Great, written in about 1250 in old French and with remarkable illustrations. It is a great rarity, and I do not have one. I want theirs. When you have it, write to me and I will come and collect it from you.'

'And in return you will get me a teaching post at Trinity.'

'I will do my best.'

'Well, after you have done your best, I will do mine. It's a deal.' How hard could it be to steal a book from an 18th century library. No guards. No CCTV. No problem.

The two men shook hands and Cooper said he would return to the library the following day to collect his letter of introduction. That afternoon Cooper bought a warmer, smarter coat from a market stall selling a variety of second-hand goods. He returned to the Ram with a spring in his step. He had a plan – with some risks attached – and would soon be leaving Lincoln behind. Maud told him where he could catch the coach to Cambridge, and looked genuinely disappointed when he said he would be departing the next day.

'But we haven't got to know one another properly,' she said with a glint in her eye.

'I'm sure I will be back one day, my dear,' he said, in what he hoped was an avuncular manner. 'But I have to earn a living and my future lies in Cambridge.'

'Very well then,' she said breezily. 'Your loss.' She should be on the stage, he thought.

Early the following morning he collected his letter from Potter and made his way to the coaching inn at the bottom of Steep Hill. The coach and four was already being prepared for departure and Cooper paid before taking his place on one of the cheaper outside seats, glad of his extra coat.

Cambridge – 2030

'Do you really think it's possible for us to help them get back?' asked Joel, through a mouthful of scone. His second. 'It sounds ridiculous. For a start we have no idea where or when they are, so it'll be impossible to send them a message. And if they have been transported back in time – which sounds madder every time I even think it – they might all be in different times, different places or even dead. With so many unknowable factors a viable rescue seems nigh on impossible. These scones are bloody great, by the way.'

Mrs Carter leaned towards him. 'I agree, not about the scones, although they are my grandmother's recipe, but about the seemingly impossible nature of a rescue. Which is why we should stop thinking of it that way.'

'Then how should we think about it?' asked Angela.

She said they should assume that cosseted 21st century scientists would find it pretty uncomfortable living in the past – if indeed that's where they are. No shiny workplace, no centrally heated home, no easy access to money, no efficient healthcare. Open to dangers we have long since forgotten about in our comfortable lives. They might not even be in Britain, so there could be language barriers too. 'If it was me battling against all of that, I would want to find a way back, wouldn't you?' asked Mrs Carter.

'Yes, I bloody well would,' said Angela. 'So what's your quarter of a plan? What can we do to help them?'

'Quantum physics got them into this mess, so we'll use quantum physics to try and get them out of it. Now ask me how.'

'How!' Angela and Joel shouted in unison.

'We give them a beacon, located at the site from where they disappeared, that will send a signal back through the ages. The further back it goes, the weaker it will get, so we will have to hope that they haven't gone back further than say 500 years. It would be almost undetectable then.'

Joel asked Mrs Carter if she knew how to build this beacon, and how long it would take, and how much it would cost, and who would pay for it? 'It's not my field. I just look at stars and planets, and stuff up there. I haven't a clue how you would do this,' he said.

'No, but I think Angela might,' said Mrs Carter, looking at the young scientist. 'And I could possibly be of some help.'

Angela was quiet for some time and looked deep in thought. Joel and Mrs Carter allowed her to be deep in thought for a while.

'It's impossible,' she said eventually. 'First of all the beacon would have to be on the site where their lab was, and we would never get permission to do that. Secondly, we would need lab space to design and build a device, and nobody would provide that if they knew what we were trying to do, because it's completely insane. Thirdly, it would cost millions, lots of millions, and would need power to run it, possibly for years.'

'You're right,' said Mrs Carter, clearing the cups and plates away. 'Let's not bother.'

'Hang on,' said Joel. 'What if we could overcome all of these hurdles. The permission, the money, the lab. Would it work?'

'It might,' Mrs Carter said. 'It might give us a chance to get them back.'

Angela, casting aside her initial doubts, suddenly looked excited. 'And it might open up a whole new field of quantum science. Communication through time. It's got Nobel prize written all over it.'

Mrs Carter smiled and carried the tray through to her kitchen, where she was followed by Angela and Joel. 'I knew we'd get there in the end,' she said.

'But where do we start?' asked Joel.

'The money, of course,' said Angela. 'We need someone with so many noughts on their bank balance that you'd need to take your shoes and socks off to count them. An entrepreneur who's into science and who would love to have their name attached to a project that would not only break boundaries, it would shatter them into smithereens.'

'If we get the money, we'll get the permission,' said Mrs Carter. 'What are you both working on at the moment?'

Joel looked thrilled to be asked and said he was leading a gravitational lensing and spectrography project to view galaxies that existed just 2.6 billion years after the Big Bang.

'2.6 billion years?' asked Angela. 'I hope our friends haven't gone that far back.'

'It's interesting work,' insisted Joel. 'It really is.'

Mrs Carter asked what Angela was working on. 'I'm part of a team looking into superconducting nanowires. Honestly, it is more gripping than it sounds. But I'm sure I can be spared if we can put together a funding case for our time beacon. Doesn't that sound great when you say it out loud. Time beacon.'

Joel shuffled in his seat, looking unsure if he should say what he was about to say. But he said it anyway. 'I know who we can ask for the money.'

'Go on,' said Mrs Carter calmly.

'My uncle. Sir Franklin Pierce-Dronfield. He's a monster, an egomaniac and I'm scared to death of him . . . but he's so rich that he would make Croesus feel like a poor relation. If there was the prospect of a seat in the House of Lords, he might just do it.'

'Joel, I could hug you,' said Angela.

Joel's face went red. 'If you two can put together a case on a single side of A4 – that's all he'll read - I'll make the initial contact through my mother. She's the only family member he will talk to. Then you can go and see him. Just you. Deal?'

Mrs Carter said, 'Of course it's a deal, Joel. That would be amazing.'

'Did you know Joel was related to money?' Angela asked Mrs Carter.

'Of course, dear. As you've said yourself, I know everything.' And she chuckled to herself as she ran the taps to do the washing up.

Sir Franklin Pierce-Dronfield was not what Angela and Mrs Carter had expected. Dressed in scuffed brogues, baggy brown corduroy trousers, faded checked shirt and a beige cardigan that engulfed his tall, wiry frame, the businessman and former Government scientific adviser looked more like a hobby gardener than a billionaire. Mrs Carter and Angela were sitting on a well-worn Chesterfield while Sir Franklin, unshaven and approaching 80, was hunched in a leather wing-backed chair, skinny legs crossed, silently reading their proposal. It was taking him some time and Angela suspected that he was going over it several times. His wild, grey eyebrows twitched occasionally as he scanned the page.

Angela cast stealthy glances around the man's study while he read. To call it untidy would be redefining the word. They had to remove scientific journals and books from the sofa in order to sit down. The antique rug in front of the fire was more hole than fibre. One of the curtains over a door leading to a conservatory hung lopsidedly off its rail and a half-smoked cigar had overbalanced from the edge of its ashtray and scorched a black-edged mark into the veneer of a side table. Most intriguing and unpleasant of all was a large empty parrot cage, beneath which was a litter of seed and crusty bird poo. Angela looked around the room to see if the bird had settled somewhere but there was no sign of it.

'It died,' Sir Franklin growled, looking up from the sheet of paper. 'Couple of months ago. Fell off its perch. 54 years old and never spoke a word. Waste of bloody money.' He dabbed his face with a red handkerchief tugged from his pocket. Was he wiping away a tear?

'I'm so sorry to hear that, Sir Franklin,' offered Mrs Carter.

'Yes, condolences,' Angela said. 'You must miss it.'

'Don't be so damn foolish. Miss Cooky was a bird. A pet, that's all.' And he dabbed his face once more. 'So, young Joe has put you up to this, has he? Asking for money?'

'Joel,' said Angela.

'What?' said the old man.

'Your nephew's name is Joel.'

'Is it? Well I'll be damned. I've been putting Joe on his £5 Christmas postal order since he was born. Are you sure?'

'Positive,' said Angela. 'I work with him. And we're friends. It's definitely Joel.' She didn't know postal orders still existed.

The billionaire looked down at the sheet of paper once more but appeared to be thinking rather than reading. 'This looks like arrant nonsense to me. And if I didn't know that you were involved in this Mrs Carter we wouldn't be having this conversation. As you know, my field is rare earth metals, and my knowledge of the quantum world is somewhat sketchy. But there appears to be one major issue with your proposal. Even if you were able to raise the money and build your beacon, how would the lost scientists be able to detect its pulse? Perhaps hundreds of years in the past, if indeed that's where they are.'

Angela responded. 'I know all of these people, and they are incredibly resourceful. If they have been tossed back in time, they will almost certainly want to get back, not only to return to their 21st century lives but also to share with the scientific community, the world, what happened in their lab and the experiences they had in whatever time they have landed.'

'What happened to them,' said Mrs Carter, 'was a random act, over which they had no control. They will want to know that they can return in a more orderly fashion, if possible to a time and a place of their choosing. Why not the time and the place of their disappearance?'

She explained that the pulse of the beacon would be similar to the beat of a clock, transmitted through the lithosphere, the earth's crust and upper mantle. Quantum physicists will use quantum physics to try and get back, and the beacon will be there to guide them.

'You're asking for an awful lot of money for an experiment that stands an infinitesimal chance of success. The assumptions you're making – they're still alive, they've gone back in time, but not too far, they can build a device for controlled time travel, the beacon will guide them, they will arrive back in one piece. The chance of all this working is so small that I would struggle to see it through a Titan Krios microscope.'

Mrs Carter smiled. She had been through all those arguments many times in her head. 'But. What if it did work? You will have saved the lives of five brilliant people, funded the research that discovered time travel and, who knows, earned a well-deserved seat in the House of Lords. Wouldn't that be worth gambling a small percentage of your vast fortune on?'

Sir Franklin harrumphed, got up and said he would take a walk in his garden. Mrs Carter and Angela stood and moved cautiously around the room, careful not to tread on any of the detritus littering the floor. 'Oh. I've found Miss Cooky,' said Angela, looking in the birdcage. 'Still lying beneath the perch she fell off. Yuk! She's not looking her best.'

'I did wonder about the smell but to be honest I thought it was our host,' said Mrs Carter.

'Do you think he'll do it?' asked Angela.

'Unlikely,' replied Mrs Carter gloomily, but we had to try.

'I'll do it,' shouted Sir Franklin, bursting in through the conservatory door. 'But I don't want it made public that I'm funding the project. If it's a success you can tell the world. In fact, I'll insist on it. Is that agreed?'

Angela and Mrs Carter glanced at one another and then Sir Franklin. 'Agreed,' they said together. If he had been a nicer, cleaner old man they probably would have hugged him, but both resisted the urge. They thanked him profusely and said they would let him know the banking and project details once they had secured university approval and lab space. Angela was bursting to tell Joel the news but waited until they got back to Mrs Carter's Audi before she rang him and put him on speaker. Startled pedestrians looked at the car as Joel screamed out in joy. 'I knew I'd get more than a fiver out of that old goat one day. Christ, he can't hear me, can he?'

It took a few weeks to secure the necessary permissions and lease a small laboratory on the Science Park. They also recruited two bright students – Geraldine, known as Gerry, and Sylvester, known as Rocky. In fact, they were the only ones they interviewed who didn't think their careers would be blighted by the words time travel.

When the five of them gathered together for the first time in the brightly-lit lab, Mrs Carter arrived with coffee and copies of H. G. Wells' 1895 classic The Time Machine. For fun, she said. They wasted no time in getting to work, viewing their task as a rescue mission. Mrs Carter had been busy and as they sat around a meeting table, she gave each of them a thick printed file of text and calculations. 'I've been through the back-up drive I made. Read this and tear it apart. And then let's build a beacon like no other.'

London – 1719

They were still passing fields, gardens and tidy cottages as they approached London from the north-east, along what Jax thought was probably the route of the modern day A11. She told Calvert that she knew that once they had passed through the city's medieval wall the sights and smells would bring back terrible memories of her arrival in 18th century London. 'You haven't really told me how you survived those first few weeks and months,' he said. 'It must have been tough, and I haven't dared to ask you about it.'

She was quiet for a while. 'It's difficult to know where to start. I think I sussed straight away that the accident had somehow thrown me back in time. I cowered in the alley I had arrived in and everything I saw, heard and smelled felt so visceral. So real. I sat on a rickety wooden crate for quite a while trying to work out what I should do. I stole clothes drying over the window ledge of a tatty-looking terraced house that made me look like a beggar, so I decided to beg. Although busk might be a better description. I used to busk with a guitar when I was a student, and though I say it myself I wasn't too shabby. I was also in the uni drama club, so knew a lot of show tunes.'

'What sort of stuff did you do,' asked Calvert.

'Oh, the usual. Bit of Lloyd Webber, Ed Sheeran, some Beatles. I was a bit wobbly at first. Nervous as hell wondering what sort of reception I was going to get.'

'And . . .'

'Nothing. Not a penny . . . for a couple of days, anyway. I was starving, and I knew I would get ill if I didn't quickly earn money for food and drink. So I moved away from the entrance to the alley and found a busier area, in a nearby square where the people looked more prosperous. Within a couple of hours pennies were being tossed at me. I collected them up, paid for a bed for the night, and did it all over again the following day at the other end of the square.'

Calvert looked full of admiration. 'Wow, that was resourceful. And from there . . . ?'

'I just carried on, and soon I had enough to buy some better clothes from a stall on the market and for a shared room in a lodging house. I was also drawing a bit of a crowd. It was too good to last, of course. After about a week, a big bloke armed with a cudgel came up to me at the end of a pretty successful day and ordered me to hand over my money.'

Seth looked across. 'Lord, what did you do?' he asked.

'I gave him the money and afterwards he shoved me to the

ground with a black-toothed sneer on his face. I had two choices. I could move to a different spot or I could deal with him.'

'I can't imagine which option you took,' said Calvert with a shake of the head.

'I followed him across the square, along a couple of dodgy-looking roads and down an alley where he pulled open the heavy door to a building that looked as though it could fall down any minute. I waited for him to go inside then quickly knocked on the door. When he poked his head out I slammed the door on it and he fell down. Knocked out. I felt in his coat pocket and took his money pouch, which contained quite a bit more than my few coppers, and legged it.'

She said the experience had turned out to be a fortunate one. She knew she could not go back to her busking spot so walked about the city during the morning, when it was safer, looking for somewhere else to sing. 'Then I saw it. A street sign for Drury Lane and not far along it an impressive looking Theatre Royal. So I sang outside there . . . and got discovered. By an actor-manager called Colley Cibber. Horrible, arrogant man, but he gave me a job.'

'What! How the hell did that happen?' asked Calvert. He was beginning to wonder if Jax was making all this up to pass the time on the journey. It just seemed too far-fetched. 'You're not having us on, are you? Why didn't you tell me all this in Bigby?'

'You never asked. We just got bogged down in the weirdness of your life in that amazing village.'

Calvert said he was sorry and asked her to continue. Seth simply looked at the road ahead and smiled as the story unfolded.

'I was singing Eleanor Rigby, making up some of the words

because I didn't know it all the way through, when a man in a flamboyant wig burst out of the stage door and grabbed hold of me. I thought he was going to rob me so I kneed him in the balls and he went down gasping for breath. Then I noticed he was quite well dressed, had come out of the theatre and so probably wasn't a mugger. I helped him up, said sorry and gave him my famous winning smile.' She demonstrated the smile and drew laughter from her two companions.

'He asked me if I was the one making all the racket. I quickly transformed my winning smile into an indignant scowl and said I was singing. And I called him a rude man. A crowd was starting to gather and they seemed to know who he was, so he said I should follow him into the theatre.'

The cart trundled on and gradually the rooftops of London appeared on the horizon. Seth said he felt nervous as he didn't like crowds and always imagined London to be a den of thieves and cutthroats. He was a big, strong man and Jax said he would stand out as someone not to be trifled with. She said she would look after him and flung an arm over his shoulder that made the big man grin boyishly. He asked her to finish her story.

Jax told him that Colley Cibber, the man who had dragged her into the theatre, was well known as an actor, playwright and theatre manager. 'He took me into his office and inspected me, like I was a prize horse. If he'd tried to look at my teeth I'd have bitten his fingers off. He asked me who I was and why I was caterwauling outside his theatre. He looked quite agitated so I let his insult slide and asked him why he had hauled me into his office. Well, I'll cut a long story short. He'd written a new play called The Misadventures of Captain Perkiss and his leading lady, Letitia Cross, had pulled out because Peter the Great of

Russia was in town and she was "entertaining" him.'

Calvert puffed out his cheeks. 'What! This Cibber fellow was so desperate for a stand-in for his leading lady that he was auditioning you for the part after hearing you screech for pennies in the street.'

'None taken,' said Jax at the implied offence.

'Sorry, but I think what I said accurately summed up what happened. So did you get the part?'

'Of course not. But I did get a part in the play after he promoted one of the other actors. The money wasn't great but it was more than I was earning "screeching in the street" and I got to eat properly and wear some nice clothes from the costume department. I shared some digs with two of the other women in the play and they taught me how to fend off the advances of the sort of letches who go to the theatre. On the whole, it was fun and I had work in various productions for the best part of a year. Until . . .'

'Until?' asked Calvert.

'Until the thief I knocked out found me. He waited outside the theatre one night and beat the crap out of me. My two actress friends nursed me back to health but I realised I could have died and decided to leave London. I cut my hair, bought some men's clothes and headed north with the aim of getting to a nice, safe town or village. I thought I might be able to teach.

'I walked or got lifts on carts and met some amazing characters on the way. And I stumbled on this friendly, shabby little town called Crassacre, where I supped a brew with the locals and took a bed for the night. I heard talk of a mysterious village off the north-south road where a stranger had materialised out of thin air, like a fallen angel, and turned the place into a paradise.'

Calvert feigned a look of smugness. 'Like an angel, eh?'

Seth looked at him. 'Fallen angel, I think Miss Jax said.'

'I thought that sounded a bit like my arrival, so the following morning I hit the north-south road. The village is indeed very hard to find and I would have missed the track if I hadn't heard Eli's cartwheels turning and the clip-clop of Clarence's hooves in the forest.'

The sound of Seth's wheels suddenly changed as the cart moved from dirt road to cobblestones, and London's town wall appeared before them. 'We still don't understand why your arrival in Bigby caused Joe Dings to disappear,' said Calvert. 'That may be a mystery we will never solve, but I hope where ever he is he's behaving himself.'

As they passed through the Aldgate arch Jax directed Seth to turn left, towards the Thames and the Tower of London. The blacksmith's face reacted to the stench of the streets and the squalor he saw. His eyes darted left and right, suspicion etched on his face as though expecting to be attacked at any moment. Jax rested a reassuring hand on his arm as Solomon, as unruffled as he had been throughout their journey, drew them towards their destination.

Seth sat up straight when he saw the Tower. 'What a fearsome construction that is, my friends. A place that appears purpose-built for intimidation, torture and execution.'

'And money,' offered Calvert.

'And lions,' said Jax.

'Lions!' said Seth with his enthusiasm suddenly revived. 'What an adventure this is turning out to be.' He tapped Solomon gently with his reins and the horse, perhaps appreciating that journey's end and a bag of oats was near, broke into a slightly quicker walk.

Cambridge – 1719

The journey from Lincoln to Cambridge took all day, with the horses changed twice at coaching inns along the way. Cooper had tried striking up conversations with his fellow passengers in the outside seats but the noise from the hooves, the wheels and the wind made it impossible and he quickly gave up. He nodded off once and the passenger beside him thrust an arm across his chest to prevent him toppling forward. Cooper nodded his thanks and they continued their speechless journey, arriving on the outskirts of Cambridge in the middle of the afternoon.

The city in which he had spent five happy years of his life gaining his degrees and doctorate was an unsettling package of familiarity and strangeness. They arrived via the Huntingdon Road, Castle Street, Magdalene Street and over the bridge crossing the Cam, passing St Clement's Church and the Round Church beloved of snap-happy 21st century tourists. The coach pulled up in Market Hill at a substantial inn called the Fox, which didn't exist in his time but would have been a popular student haunt, he thought. His bag was thrown down to him by the coach driver and he headed straight to Sidney Sussex College to introduce himself to Potter's friend, an academic called Peabody who might be able to wangle him a job.

He had no trouble finding his way around the city. The ancient colleges he saw about him had hardly changed in his time and the layout of the roads was practically the same. Most of the other buildings – the houses and businesses – were different but this was a place he felt at home in. It had an even more prosperous feel than Lincoln and there was a bustling confidence on the streets as he jostled his way towards the Elizabethan college he and his fellow students had known simply as Sidney. One of the large doors in the ornate gatehouse was open and when he stepped through it he was met by two black-coated men of short but sturdy stature who were clearly the equivalent of the porters of his day. They could have been brothers, standing there in identical poses, their hands clasped almost protectively in front of their genitals. One of them offered Cooper a cold smile and wished him a good afternoon.

'Good afternoon, gentlemen. I've come to see Professor Peabody.'

'Is he expecting you, sir?' asked the one who hadn't smiled.

'No, but I have a letter of introduction from the librarian at Lincoln Cathedral.'

'Ooh, a librarian, Hubert,' said the smiler, with a dollop of sarcasm.

'Well that makes all the difference,' said his colleague.

Cooper, who was substantially bigger than both of them, stepped forwards with the intention of showing them his letter. The movement took the two by surprise and the snooty demeanour fell from their faces as they took a step backwards.

'Will you take this gentleman to the professor's room or shall I?' asked the former smiler.

'You can do it, Humphrey, if that's acceptable. I'll make a note of sir's name in our ledger shall I?' He picked up a quill, leaned over his book and looked expectantly at Cooper. Their visitor curled his lip into a sneer and said, 'Arnold

Schwarzenegger.'

The man dipped his pen into the inkwell and shouted, 'How do you spell that?' as Cooper strode off into Sidney's courtyard with the other gatekeeper trailing in his wake. The man hurried to catch up with Cooper and called for him to slow down. He didn't know where he was going. Cooper stopped, leather bag over his shoulder, letter in hand. 'Well show me then, before I lose my patience entirely.' The man took the lead and a broad smile broke across Cooper's face. In all his years at Cambridge he had never had the nerve to cheek a porter.

He was led to a corner staircase and up to a sturdy wooden door, which the gatekeeper rapped on firmly. There was no reply. He rapped again, harder. Silence. He raised his fist reluctantly to knock once more when a reedy voice squawked, 'What do you want?'

'It's Humphrey, Professor Peabody. You have a visitor, sir.'

'I don't want a visitor.'

Cooper looked down at Humphrey, who said, 'He's quite insistent, sir. And quite large.' There was muttering behind the door, and the scraping of a chair across a bare wood floor. The iron handle turned and the door was yanked open by a bony hand belonging to a thin-faced figure even shorter than Humphrey. He was dressed in thick, faded black robes worn colourless where they brushed the floor. 'Who are you?' he wheezed, not bothering to look further than the letter Cooper held out.

'Thomas Cooper, professor.'

Humphrey looked shocked. 'You said you were Arnold Somethingorother. Hubert'll have to put a line through that now. Mess his ledger, that will. He won't be pleased.'

'Go away, Humphrey, you odious creature,' said Peabody,

turning and beckoning Cooper to follow him into his room before slamming the door behind him. He sat in a chair beside a desk, his feet not quite reaching the ground, and motioned Cooper to take the only other chair in the room. It was a very brown room, and quite large for a man who took up so little space. Books were piled up everywhere, including on a table that was probably also used for dining. A once crimson curtain was suspended on rails along two sides of a corner, behind which Cooper could glimpse Peabody's bed.

'So why has that miserable oaf Potter sent you to me?' the professor whined, looking at his guest for the first time. 'He describes you as a man of wit and intelligence. And calls you Dr Cooper. What are you a doctor of, and where did you earn this distinction, may I ask?'

Cooper had anticipated this. It needed to be something of relevance to this time and from a university where it would be difficult to check his qualifications. If he had said Trinity College, Cambridge, Peabody would have had someone running up the road within minutes to find him on the register. He plumped for mathematics at Trinity College Dublin as this would involve the longest journey, and include a sea crossing.

'Oh, there,' said Peabody disparagingly. 'Couldn't get into an English college then. So what does Potter want me to do with you? I'm a classicist, I have no need of a numbers man. I think he has wasted your time and, more importantly, mine.' He stood up and handed back the letter of introduction. 'Good day, sir.' He waved at the door and sat down to study some papers spread out on his desk. Cooper remained seated with an uncomfortable look on his face.

'Our mutual friend did say that you might exhibit some

reluctance to help,' he said. 'And if that were the case he told me to say to you, "The Countess." It might provide some encouragement, he said.'

'What?' gasped Peabody. He turned quickly in his chair, his face ashen. He folded his hands into his lap and looked down at them, as though an old pain he thought long since cured had suddenly smitten him again.

'That was a mighty cruel blow,' he said quietly. 'Did he tell you more?'

'He did not, professor, I promise you. And were I not desperate for a position here I would not have used the painful instrument of persuasion that those two words clearly were.'

Peabody nodded slowly. 'Return tomorrow morning. I will see what can be done.'

Cooper was wracked with guilt as he made his way back to the Fox to seek lodgings for the night. He had blackmailed the man and the resulting agony was written across Peabody's face. Potter hadn't told him the story behind those two powerful words from Peabody's past but they had pierced him deeply.

Cooper paid for his bed and took a walk around the city, noting the buildings that had survived into his time and those that had been flattened or remodelled by the Georgians and Victorians. He ate and slept well at the inn and at mid-morning returned to the Sidney Sussex gatehouse, where he donned a threatening expression and received a more courteous reception from Hubert and Humphrey. Hubert escorted him to Peabody's room. The professor rose when Cooper entered but didn't invite him to sit, hoping to get their meeting over with as soon as possible. He held a piece of paper in his hand.

'I wish to have your assurance as a gentleman that you will

not mention the words you uttered yesterday to anyone, ever again,' he said looking intently at Cooper. 'Do I have that assurance, Dr Cooper?'

'You do, professor, and you also have my sincerest apologies at deploying such a low tactic in order to secure your help. If it is any consolation at all, in exchange for your assistance Master Potter has required me to do something that will provide him with a considerable hold over me too. He is a friend to neither of us, sir, and I swear that your secret is safe with me.'

Peabody shook Cooper's hand and handed over the paper. 'You have an interview at Trinity at 12 noon with Nicholas Saunderson, Lucasian Professor of Mathematics.'

Cooper looked stunned. 'Surely the Lucasian Professor is far too senior a figure to interview a humble mathematics teacher.'

'Nicholas is a friend. I have done my part in making the introduction. Securing the position is down to you. I wish you well, sir. Please do not visit me again.'

Saunderson's name seemed familiar. He must have come across it in his time at Trinity, perhaps in a portrait. He couldn't believe that he would be interviewed at his old college. He walked down to the banks of the River Cam, which was littered with students, all young men. Cooper knew that women wouldn't gain degrees at Cambridge University for another two centuries or more.

He talked to several small groups, asking if any of them were mathematicians. He eventually found two men who were chatting and throwing stones at ducks minding their own business on the river. They admitted that they were studying mathematics and one of them, who introduced himself as Charles, took pity on Cooper when he said he was being interviewed for a post. 'Working with numbers is the most exciting thing imaginable, but the dons are a deadly dull bunch and few of them are open to the new ideas that are emerging elsewhere,' he said. His companion lay back on the grass, pulled his cap over his face and groaned in agreement.

'I'm being interviewed by Professor Saunderson,' said Cooper. 'What should I know about him?'

'You're honoured, my good fellow. He's the top man, and different from most of the others. An energetic cove, and a wonderful teacher and explainer of ideas.'

'Is he interested in any particular areas of mathematics?' asked Cooper.

The man under the hat, Christopher, lifted it from his face. 'Optics, astronomy, probability theory, perhaps, and Newtonian natural philosophy. He's a great champion of Sir Isaac's ideas, and something of a reformer when it comes to teaching mathematics here. So not popular with tutors who like things done how they've always been done. Oh, and he's blind, but then you probably already knew that.'

Charles could see that Cooper looked concerned. 'I'm sure this stuff is bread and butter to you. Why not impress him with something he may not have come across before.'

'Hmm. Thank you, gentlemen,' said Cooper, getting up and wiping damp grass from his backside. 'I'll go and think about what that might be.'

'I wouldn't think for too long,' said Christopher, nodding towards the King's College clock tower. 'Didn't you say your appointment was at 12?'

He had less than a quarter of an hour to make it but a brisk walk saw him arrive at Trinity's turreted gatehouse with a few minutes to spare. One of the gatemen looked at his paperwork and led him silently to the door of Professor Saunderson's rooms. A voice on the other side shouted enter and the porter opened the door and closed it behind Cooper, who found himself in the presence of a man of about 40 but who looked older in his long brown wig and layers of dark clothing. The forked Geneva band at his throat gave him the appearance of a clergyman.

'Welcome, Dr Cooper,' said Saunderson. It was a friendly, mellow voice, and his face bore a warm smile beneath eyes that were not only sightless but not present at all.

'Thank you for meeting me, professor. It's a very great pleasure.' Cooper looked around him and saw the large, well-ordered room of a man who needed to know exactly where to find everything by touch. Some of the shelves and tables had on them devices that Cooper had not seen before, possibly specially made to assist the mathematician.

'I always allow a little silence so that new visitors to my rooms can take in what they see,' said Saunderson. 'The space is somewhat tidier than that of many of my colleagues, and I can place my hand on anything I need, including the items which have no doubt attracted your attention. Can you guess what they are for?' The professor got up and strode confidently to a desk, where he picked up a board with a square array of holes into which pegs of differing sizes could be placed.

'It's a calculator,' said a stunned Cooper. 'It's a damned calculator. Did you invent this, professor?'

'I did. And what about this?' He handed Cooper another board with holes for pegs, around which string could be tied.

'For geometry. You use it so that you can feel the shapes. Amazing, sir.'

'I have another which allows me to examine three-dimensional geometry by touch, but I won't bore you further with my little assistants. I understand you are seeking a teaching position at the university. And your arrival comes at a fortuitous time as I am struggling with teaching seven or eight hours a day and must reduce my workload if I am to undertake more research. What experience do you have, Dr Cooper.'

Cooper decided to be honest. Well, as honest as possible. 'None, sir. I have never taught mathematics and have spent my career, until fairly recently, totally in the field of research.'

'Then let us deal with the recent past first. Tell me about that.'

Cooper gathered his thoughts. 'I found myself in Great Yarmouth in 1718, where I was press-ganged into the Royal Navy, spending about a year chasing the Spanish and being terrified in battle. When my ship went into dock for repairs I left the Navy.' The truth would not have got him the job.

'Absconded, do you mean?'

'Yes, sir.'

'Good for you,' said the professor with a smile. 'Proceed. This is most entertaining.'

'After some time travelling . . .' A hyphen between those last two words would have made that more truthful but it's difficult to introduce in speech. '. . . I found myself in Lincoln, where I was befriended by the librarian at the Wren Library, who kindly provided me with an introduction to your friend Professor Peabody.'

'That's all very good, and most exciting,' said Saunderson

with a wry smile. 'Absolutely first class. You are a very good communicator, sir. The senses which compensate for my blindness detect a great many holes in this story but I will assume that you have provided me with such a precis because you know that my time is precious. However, if you are up to the job this will be time well spent. Tell me about your research. Have you published anything?'

Cooper had published numerous papers on his work that would make no sense to Saunderson. But he knew he had to come up with something that would intrigue the man and not make him sound like a fruit cake.

'My research is in a field known as quantum physics.'

'Quantum. From the Greek for "how much"?' asked Saunderson. 'How peculiar.'

'The quantum world is indeed a peculiar one, professor. I will explain. Quantum physics studies matter and energy at their most basic level, objects such as protons, neutrons and electrons. Objects smaller than atoms that affect the behaviour of everything around us. This desk, the building in which we sit, human beings, the sun itself.'

The smile had dropped from the professor's face and he listened intently to Cooper, who paused. The silence was broken by Saunderson. 'I am listening to what you are saying, Dr Cooper, but also to the manner in which you are saying it. You are either speaking the truth or are a shameless spinner of very tall tales. Let me hear more.'

'It is, of course, impossible to view atoms through a microscope but mathematics can explain the behaviour of the electrons that orbit an atom's nucleus in surprising ways. An electron can, for example, exist in more than one location at any particular time. Is there a way in which I can illustrate this for you?'

Saunderson rose and walked to the door. Cooper thought he was about to be thrown out. Instead, the mathematician shouted loudly for someone called Briggs and within seconds an eager-looking young man scampered into the room. 'This is my assistant Briggs. He's very bright and he will hopefully help me to visualise the things you are about explain to me. Give Dr Cooper some paper, Briggs, and prepare to question and interrogate. We must decide what to make of our guest and his ideas if we are to offer him a position here.'

The three men sat side by side at a large, uncluttered oak table, with Cooper in the middle. He struggled using the quill and ink he was provided with, but with Briggs' help sketched diagrams and formulae on sheet after valuable sheet of paper, explaining to Saunderson what he was doing. Briggs often repeated the description in slightly different terms, and the professor occasionally let out a thoughtful hmmm as he absorbed the information. Once or twice he touched the paper as if to trace with his fingers the scratched markings Cooper had made.

What Cooper had set out to present was a sort of everyman's guide to quantum physics, attempting to make it relate to the science of the time he was in. He knew that this was an era of curiosity and discovery, an era in which people were open to new ideas.

Saunderson sat quietly for a time, numbers tumbling around and reordering themselves in his brain. 'Briggs,' he suddenly said. 'Will you help me to build some models so that I can feel this new quantum world?'

'Of course, professor.'

'And you, Dr Cooper, will you talk to me in the days and weeks to come about other matters of which I feel so ignorant?'

'If that means I have a position here, then I will gladly talk to you as often as you wish about the quantum world.'

Saunderson smiled. 'I will sit in on your initial lectures to reassure myself that you have the ability to deliver information at, shall we say, a more basic level to our students here. And you are more than welcome to observe mine. Consider yourself on probation, Dr Cooper, at say £4 per month. Do you have any questions?'

'May I use the Wren Library, sir?'

London – 1719

Entering through the main gate of the Tower of London was more daunting than Jax had expected it to be. She had visited the place once before on a school trip and the Beefeaters had been a smiley bunch, laughing and joking with visitors, and making light of the most gruesome events in the Tower's history. The yeoman warders who greeted them now were, despite their cheerful red livery, a stern lot. They led the three of them and Solomon, who was clearly unsettled by the smell and roaring of captive animals, towards the Royal Mint.

They were expecting to see Bill Jenks, who had posted that clever message in The Courant, but when Daniel Allstein also shot out of the door to greet them they were stunned. They took in the delighted faces of their friends before leaping down and hugging them. A smiling Seth descended in more sedate fashion, handing over Solomon's reins to a stable boy and instructing him not to unload the cart.

'This is our friend Seth, without whose help we would not be here,' said Jax. 'He's an absolute hero.' Jenks and Allstein stepped forward and shook the man's hand.

'And let me introduce the man whose brilliant idea brought us together,' said Jenks. 'It was Sir Isaac's idea to place the advertisement.' Jax and Calvert looked starstruck at the sight of the famous scientist holding out his hand to them.

'You are most welcome, my friends,' said the great man, who invited them into his quarters. 'I will show you around later, but first you must take some refreshment with your colleagues. I am sure you have much to talk about.'

Seth said he would like to stretch his legs and asked Sir Isaac if it would be possible to walk freely within the Tower precincts, and perhaps visit the armoury. The scientist called for one of his assistants and asked him to show the blacksmith everything he wished to see.

The four scientists sat around a solid oak table laden with food and just looked at one another. At faces they thought they would never see again. At friends they thought had died. And all of them wondering two things – was Tom Cooper on his way, and would they ever get home?

'This means that Tom probably didn't die, at least not in the explosion,' offered Allstein. 'If we all made it, he probably did too.'

'Although, knowing his talent for getting into scrapes . . .' said Jenks, unwilling to finish the sentence in case he was talking ill of the dead.

'Yes,' said Calvert slowly, ripping off a chunk of bread. 'The dean's daughter . . .'

'. . . and that incident with the punt,' added Jax. 'And that incredible dinner he laid on for us all.'

'Oh my god, yes. Where on earth did he get a swan?' shouted Jenks.

They spent several hours catching up, each of them in turn relating their stories, the dangers they faced and the people who had helped them, one of whom had just joined them at the table. Seth said he had hammered out the blade of a sword during his visit to the armoury and looked tired but contented as the group chatted and ate. As the talking subsided and they absorbed the reality of their new situation, the newcomers silently took in their environment. The rug-covered stone floors and dust-encrusted windows. The guttering candles and age-black furniture. The leather-bound books and ink-stained pens.

Calvert was first to speak. 'We're a pretty smart bunch of people, and I'm including Seth in that statement. Without him, and the people of Bigby, we wouldn't be here. But looking around us, at what is, frankly, a largely medieval environment, I have to say that I don't feel very positive about us designing and building something that will get us back to the 21st century.'

'Although we did bring bits of the 21st century with us,' said Jax.

'As did Allstein and I,' said Jenks. 'Perhaps we should take a look at what we've got between us.'

The four scientists were about to get up to retrieve their items when Sir Isaac joined them. 'I have instructed some of my team to clear out one of the large stables for you to use as you wish. Advise me of any other requirements and I will do my best to assist you. And if you will permit me to observe your methods, I would be most honoured,' he said.

'The honour would be ours,' said Calvert as they dashed off to gather together the items that had travelled back with them. Minutes later they placed them on the table, half a dozen artefacts of metal and glass that looked alien in the gloom of Newton's centuries-old apartments.

'Well, it's a start,' said Allstein.

Calvert and Jax looked at one another. 'Oh, we've also got the Wells chamber on the back of our cart.'

'Of course you have,' said Jenks, disbelievingly.

'It's true,' said Calvert. 'It came with me, and Seth and the good people of Bigby kept it safe. The group hurried to the stables where the cart had been stored and Calvert leapt on to it to clear away the hay surrounding the chamber, lying on its side and tied down with ropes. Jenks touched it reverently. 'It's beautiful,' he said. 'So beautiful.'

'It's just a titanium box,' said Allstein, dispassionately. 'But it's packed with stuff that might just expedite our little trip. I wonder why some of the technology came with us, and not, say, the bricks and mortar. Perhaps we just didn't notice ordinary stuff like that and collected up what we thought might be useful. The shiny bits. We were all in roughly the same part of the lab when the flash happened, which probably explains why we ended up in the same time but in different places.'

'OK,' said Jax. 'Let's go and see our new laboratory and start planning how we're going to make a time machine, preferably one that's going to take us where – and when – we want to go.'

The stable Newton had allocated was bigger than they expected. It had stalls for four horses, which workmen were already dismantling to create one large room. Poo-filled straw had already been barrowed out and the stone floor swept. The rough walls were made of stone and Jax asked Sir Isaac if these could be painted white to reflect more light. The roof was watertight but Jenks requested a lower ceiling be installed to better seal the space. Seth looked like he was dancing but he was actually moving his feet over a wobbly floor slab.

'We'll need a level floor, guys,' said Allstein, who turned to Newton. 'Sir Isaac, would it be possible to have some timber to create a raised floor.'

Newton nodded to one of his staff and asked him to measure the space and order the materials. 'Would you like to paint that white too?' he asked with a smile.

'Definitely,' said Jax, hooking her arm through that of the great man, who looked rather pleased at the manoeuvre.

Cambridge – 2030

Joel was doing his day job in gravitational lensing and spectrography but made sure he popped into the beacon lab at least once a day. To check on progress, but mainly to spend time with Angela. Granted six months' sabbatical from her other projects, she was a different person to the one whose spirits had slumped so low. She absorbed the energy that radiated from Mrs Carter. The two women and their assistants had formed a family-like bond that made him a little jealous.

As usual, he arrived mid-morning with coffee and pastries and asked how things were going. They would usually just say fine and leave it at that. But this time Angela said, 'We're struggling, Joel. We're confident we can build a device that sends a pulse. It's a physical thing that's basically electronics, and we're pretty much there with the design of it.'

'So, what's the problem?'

'Emitting the pulse is one thing, but even if they manage to detect it, how do they know it's coming from us. We need a simple way of signalling the location and the year.'

'Something like Morse Code, you mean?' asked Joel, his mouth full of doughnut.

'What?' said Mrs Carter.

'You know,' said Joel. 'Dot dot dot dash dash dash, sort of thing. Learned it in the Scouts.'

Angela gave him one of those slow, appreciative nods that he knows means he's been a good boy. 'We were overthinking it weren't we? But it is slightly annoying that an astronomer solved the problem for us.'

'Well, a Boy Scout, actually,' added Mrs Carter.

'They're just called Scouts now,' said Joel. 'The appreciation didn't last long, did it? About a nanosecond, I'd say.' And with that, he grabbed the bag of doughnuts and huffed out of the room.

'Sorry, Joel, I'll make it up to you,' Angela managed to shout before the door slammed shut. 'He'll be OK. I'll take him to the pub.'

'It was a stroke of genius though,' said Mrs Carter. 'So, what do we send?'

'How about CAM30? Location and year. I'm not sure what it will sound like in Morse Code but it's worth a try. And if it's rubbish we can blame Joel.'

'Here it is,' said Rocky, the fastest Googler in the east.

DASH DOT DASH DOT DOT DASH DASH DASH DOT DOT DOT DASH DASH DASH DASH DASH DASH DASH

'Sounds complicated. Would they get that?' asked Angela. 'Were any of them Scouts?'

'I'd put money on Jenks being a Scout. I can picture him in shorts and a woggle,' said Mrs Carter with a laugh in her voice. 'We have to give Morse a try but we should keep thinking. We might come up with something a bit more . . . scientific.'

'I'd better go and mollify Joel. I don't like hurting his feelings and, who knows, we might need his Scout knowhow later on.'

Angela, coffee in hand, found Joel sitting on a bench finishing the last of the doughnuts. 'Sorry, we didn't mean to make fun of you. It was a bloody good idea,' she said, settling down beside him. 'In truth, we were probably a bit annoyed for not thinking of it ourselves. It was very clever of you, Joel.'

'Really?' he said, making the transition from gloomy to smug in the blink of an eye. 'It just seemed obvious to me. There is one thing I'm curious about, but I'm sure you've got a solution.'

'What is it?

'You're transmitting a pulse from the beacon in 2030. How are they going to detect it perhaps hundreds of years into the past?'

'They're not,' said Angela, sipping her coffee. 'If they are trying to get back, we are assuming that they'll be building a device similar to the one they were working on when things went wrong. The big differences are that they will be trying to jump forward in time and arrive at a specific date and location. If it was me back there, I would be trying to tune in to that date and location.'

'Like trying to find a station on an old transistor radio,' said Joel, looking pleased with his analogy.

'Exactly. The beacon will give them something to tune into, if they can work out the Morse Code. We reckon it will take three or four months to build and install it on the site of the old laboratory. Then, we'll just have to wait . . . and hope that they can create a suitable device with whatever resources they have in the past.'

'Piece of cake for five brainbox physicists then,' said Joel.

Bigby – 1719

Peter Perkins was writing his sermon when Joe Dings knocked on his door the day after arriving back in Bigby and asked if he could speak to him privately. He had had a dream. Or at least he thought it was a dream, and needed to discuss it with someone who wasn't Enid Whipple, who frightened him. The parson ushered him into his study and the two men sat facing one another either side of the hearth.

'A dream, you say, Joe.'

'A most strange and vivid one, parson. Containing things that I am reluctant to say out loud in case it gets me permanently locked up.' Joe shifted uncomfortably in his chair. Perkins settled back and decided to give Joe the time and space he needed to tell his tale, which would almost certainly have something to do with his disappearance.

'I dreamt I was somewhere very, very bright,' Joe said

slowly. 'Does that make sense? No, probably not. Let me start somewhere else. I dreamt I was in a wood or a forest. Not the one outside Bigby. All the trees were the same, huge fir trees, in straight lines, like corn. And I walked until I found a perfectly straight lane that looked like it led for miles both ways, so I chose one way and started to walk. Then I hears a humming sound that gets louder and louder until the lane is filled with a green-coloured four-wheeled carriage of some sort . . . with no horses. I must have gone a bit wobbly then because a man got out and helped me into the carriage. And it moved off. On its own, parson. On its own.'

Joe was beginning to look agitated so Perkins told him to relax and take his time. 'The dream got a bit hazy then and the next thing I remember is being in a palace. All white, with bright lights in the ceiling and lots of people lying in beds, some of them not looking too well. I struggled a bit when they tried to take my clothes off but then they stabbed me in the arm and it made me feel quite nice.

'I must have fallen asleep – which is a strange thing to happen in a dream, ain't it, parson – and when I wakes up I'm in a different palace, with people telling me I'm safe in very calm voices, and asking me where I've come from.'

'It must have been quite a frightening experience for you, Joe.'

'For some of the time it was. But then they would give me a pill to swallow and everything seemed nice again, and I could look out of the window and see smooth grass and beautiful flowers and people being pushed along paths in chairs with wheels. It felt like heaven, but I knew it was a dream. It was a dream, wasn't it parson? I haven't gone mad, have I?'

Perkins couldn't decide whether to tell Joe that he had probably glimpsed the future. He was clearly fragile, having been told he had been missing for six weeks, and might struggle to comprehend the idea that he had witnessed the world as it would be in 300 years' time. But he decided the poor man deserved the truth. A truth that most of the other villagers had seemed to accept.

So he told him about Jax and Calvert and their colleagues having been transported back in time because of an accident. And about their intention to return. He told him about the meeting in the church, where villagers had expressed their gratitude to Calvert for what he had done for Bigby, and how Seth had accompanied them on their journey to London.

Joe sat there open-mouthed for several minutes, and Perkins let the information sink in. The vacant expression on the big man's face remained there as he stood and made his way silently and slowly to the front door of the parsonage. He turned to Perkins. 'So, not a dream then.'

'No, Joe. You've been to the future and back.'

Joe smiled. 'It was lovely,' he said. 'So clean.'

Cambridge – 1719

Trinity's Wren Library was larger than the one in Lincoln Cathedral. Well-ordered bookshelves filled both side walls of the long room and additional shelves jutted into the space at right angles. Light streaming in through large, arched windows above the shelves gleamed off the library's chequerboard floor.

The librarian there could not have offered a greater contrast to his counterpart at Lincoln. Dr David Troughton instantly recognised Cooper as a new face at Trinity and greeted him warmly. Cooper gave him Saunderson's letter of introduction and Troughton offered him a tour of the library, of which he was obviously proud. He told Cooper that he had seen Lincoln's library and liked it very much, but found its librarian to be "disagreeable". Cooper agreed with him.

Troughton was in his late thirties and had read classics at Trinity. He told Cooper that he was free to use the library whenever he wished and that he would be pleased to locate any books that he wished to see. Cooper decided against mentioning the copy of The Romance of Alexander that Potter had asked him to steal. He would have to bide his time.

Cooper took a room in a lodging house not far from the college and Saunderson agreed that he could spend a week observing a few of his lectures before taking his own classes. Saunderson, usually accompanied into the classroom by Briggs, was an engaging and entertaining speaker who was respected by his students, mainly well-to-do sons of the gentry. The subjects covered - from calculus and algebra to optics and geometry – seemed pretty basic to Cooper. The test would be in how well he would be able to deliver the information in order to secure a permanent position beyond his trial period. He need not have worried. Briggs helped him prepare his lessons and Saunderson sat in on his first lecture, declaring Cooper a natural teacher and never bothering to bring his trial period to an end. Cooper was hired.

He visited the library often, getting to know the way the books were catalogued and one day hearing a student asking Troughton if he could view The Romance of Alexander. Cooper discreetly noted where the librarian took it from before returning to the copy of Newton's Philosophiae Naturalis Principia Mathematica he was pretending to read. One thing he was able to read was a letter from Potter handed to him at the Trinity gatehouse asking him where "the book" was. 'I have met my part of the bargain. Now it is time to fulfil yours,' the letter said. 'I will allow you one more month before I start casting doubt on your background, your credentials and your honesty. Trinity College Dublin indeed.'

He had grown to like Troughton and the two had occasionally eaten together. Cooper told him about his time in the Royal Navy and even his spell in the household of Lady Muckleborough, avoiding too many details that would raise questions. He knew that he would feel guilty about carrying out the task Potter had assigned him, but what was the alternative? If he didn't steal the book, he would be exposed and lose a job he was beginning to enjoy.

He arranged to have dinner with Troughton at the Fox that evening and had decided to explain his dilemma. It was risky but he now regarded the librarian as a friend and felt he could trust him.

'May I take you into a confidence?' Cooper asked the librarian after each had picked their way through a substantial meal. 'I find myself in something of a bind.'

'Of course,' said Troughton. 'Providing no crime is involved, I am content to be your confidante, Thomas. Is it a lady, perchance?'

'Oh no, nothing as simple as that, David. This matter involves a crime, but not one that has yet been committed, so I think we are safe in discussing it.' He ordered more ale.

'Let us start slowly, Thomas, and see where it leads us.'

'I have been asked to steal a valuable book from your library.'

Troughton's expression didn't change. 'Can we take it a little more slowly still? That sentence came at me a trifle fast.'

'Very well, David. I am not going to steal a book from your library. I was going to steal it but I know how much that would distress you, so now I'm not going to.'

Troughton took several gulps of ale. 'Not only would it distress me, Thomas, it would also cost me my job,' he said in a matter-of-fact way that camouflaged a thudding heart and a racing mind. 'So what is the other concern? A murder, perhaps, or the bringing down of the monarchy?'

'I am not all I seem, my friend, and the man who asked me to steal the book is going to expose me if I don't carry out the task. He was instrumental in me gaining my position here and can just as easily see me dismissed or even prosecuted. Perhaps imprisoned. I know I am a good teacher but I am here under false pretences.'

Troughton leaned across the table and grasped the arm of his dining companion in sympathy. 'I am afraid you have but one course of action open to you, Thomas,' he said sympathetically.

'And that is?'

'Get the hell out of here before they lock you up.'

'I know,' said Cooper, dejectedly. 'But where can I go?'

'London, of course. You can easily lose yourself in one of the largest cities in the world. You're resourceful. You will find your way, Thomas. And my books will remain safe.'

Cooper would be paid in a week, well before Potter's deadline, and would use the money to get him to the capital – 60 or so miles by road and a little over half a day's journey by coach. Then he would have to survive on his wits. Again.

He had hoped that Potter would forget about him once he had got to Cambridge but the man was a weasel and may even have had Peabody spying on him. It's a shame because he was enjoying teaching and the academic life, and was disappointed at having to move on after such a short time in Cambridge.

The morning after he was paid, he packed up his belongings and caught the 6am coach to London and would be out of Potter's clutches by early afternoon, lost in a city of more than half a million people.

The coach approached London from the north and into the western side of the city, along the route of the modern M1. Pleasant open countryside was gradually replaced by the relatively new stone and brick buildings that had replaced the wooden structures destroyed just over 50 years before in the Great Fire. There was investment here, in smart homes, civic buildings and commercial property.

But how would he earn money? He didn't know anyone, there were no universities to teach at, and in any case he had no references or qualifications. Perhaps a posh school would take him on, if they were desperate, no questions asked. Or was there another way mathematics and science could provide him with a living?

He turned to and nudged the passenger beside him on the outside seats. The man, in his forties and swaddled in a huge coat, had been asleep for the last few miles and woke with a start. 'Are we there?' he asked, suddenly wide-eyed.

Cooper apologised for waking him. 'We're in London, sir, so nearly at our final stop. Do you happen to know where the

Royal Society meets?'

The man looked around him to get his bearings. 'That pompous talking shop of medical types and so-called natural philosophers? If that's who you're referring to I believe they gather at Gresham College in Bishopsgate. I went to one of their lectures a few years ago and was one of a number in the audience who dropped off at the droning voice of the presenter. The sound of snoring eventually drowned out the speaker's voice. I felt quite sorry for him in the end. If you have business there, I feel sorry for you too, sir. They are a tedious bunch. What is it you do?'

'I'm a mathematician and natural philosopher, sir, but not one of the tedious ones, I hope.'

The man declined to look chastened and had the decency to wish Cooper good luck. The coach finally stopped at an inn in the Strand. Although Cooper hardly recognised the famous road, he knew that from there he would be able to locate Bishopsgate to the east. He estimated that it would take him about an hour to walk, along the north bank of the Thames and through the City of London. He kept tight hold of his bag, walked along the busiest streets and fixed a menacing look on his face to deter robbers.

If he was afraid that he might not be able to find Gresham College, he need not have worried. It was housed in a huge, unmissable Elizabethan mansion. There was an inn opposite so he crossed a mud-slick road busy with carriages and handcarts and ordered food and ale, his first meal of the day, he realised. The place was full of men. The only women there were serving ale.

As he considered how he was going to approach the society,

he picked up snatches of conversation from around the room. Talk of commerce and trade, ships due into port, money to be made, debts to be recovered. But what interested him most was a reference by a prosperous-looking man at a nearby table of a lecture to be delivered at the Royal Society that evening. He was talking to a similarly well-to-do man, whose bored expression said he could think of a hundred better ways to spent his time than attending a lecture.

As his food arrived, Cooper leaned across to the man who had mentioned the talk. 'I am so sorry to intrude, gentlemen, but may I ask who is presenting the lecture and what the topic might be.'

The two men studied him closely for several seconds. He realised his appearance was in stark contrast to their own fine attire, covered as he was in dirt and grime from his journey. 'Please forgive the way I appear, good sirs, I am a natural scientist. I have just returned from a research expedition and was in dire need of sustenance before changing,' he said. In truth, he hadn't anything to change into but resolved to brush himself down and tidy his appearance later. He would try and get a room for the night.

'What was the nature of your expedition?' asked one of the men, catching Cooper off-guard.

'The behaviour of the herring shoals in the German Sea,' he said, falling back on a tried and tested – although ultimately unbelievable – tale. 'Development of the commercial aspects of the trade are of considerable importance to our nation,' he added with enthusiasm.

'Then I doubt that this evening's lecture will be of much interest to you,' the second man said snootily. 'I understand that a man named Joseph Williamson is talking – probably at great length, knowing him – about a new clock he claims he has invented.' The man looked at the gold watch tucked into his waistcoat pocket. 'This is all I need to know about time – that we must be on our way to the meeting of the South Sea Company.'

'Ah,' said Cooper, 'whose bubble is soon to burst, I believe, gentlemen. I hope you do not have too much invested in it.'

The two men stood before him, adjusting their wigs. 'What the devil do you mean by that, sir?' said the first.

'I'm afraid you will find out . . . in time.' Cooper's food arrived and the men turned on their chunky heels and departed. Cooper called back the young woman who had delivered his meal and asked her where he could buy a ticket to the lecture across the road. She said she believed all events at the Royal Society were free.

He paid the landlord for a room for the night, dumped his bag and tidied himself up. When he noticed people arriving at Gresham College, he joined the throng and took his seat at the back of the lecture hall.

At 7pm precisely, according to the wall clock in the hall, Joseph Williamson stepped up to the dais and placed on the small table beside him a device about the size of a carriage clock. Without preamble of any sort he announced in a broad Irish accent the invention of his equation clock, a device he said displayed not only standard time but also the solar time, claiming that it made the clock the most accurate ever invented. Clearly a respected clockmaker of considerable inventiveness, Williamson went on to describe the cam and differential gearing that made his clock so revolutionary, and received generous applause.

But Cooper wasn't there to hear about the latest trends in

clockmaking, he wanted to meet people and look for a job. He chatted to several physicians, keen to talk about the rapidity of their most recent amputations, but then he spotted a man who appeared to be attracting a great deal of attention. Obviously a mover and shaker in the 18th century. He edged towards the man, attempting to listen in on the conversations he was having, but these appeared to be wide-ranging and somewhat unfocused. Nature, the planets, optics, money. What on earth was the man's speciality?

Cooper eventually found himself alone with the man and introduced himself. Said he was new to London and looking for a position suitable for a mathematician and natural philosopher. There was no point beating about the bush.

'Thomas Cooper, you say?' asked the man in a voice that was both droning and agitated. 'Dr Thomas Cooper, of Cambridge?' The man was studying him closely, and Cooper found it unnerving.

'Indeed, sir, but I don't think we have met before,' said Cooper feigning a confidence that was fast ebbing away. 'Mine is an extremely common name.' He began to back away from the man, fearing that he was a friend of Potter and had already heard about his departure from Cambridge in order to renegue on his agreement with the duplicitous librarian.

A smile had crept onto the face of the man, who ushered away those who had started to congregate around him once more. He held out his hand and introduced himself as Isaac Newton. He gripped Cooper's hand firmly and said, 'I wonder if you have some time to spare, Dr Cooper.'

Cooper was stunned into silence. He had shaken the hand of one of the most influential scientists of the age but all he could think of doing was fleeing the room. As he tried to increase the gap between then, Newton held on to his hand. 'I don't believe you heard me, sir,' he murmured, looking Cooper squarely in the eye. 'I asked if you could spare me . . . some time.'

Was the great man threatening him? The tone of his voice did not suggest that he was. But why would he want to engage in conversation with a stranger, someone he knew absolutely nothing about, a nobody looking for a job.

'There are some people who would like to see you again.' This again sounded a little threatening. 'If you have . . . the time. But I must ensure that my instincts are correct and that I have the right Thomas Cooper. I can do this easily enough by giving you a date . . . say 2030.'

The room wobbled unsettlingly. Cooper thought he was going to pass out. But Newton held on to him. 'Please come with me, Dr Cooper. I have a carriage outside that will take us to my offices at the Tower of London where you will find your colleagues.'

'They're in prison?' asked Cooper. 'In the Tower, for goodness sake? What have they done?'

'They're my guests, good sir. They are working there on a way to get you back to where you belong.'

'But who?

'All of them – Jenks, Jax, Calvert, Allstein. The brightest brains in our world today. They had all but given up hope of you joining them. But here you are. Thrown here by fate.'

Cooper dashed across the road to the inn and recovered his bag before leaving with Newton for the carriage journey to the Tower. During the 15-minute drive Sir Isaac explained how Jenks had found him and about his suggestion to place an advertisement in the Courant, which had resulted in Calvert, Jax and Allstein travelling to London. He said he would leave his colleagues to share their adventures and experiences with him.

The four scientists were busy when Newton's carriage clattered across the cobbles outside their workshop beside the Mint just after 9pm. Cooper followed Sir Isaac into the white-painted candlelit interior, where he saw the Wells chamber in the centre of the room and other 21st century parts laid out on benches. Allstein was studying plans attached to one wall. Jax and Jenks were carefully reconfiguring two of the units on the bench and Calvert stood with a drink in his hand gawping at the new arrival.

'Evening, everyone. Sorry I'm late,' said Cooper setting down his bag. They stood there transfixed. Jax was the first to react. 'You always were a rubbish timekeeper,' she said, rushing up and throwing her arms around him.

'We'd pretty much given up hope of you finding us,' said Jenks.

'I hadn't,' said Jax. 'We'd all got here, why not Tom? I knew you'd do it. Eventually.'

'I thought you'd probably died,' said Calvert with a smile. 'Shot in a duel by a jealous husband would have been my guess.'

Allstein stepped away from the plans and slapped Cooper on the back. 'I couldn't be more pleased to see you, Tom. Another brain on our little problem.' He looked at Cooper's bag. 'Did you bring any goodies with you?'

'Such as?' Cooper asked.

'Well, we all arrived with bits of the tech that landed us here,' said Jax, indicating the Wells chamber and other items.

'Ah,' said Cooper. 'I might have done. But I arrived in the

middle of a river, so if anything came with me it's at the bottom of the Yare.'

'It sounds like you have a good story to tell,' said Calvert. 'So shall we adjourn to the Queen's Arms round the corner and catch up.'

'And celebrate,' said Jax. 'We've got the band back together!'

A smiling Newton declined their invitation to join them and sat down at his desk and looked grimly at the group. 'I fear that you are all facing the most difficult part of your adventure. I cannot see how even your considerable abilities are going to conceive of a way to get you home with what poor resources this age can offer. If I can help in any way I will, for this is an undertaking I had not expected to witness at my advanced age.' He offered them a wan smile. 'Enjoy your celebration this evening. I will be waiting tomorrow to assist in any way I can.'

At the inn, and later at lodgings the four shared in a narrow street behind the Tower, the group discussed their experiences. Jax said she was sorry that Cooper had not met Seth and Solomon, who had returned to Bigby. 'I'm going to miss that lovely village and its amazing people. Especially Seth,' she said. 'He has a giant's heart.'

They all agreed that Cooper's tale of press-gang, battles, country house living and blackmail at the hands of a malign librarian took first prize. But Jenks came in for the most praise, for seeking out Sir Isaac Newton and convincing him of where they had travelled from. 'I recalled from my school days that although Newton experimented widely in many different fields, he was often reluctant to acknowledge new thinking from other natural philosophers,' said Jenks.

'But I knew that he had considered the concept of time and attempted to give him a glimpse of the future – air travel, computing, space travel – in a way that would excite him. His idea of placing an advertisement was a stroke of . . . well, genius.'

Cooper looked around the bedroom in which they were seated. It was gloomy in the candlelight and sparsely furnished. It had two biggish beds, however, and Cooper was invited to share one with Jenks. Allstein and Calvert shared another, and Jax had a room to herself. The landlady, Mistress Trott, was delighted with her well-mannered lodgers, who paid their rent in advance and didn't get up to any funny business under her roof.

'How do you pay for this?' asked Cooper. 'In fact, how are you paying for any of it?'

'We're working for the Royal Mint, of which Sir Isaac is Warden. We are coining it in,' said Allstein, delighted with his joke. Cooper was the only one who chuckled. He was the only one who hadn't heard it before. 'We spend an hour or so a day on Mint work – improving the efficiency of the machines, the quality of the dies used for striking the coins, the security of the storage facilities.'

'We've even used an idea of Sherlock Holmes to clamp down on clipping and counterfeiting,' said Calvert. 'You've heard of his Baker Street Irregulars, the youngsters who brought him information. Well, we've got the Tower Territorials, a couple of dozen kids who tell us about dodgy coins, who's making them and where they can be found. They're paid for the information and paid again if Sir Isaac's men catch the crooks. He's delighted with it and wanted to know if we had met Mr Holmes.'

When the last of their candles sputtered out they decided to turn in and make an early start on their project. 'He's right, you know,' said Allstein. 'This is going to be the hardest part. Being dumped here by accident is one thing. Getting back in a precise way is something else entirely.'

'Well that should help me sleep better. Thanks, Dan,' said Cooper.

As they walked silently to the Tower the following morning, the rising sun cast a deep shadow beneath its western wall. It was a gloom they shared. The joy they had experienced at all five of them having survived the accident, and the stories they had shared of their time in a foreign age, had left them overnight. Reality had dawned with the thin sunlight creeping over the Thames.

Their workshop was not as it was when they left it the previous night. All their equipment was missing and the plans had been removed from the wall.

'Perhaps Newton has relocated us to a larger stable,' said Jenks. 'I'll go and find out.' He returned five minutes later with Sir Isaac scurrying behind him looking shocked at the news.

'I gave no instruction for these items to be taken away,' he said, flustered.

'No, but I did,' said a voice from the doorway. An overweight man in a long brown wig stood there with his right hand clasping a silver-topped cane. Two Beefeaters stood behind him. 'I asked these gentlemen to remove that ghastly box and the other baubles you had lying about. This may not be a very modern thing to say but they had the whiff of witchery about them.'

'Ah, my lord. How very good it is to see you here at this

early hour,' said Newton, not meaning a word of it. He turned to the scientists and said, 'May I introduce the Earl of Carlisle, esteemed Constable of the Tower and, as you will know, briefly First Lord of the Treasury.'

There was clearly no love lost between the men. 'My colleagues and I are engaged in a scientific experiment, not witchcraft. Return our equipment immediately, sir.'

'I will not. I am in charge of the Tower, not you. And I will not tolerate your impudence and irascible attitude. The roguish items will remain under lock and key until I have decided what to do with them.'

'The King will hear of this,' said Newton.

'He is in Hanover. Have a safe journey, Newton,' said Carlisle, turning briskly and marching off with the yeoman warders in his wake. Sir Isaac called to the Tower's Ravenmaster as he passed by a few seconds later and asked him if he knew where the equipment had been taken. Had Carlisle destroyed it?

'I don't know, and I don't want to know, Sir Isaac,' he said loudly, waiting for Carlisle to disappear from view before quietly adding, 'I'll find out and let you know.'

'That damnable man. He's done everything possible to make life difficult for me since he became Constable here. He was a friend of Robert Hooke and felt that automatically made him my enemy. I feel sure he would not have dared destroy the items, but if they are still within the castle grounds they will be well guarded. Even if we managed to recover them they may never be safe here.'

'Is there no way we can win him over,' asked a disconsolate Jax.

Newton fell silent. 'We may not be able to win him over but

it might be possible to win back your equipment. Do any of you good people play cards?'

It seemed such an odd questions that none of the scientists could think how they should answer. 'Are you suggesting that we might be able to get back the Wells chamber and the other items by beating him at cards?' asked an incredulous Calvert.

'Precisely. Whoever played Carlisle would have to be very good for he is an extraordinarily successful gambler. I understand that his winnings at the gaming table account for as much as a third of his annual income, a great deal of which is going into the building of his enormous house in Yorkshire, Castle Howard. It has probably fallen into disrepair in your time,' he said hopefully.

Calvert smiled. 'I've visited the house, sir. It still stands, and is magnificent.'

'Shame,' said Newton.

'What chance would any of us stand against such an experienced and successful card player?' asked Jenks. 'And what would our side of the wager be? It would have to be significant enough to tempt him into playing.'

'Simple,' said Newton. 'If he wins I will stand down as Warden of the Royal Mint. I am old, I have served my time here and the King is pleased with my achievements. I can leave with my head held high. If you win he will have to return your equipment and provide you with everything you need to complete your task here.'

The group looked stunned. 'We can't ask you to do that. We'll find another way,' said Jenks.

'There is no other way. He is a man of his word, I'm sure. If he loses he will honour the agreement. So, while I go and put this proposal to him, you must decide which of you is going to take on this challenge. Cards isn't just about chance, it's also about mathematics, so might I suggest that you to choose the most capable opponent for his Lordship.'

As Newton left the workshop, the group turned as one to Cooper. 'It's got to be you,' said Jax. 'I don't know anyone who can do calculations quicker than you. And you've got plenty of . . . what's it called?'

'Front,' said Calvert. 'You've got more front than Blackpool. If anyone can pull this off, it's you. We just have to find out what the game is and help you prepare. Newton has put himself on the line for us. We can't let him down.'

Sir Isaac returned after half an hour with a satisfied smile on his face. 'He has agreed. Said he couldn't wait to see the back of me. He confirmed that the items have not been destroyed but wouldn't tell me where they were. But on the way back here Ravenmaster Phipps told me they were secured and well-guarded in the armoury, so there is little chance of us recovering them without undertaking this challenge. The game he has chosen is played in pairs. It means two of you will have to take on Carlisle. He is to be partnered by one of the regular players at the Crown Coffee House in Bedford Row, who will be chosen by ballot. It is to be whist, which I understand is very popular.'

Cooper looked surprised. 'Whist? As in whist drive? The game old people play in village halls?'

'I do not understand your description of the game but whist it is to be,' said Sir Isaac. 'The game will take place at 9pm in five days and will comprise nine games.'

The Ravenmaster strolled into the workshop. 'Master Phipps here is no slouch at the gaming table and has agreed to tutor you in the rules and certain strategies that you might employ,' said Newton. 'These might be subtly different from the game you know, so I would suggest you pay close attention. I would very much like to finish my work here, but more importantly I would like to see Carlisle humbled. So, who will your partner be Dr Cooper.'

'Me,' said Jax. 'I played whist on family holidays but we preferred to call it trumps because it was another name for farts.' She looked at their amused faces. 'We were kids, OK?'

Everyone agreed that Jax should partner Cooper. She was a brilliant scientist and, in finding Bigby, clearly resourceful. Newton looked uncomfortable, as though he wanted to say something but couldn't find the words. Jenks noticed and asked him if he was having second thoughts about putting his position at risk.

'Not at all,' said the great man. 'It's the only wager that would entice Carlisle into the challenge. My concern – and I am most reluctant to say this Miss Jax – is that a woman may not be permitted to play cards at the coffee house.'

Calvert had expected her to erupt at this but she remained calm. 'That's fine. I'll go as a man. It's how I got to Bigby, after all. I'm sure I can pull it off again.'

Cooper walked over to Phipps, a squat man with a pockmarked face, and thanked him for his offer of help. The Ravenmaster told the group that Newton was paying him handsomely for his tutorage and that it should start as soon as he came off duty that evening. 'There's a lot to learn if you are to beat his Lordship,' he added. 'I've never played him but I understand he is a clever and ruthless cardsman. The two of you will need your wits about you if you are to win. But let's see what we can do.' The Ravenmaster left to put his squawking charges to bed for the night. Newton returned to his office and immediately began scratching away with his quill.

'I still can't believe we are putting at stake Sir Isaac's position here, and our chance of getting home, on a few hands of what I've always thought of as a game for children or old ladies,' said Cooper. 'It seems such a big risk to take.'

That evening Jenks, Allstein and Calvert continued with their calculations on the assumption that their equipment would be won back. Cooper and Jax settled down at a table in a corner of the workshop with Phipps, who was accompanied by Warder Graine to make up the practice four.

For the first half-hour Phipps explained the rules and conventions, which were very much as Cooper and Jax understood them. The entire pack of 52 cards is dealt out, giving each player 13 cards. Partners sit opposite one another and are not allowed to communicate in any way. No sighing at the sight of the hand, no raised eyebrows or winks, no coughing that could be construed as a signal. The dealer is decided on a cut of the cards, which are then shuffled by the player on the dealer's left and then cut by the person on the dealer's right.

The dealer distributes the cards clockwise face down, starting on his left, and the final card is turned up to indicate which suit is trumps on that round. It remains on the table until it's the dealer's turn to play when it is returned to his hand. The winner of the round, known as a trick, is the person who plays the highest card of the suit led or, if they don't have a card of that suit, the one who lays the highest trump card. Whoever wins the trick lays the first card in the next trick.

Scoring after all the tricks have been played is different to how Cooper and Jax recall it, with points being awarded for every trick won above six tricks per game. The winner of the game is the first pair to nine points.

The scientists played a few hands with the warders, quickly appreciating that although fate dictated which cards you were dealt, strategy and memory also played a big part. Jax recalls being constantly rebuked when partnering her father for not remembering what had been laid before putting down a card. She had a sharp brain even as a child and learned fast. Their initial losing streak to the Beefeaters was quickly turned round and as the night wore on they won game after game. The warders agreed to return the following night to continue their tuition.

In the far corner of the workshop Allstein, Jenks and Calvert were deep in discussion, bent over hand-drawn sketches and page upon page of calculations and equations created in quill and ink. Cooper could see that their discussion had degenerated into grumpy disagreement and suggested that they return to their lodgings.

'Perhaps we can have a game of cards when we get back,' said Cooper.

'Sod off,' said Allstein.

Newton was studying their workings when the five scientists arrived the following morning looking refreshed but concerned. 'What is this device here?' he asked, pointing at an area of the drawing.

'It's a dynamo,' offered Jenks. 'A machine that converts mechanical energy into electricity by rotating coils of copper wire in an electrical field. Electricity will provide the energy necessary to power our device once we put it all together. Unfortunately the dynamo will only allow us to test the system.

It won't be powerful enough to get us home.'

Jenks turned to his colleagues. 'It's one of the things we were getting so fractious about last night. We should be able to source materials to make a simple dynamo but we need a reliable mechanical means of driving it.'

'Like a windmill?' said Newton. 'Or a waterwheel, perhaps?'

'Precisely,' said Calvert. 'We were arguing last over which might prove more efficient. Or indeed, the easier to build.'

'The windmill without a doubt,' said Newton. 'If we build it on the roof above the Mint it will be simple to connect it to your device. A waterwheel in the Thames would take longer to build and an extremely long rotating connector running through the grounds, which might get Carlisle asking difficult questions.'

The scientists looked at one another, relieved at the decision having been made for them.

'Tell me what you need and I will order the materials,' said Newton. 'Then tell me more about electricity. How else might it be used?' The scientists had discussed how much future technology they should reveal to Sir Isaac and he could see from their expressions that they were uncomfortable in revealing too much. 'I understand,' he said. 'My time is perhaps not ready for such advancements.'

Cambridge – 2030

'I can't find this one on the list,' said Dawn to her friend Lesley midway through the sculpture trail on the Science Park. 'What do you think it's supposed to be?'

'What are any of them supposed to be?' said Lesley. 'I'm sure some of these artists just cobble this stuff together out of rusty metal and give it the first name that pops into their fluffy heads.'

They looked at the object for several minutes, sustaining themselves with sausage rolls they had purchased for their art experience. About four metres tall, it pierced the ground like a skinny, upside down pyramid. An array of solar panels lay across the flat top, illuminating tiny LED lights dispersed across its four otherwise dull grey surfaces.

'It looks a bit . . . ominous. Like the thing those monkeys found in that space film,' said Dawn.

'I can see where you're coming from,' said Lesley, nodding, deep in thought, trying to get the artist's message. But failing. 'There's some writing. Do you see it. It's in a slightly lighter grey than all the other grey. Beacon of something-or-other, it says. And there's five names, but they're too small to read.'

'That tree's had it,' said Dawn, pointing at the amelanchier planted nearby, having abandoned all hope of discerning the artist's message. The two women moved on to find the next sculpture on the tour as Angela and Joel arrived with coffees and a lunchtime bag of jam doughnuts.

'Think it will work?' asked Joel, sugar glistening on his lips.

'It is working,' replied Angela indignantly. 'It's firing a pulse of Morse Code – which was a great idea, Joel – incredibly deep into the ground, indicating the location and date.'

Joel reached for another doughnut. 'It still feels a bit random to me. It's like a billion to one chance they're going to locate this thing.'

'I agree the chances are incredibly low, but they're better

than no chance at all. Think of this as a lighthouse. If you were the captain of an old sailing ship seeking a harbour at night, you would look for a light to guide you there. Our friends, if they're alive, will be looking for a way of finding their harbour using what they know best – physics.

'We designed it to look like a piece of sculpture, a memorial. Only a handful of people know what it's here for, and most of them think that Mrs Carter and I are totally nuts,' said Angela.

'They're probably right,' said Joel, casting a gentle arm across Angela's shoulder. As they walked away from the beacon and back to work she responded by looping her arm around the small of his back. It made Joel smile.

London – 1719

The hammering on the Mint's roof was driving Allstein mad. He had become used to a quiet life in bucolic Suffolk and the thudding of nearby money-making machinery combined with the hammering of workmen overhead was making him tetchy as he pored over complex calculations. The turbine work had also attracted the attention of an equally tetchy Carlisle. He stormed into Newton's office while he was writing and asked him what the devil he thought he was doing. Diversifying into milling corn? Turning his legendary butterfly mind into baking bread? He was clearly going mad, so wasn't it time he retired?

Newton didn't look up and continued scratching at his paperwork. 'I'm going to use wind power to make my coin-making engines work more efficiently for His Majesty. Is there anything else I can help you with, my lord? No? Then good day.'

Sir Isaac smiled to himself as Carlisle pivoted on the heels of his broad-buckled shoes and stormed off. It would take three more days to complete the wind turbine and cobble together a dynamo that would provide them with just enough power to test their equipment. If they got it back.

Jenks took the lead on the project. He and Allstein would try to work out what had gone wrong with their experiment and come up with a plan that would enable them to replicate it. They would also assess how much of the equipment that came with them would be usable, doing as much of this on paper. Calvert, Cooper and Jax would focus on the equally tricky task of getting them back to approximately the right time and location. In the evenings, Cooper and Jax would play whist, with their colleagues, with friendly yeoman warders and with well-rewarded Mint workers. They had considered trying to use subtle hand or eye signals in their game against Carlisle but were warned by Phipps that they would be closely observed and if caught would instantly forfeit the match. The stakes were too high. It would mean losing their equipment, costing Newton his job and squandering any hope of returning.

Cooper looked lost in thought while Phipps was reminding them of all this. He peered at the Ravenmaster. 'Would it be possible to acquire a pack of the same cards that are to be used in our match against Carlisle?' he asked. 'Purely for practice purposes, of course. You will be well paid. Won't he Sir Isaac?'

Newton had just walked in on the conversation. 'If it will help us to defeat the rogue Carlisle, how can I refuse? But please be aware, I may be Warden of the Royal Mint, but I am not made of money,' he said, cackling and shrugging his shoulders in glee at having uttered what was probably the first witticism of his life. He walked back to his office still chuckling.

'If I hadn't heard that with my own ears I would not have believed it,' said the warden. 'Don't worry, I'll get a deck of coffee house cards for you. But please don't do anything rash, Dr Cooper. There is too much at stake. Just play nicely and all will be well. Probably.'

Jax looked worried. 'Are you going to tell me what's going on in that mendacious mind of yours?'

'It's probably best you don't know,' said Cooper brightly. 'OK, shall we play a few hands.'

What struck them first was the noise. Men in fashionable wiggery shouting and banging the tables with their fists and glasses as they argued and debated, and someone trying to sing a raucous ditty without the talent to carry it off. The second thing was the assault on their noses. The Crown Coffee House stunk of body odour, smoke from long-stemmed pipes and cheap candles, and the smell of stale wine drifting up from the sticky floor. The aroma hit Cooper and Jax as they entered the front door behind Phipps and Newton. The sight of the revered man silenced the room. Word had spread of Carlisle's challenge and what was at stake for Sir Isaac – mainly because Carlisle had spread it - and the coffee house was full of intrigued observers. A square table had been left unoccupied in the middle of the room and as the scientists and their supporters approached it, it was clear that Jax, in her masculine guise of breeches, long coat, waistcoat and periwig, was attracting all the attention. Most couldn't quite put their finger on exactly what the attraction was.

She was trying not to smile at the silliness of the pretence and wondered if it might not have been simpler if one of her male colleagues had partnered Cooper. But now she came to think about it, none of them had even tried to volunteer. If there wasn't so much at stake, this would be fun, she thought as she took her seat at the table and self-consciously adjusted her hairpiece. Cooper had turned down the offer of a wig, telling Phipps that there were probably creatures living in it. Instead, he had tied back his hair and chosen sober, practical clothing that he hoped gave him an intimidating appearance in this room of foppish, colourful finery. He took his seat opposite Jax and she smiled encouragingly at him. He offered her a twitch of the eye that could have been a discreet wink.

Carlisle sported a confident look at he sat down at the table, nodding to both of them. The other seat would be occupied by a member of the coffee house whose name would be drawn from a large velvet bag. About 20 men had put their names forward for the match.

A large woman in voluminous clothes – the only other woman in the room that Jax could see – pulled a slip of paper from the bag and called out a name. 'Peter Carpenter,' she bellowed over the growing hubbub. 'You will partner Lord Carlisle.' Carlisle looked pleased. Carpenter was a good player, it seemed.

Phipps, dressed in full Beefeater uniform but without his pike, was standing beside the woman who had made the draw, possibly the wife of the coffee house owner, Cooper thought. After she had put the name slip back into the bag Phipps grabbed hold of it. She refused to let go but the determined warder tugged it from her grasp and handed it to Newton, who clasped it in front of him as he took his place behind Jax's chair. Phipps moved to stand behind Cooper, firmly nudging away a short, round man who had tried to settle there. Phipps had suggested that it might be wise to do this to prevent anyone from attempting to look at the hands of the scientists and perhaps subtly passing on valuable information to Carlisle and his partner.

An elderly man with a quavering voice outlined the rules of the game, which were as Phipps had told Cooper and Jax. There would be nine rounds and the winners would be the first to nine points. The contest would be aborted should there be any indication of cheating, he said firmly.

If the atmosphere in the coffee house had been fraught when they had arrived, it had intensified now that the game was about to commence. Despite an abundance of candles, the large room seemed dark and oppressive, with deep shadows in corners not reached by the dancing flames. What on earth were they doing in this menacing and alien environment, thought Jax. Playing cards for a chance to get home and save the job of the most famous man in the land. Whist for goodness sake. It would be laughable if it wasn't so serious.

She wondered what would happen in the future if Newton had to resign. Would Wikipedia update itself automatically? Would it give him more time to carry out research, perhaps based on what he had learned since their arrival. Would the future be irrevocably altered? It even occurred to her that as the dates for Newton's tenure at the Royal Mint were a historical fact in her time, they must win the match against Carlisle. Or was that wishful thinking?

Just as these thoughts were rattling through her mind she was being invited to cut the pack to decide who would deal. It would be Cooper, earned with a queen. He offered the deck to

Carpenter on his left, who shuffled the cards efficiently and handed them back. Cooper then placed the pack in front of Carlisle to his right. Carlisle cut it in two, placing the bottom half on top and returning the cards to Cooper with a look that Jax took to be the absolute definition of smugness. Boy, would I like to wipe that expression off your overfed face, she thought.

Cooper dealt the cards confidently, neatly delivering 13 cards to each player across the cloth-covered table. It didn't start well for the scientists. They lost the first three hands, conceding five points to the grinning Carlisle. He only needed four more to send Newton packing. Cooper and Jax picked up a point in the fourth hand, in which they scraped home by seven tricks to six. But the following hand saw Carlisle and Carpenter scoop up two more points to lead 7-1 with only four more hands remaining. Jax couldn't help feeling that all was lost but then she was dealt a hand stacked with trump cards and the pair won it 9-4, giving them three valuable points. They took another point in the following hand, leaving the score at 7-6 to Carlisle and Carpenter going into the final round. But Cooper and Jax won a point that tied the match.

The man with the quavering voice stepped forward and announced that an additional hand would be played to decide the winner. For the first time Carlisle looked concerned. Jax dealt. Arranging her cards in her hand she glanced at Cooper to see if she could detect a sign of either confidence or concern. He was stony-faced and held his cards close to his chest. Carlisle laid the first card. Midway through the hand, tricks were being won by both sides. It was going to be close. The room was edgy and silent.

Suddenly, a man standing close to Carlisle shouted out.

'What's this, sir?' he yelled angrily at his lordship. 'You've dropped a card. I saw it fall from your hand.' Carlisle looked down and at his feet lay the ace of hearts, the trump suit.

'That's not mine,' he screeched. 'I have all my cards. I know nothing of this.'

'He's cheating,' bellowed the angry man. 'That's how he takes all our money, the cad.'

The room became chaotic and Cooper rose theatrically, slamming his cards on the table and looking squarely at the elderly man for a ruling. He hesitated long enough to make Jax nervous but then said, 'I declare our guests the victors, and humbly apologise to them for what they have experienced in this most respected of houses. It is a matter of deep regret that our visitors have been treated so shamefully.'

Carlisle looked stunned and continued to protest his innocence as he was ushered towards the door of the coffee house. People muttered and spluttered their disgust. Carlisle's unfortunate partner looked bemused and insisted he had no part in the deception. 'I didn't even want to play with the man but I owed him money and he insisted,' he said.

Newton stepped towards him and the room hushed. "What do you mean, he insisted,' said Sir Isaac. 'Your name was drawn at random from this bag, was it not?' He tipped the slips of paper onto the card table and every one bore the name of the poor wretch. Peter Carpenter. The coffee house's best cardsman after Carlisle himself. Those gathered around the table looked shocked.

As one, the establishment's members turned their backs on the man and created a pathway to the exit. 'I had no choice,' he whimpered, tears filling his eyes as he made his way slowly to the door. 'He would have ruined me.'

Jax crept up to Newton. 'You knew, didn't you? That's why you got Phipps to grab the bag of names.'

'What?' said Cooper.

'I merely suspected and took charge of the bag from the landlady.'

'And the card on the floor?' asked Jax.

Newton looked at Cooper. 'A complete mystery to me,' said Sir Isaac, with just the merest hint of a smile. 'And me,' said Cooper, unconvincingly. 'Let's get out of here.'

The man with the quavering voice shook the hands of all four as they departed, apologising for Carlisle's behaviour and the shame it had brought on the reputation of the coffee house.

They arrived back at the Mint after a short carriage drive and Jenks, Allstein and Calvert shot out of the workshop to greet them. 'Well?' said Calvert before they had even alighted from the carriage.

'The man cheated,' said Cooper.

'He wasn't the only one,' said Jax.

Cooper ignored her. 'He got a ringer to help him win,' he said. 'The second best player in the house after him. Peter Carpenter's name was drawn from a bag full of Peter Carpenters. It was disgraceful. Got them both drummed out of the coffee house with their tails between their legs.'

Jax stared at him in disbelief with her arms folded. He noticed and paused. 'What's wrong?' he asked.

'Was he the only one who cheated?' Jax asked him.

'Probably not,' said Cooper. 'That Carpenter chap was probably sending him signals, and as Phipps made clear to us, that's just not allowed.'

Jax maintained her gaze and raised her eyebrows. 'You know what I'm talking about. Tell them what you did.'

Cooper decided that he couldn't string it out any longer. 'I flicked a card at his feet. The trump ace. It looked as though he'd had it hidden. Someone spotted it fall to the ground and the room went berserk, assuming that Carlisle was cheating.'

'So you won,' shouted Allstein. 'We get our kit back and Sir Isaac here keeps his job. Brilliant.'

Jax relaxed and joined in the celebrations. 'I knew when you asked for a pack of coffee house cards you had something up your sleeve. Well played, Tom.' She kissed him on the cheek.

Newton left the group and went to track down Phipps. He wanted to set in motion as quickly as possible the recovery of the scientists' equipment from the armoury. 'Please ensure that it doesn't come to harm overnight, Ravenmaster. And see that it is returned here by the morning,' he said. 'Oh, and thank you for your invaluable help, Master Phipps. I will not forget it.'

The old soldier stood ramrod straight and saluted Sir Isaac. 'You can rely on me, sir. I can't abide cheating. Unless it's us what's doing the cheating, of course.'

Shortly after the scientists arrived at their workshop the following morning they heard cartwheels and boots clattering over the cobbles. The Wells chamber was still intact and the other pieces of the quantum puzzle were all present on the back of the cart. They breathed a sigh of relief and unloaded it.

Newton, who had been scribbling away with his pen for several hours before the scientists' arrival, joined the group in the workshop. They were seated on an assortment of chairs and stools in readiness for a catch-up meeting, and Sir Isaac asked if it would be acceptable for him to listen to their conversation.

'We would be delighted, Sir Isaac,' said Jenks. 'And if you have any questions, please feel free to ask them.'

'Indeed,' said Calvert, And if you have any suggestions we would like to hear those too. I think we're going to need all the brainpower we can muster.'

Jenks opened the conversation. 'So, while you've been having fun playing cards, Daniel, John and I have been looking into what we did to make our experiment go tits up.'

'And what did we do wrong?' asked Cooper.

'Nothing,' said Jenks. 'We've looked at all the calculations and examined the equipment that came with us, and nothing we did caused this ridiculous anomaly.'

Jax and Cooper looked puzzled. 'But something caused it,' said Jax. 'Otherwise I'd be sitting in my lovely little Cambridge flat eating toast and marmalade. Ooooh, and Earl Grey tea with Radio 3 on in the background. I really miss that in the morning.'

'Anyway,' said Cooper interrupting her reverie. 'If we did nothing wrong, what happened?'

'A power surge is our best guess,' said Allstein. 'Possibly caused by a geomagnetic storm affecting the grid.'

Newton raised his hand. 'Explain, if you would,' he said.

Allstein outlined how electricity was generated and distributed and explained how this could be adversely affected by particles from the sun hitting the earth's magnetic field. Ultra severe solar storms, which were pretty rare, could not only produce a power surge but could also knock out communication satellites.

'Interesting,' said Newton, thoughtfully. 'Thank you. May I ask another question?' The scientists nodded. 'What exactly were you trying to achieve with your experiment?'

'Shall I take this one?' said Jax. She told him that alongside their day-to-day work they were running an experiment that would take the concept of wave-particle duality beyond mere theory. 'It has been known for some time that molecules can exist in two places at the same time. Well we wanted to demonstrate that something larger than a few molecules could be in two places.'

'And what was this item?' asked Newton, intrigued by the notion.

'A pea,' said Jax. 'A humble garden pea.'

'And did it work?' Newton asked.

'We will probably never know,' said Allstein. 'We pressed the button and everything went white and wobbly, and we ended up back here.'

Sir Isaac offered the group a rueful smile. 'I'm afraid the windmill on the roof might provide you with sufficient electrical energy to try out your equipment once you have assembled it, but from what you have said it will not be strong enough to get you back home. And it sounds like powerful solar flares are not only uncommon but also highly unpredictable.'

'We would be able to predict them with 21st century equipment but that's not possible here,' said Cooper.

The group slumped into a despondent silence before Jenks clapped his hands and said brightly, 'OK, let's get on with what we can achieve, and that's putting this kit back together to see if we can pump some life into. If we can't, that's the end of our adventure. If we can, then we'll work out the power issue.'

'And a way of making a targeted return if we can please,' said Cooper. 'I don't want to finish up in Hastings in 1066. One bloody battle in a lifetime is plenty, thanks very much. Perhaps Daniel and I can work on a way of pinpointing the time and place of arrival while you guys sort out the kit.'

Bigby – 1719

Seth the blacksmith was glad to be home. It was evening and the last ten miles of his journey had dragged. He'd found himself talking to Solomon and imagining he could hear the horse reply. So when he climbed down from his cart, he gave the patient beast a pat on the neck and returned him to Dick Cobbitt. The farmer hugged Solomon, released him from his harness and thanked Seth for taking good care of him. The blacksmith took his tools, musket and sword back to the forge and made his way to the inn.

The Rising Sun was lively and noisy, but fell silent when the big man entered. They knew there was a story to be told and waited patiently until Seth had downed three tankards of ale and eaten a large pie before someone spoke. It was Enid Whipple, of course.

'Well we're not going to wait all night, blacksmith,' she said. 'Let's get on with it, shall we?'

Seth was a good storyteller. From his seat in the corner of the inn he related a narrative packed with facts and details made lively with colourful descriptions of the people and places the four of them – he always included Solomon – had met and seen. The stops along the way. The people who had helped them. The people they had helped. The awfulness of filthy, noisy London. The thrill of meeting Sir Isaac flippin' Newton and of making a sword in the Tower of London armoury.

It was nearly midnight when he finished and he answered questions patiently before succumbing to an almighty yawn and rising from his chair. His audience murmured with vicarious excitement at Seth's adventure, several men slapping the blacksmith's back as he departed.

'I'll walk with you, Seth,' said Enid, scurrying after him. 'Do you think they'll be all right? Master Calvert, Jax and their friends? They could always come back to Bigby. If the future don't want them, they'd be very welcome here.'

'They are smart people but I fear the challenge will be too great. Even with the help of Sir Isaac,' he said glumly as they reached his forge. 'Thank you for accompanying me, Enid. Would you like me to see you back to your cottage now?'

'If you wouldn't mind, Seth. It's a mighty dark night, and I thought I heard a creature earlier.'

Seth walked her home and returned to his own cottage with a weary smile. He had met no one quite like Enid on his travels. There was no one like Enid.

Despite the late hour, she had decided to write a letter. The second she had ever attempted. She was 16 when she had written the first, to the son of the landlord of the inn at Crassacre. She had taken a shine to him on a visit to the market and, lacking the confidence to speak to the lad while she was there, decided to write to him. Unfortunately, she didn't know his name and had simply written the name of the inn on the outside of the folded letter. The landlord's wife opened it, thought the amorous message was from a mistress and beat her husband black and blue with a hefty broom handle.

Enid received no reply, of course, and consoled herself with the notion that perhaps the boy couldn't read.

The second letter she addressed to Jax and Calvert at the Tower of London.

Master Calvert and Miss Jax,
I thought I would let you know that Seth has arrived safely back at Bigby and told us all about your journey to that there London. I hope you have not been killed yet and will not be in the future. But thinking of it you should be safe in the Tower of London, unless one of those lions Seth told us about escapes, which I hope it doesn't.
Seth does not think you have a hope in heck of getting back to the future but he wishes you good luck. As do I. If your speriment does not work, and you are not killed, we would all be most pleased to welcome you back to Bigby. I say all but I heard Magnolia from the Rising Sun say good riddance when you left so she probably wouldn't care two hoots if you were killed or did not come back. But she is an old hag and her opinion does not count. The parson said he would very much like to see you come back to Bigby, especially Miss Jax, who I think he might be keen on. We have not had a wedding here for a while. The last one got a bit riotous and the big barn burned down.
Anyway, you are missed by everyone here (except the vicious old bag at the inn) and we would be pleased to see you in Bigby again. If you don't come back would you ask Sir Newton to write and tell me what has occurred.
Your friend,
Enid

Enid read the letter several times and thought about deleting the references to Magnolia but her arm was aching with holding the quill and so she folded and sealed the paper and addressed it to the scientists at the Tower. She would ask Eli the carpenter to take it to Crassacre next time he went so it could be taken to London on the next mail coach. She took a nip of her newest plum brandy, pulled a face and went to bed, where she dreamed of Calvert being chased around the Tower of London by a lion. He had his shirt off.

London – 1719

The turbine on the roof of the Mint was turning efficiently in a moderate breeze. Manufactured from tall iron uprights forged in the armoury, sturdy timber braces and canvas sales, it creaked alarmingly when the wind was strong but appeared functional and stable. A metal rod piercing the Mint's roof was connected to vertical and horizontal cogs that transferred the turbine's mechanical power to the cobbled-together dynamo in the workshop. The scientists had no meter to show how much electrical energy was being produced but they would soon know if it was going to be enough. The Wells chamber and its various attachments had been assembled, the dynamo had been connected to the power socket using copper wire and a simple on/off wooden-handled lever. The only section missing was a power modulator, which probably now lay in the mud at the bottom of the River Yare.

They stood back to admire their work. 'It looks very . . . Heath Robinson,' said Calvert, who was not brimming with confidence now that the moment to test the equipment had arrived. 'The dynamo is hardly moving, which means the wind has dropped. Shall we call it a day and try it out tomorrow?'

His colleagues agreed, partly because of the lack of wind power but also because they didn't want to flip the switch and find that nothing happened. No twinkling LEDs. No gentle hum. No screen flickering to life. Putting it off for the night would at least allow them to wake in the morning with a scintilla of hope.

They agreed that having got this far they shouldn't leave the device unattended. Carlisle, who had given the Mint a wide berth since his ignominious departure from the coffee club, might be tempted to take revenge by damaging or destroying their work. Cooper's trick with the rogue card triggered his exposure but it was the bag of names – or rather one name – that did for him. If Phipps and Newton had not acted as swiftly as they did in securing the bag from the landlady, Cooper and Jax might have forfeited the game, their equipment would have been wrecked and they would be stuck in this alien time.

Jenks and Cooper took the first shift and warders Phipps and Graine, armed with their lethal-looking pikes, offered to spend the night with them in the workshop. All four were sleeping when, at about 1am, the locked door of the workshop rattled. Low voices and the clattering of keys could be heard outside. The warders woke first and quickly positioned themselves between the equipment and the door. The scientists stood behind the two ex-infantrymen, whose weapons were now pointing towards the door. A key turned in the lock. The voices outside were silent. The door creaked as it was pulled slowly outwards. Someone said shush.

It was dark inside the workshop but there was a low light outside the Mint, where several lanterns blazed on brackets. So Phipps and Graine saw four of their colleagues before they were noticed themselves. When the Ravenmaster bellowed, 'Halt, who goes there?' at parade ground volume the four Beefeaters attempting to enter took an involuntary pace backwards. One of them bumped heavily into the significant figure of the Third Earl of Carlisle, who was attempting to crouch behind them.

'What do you lot want?' barked Phipps, addressing the Beefeaters.

The one who bumped into Carlisle was clearly quicker at thinking on his feet than his colleagues and said they were simply checking on the safety of the equipment as they did their rounds of the Tower.

'And you, my lord? Were you also keen to ensure that our device was safe from harm?' asked Cooper, stepping forward. 'It is rather late for the Constable of the Tower to be showing such concern.'

'Oh, it's you,' said Carlisle with a snarl. He pushed his way through the four warders and stood within a couple of feet of Cooper, who towered over him. 'Your vile trick has ruined my reputation. I should ask one of these men to run you through and destroy this infernal device, like you have destroyed my good name.'

Cooper raised his hand to stop the man from talking. 'Regardless of the stray card discovered beneath your chair – goodness knows how it got there – you were caught rigging the secret ballot for your whist partner by blackmailing poor Peter Carpenter and ensuring that his was the only name in the bag. You cheated. You lost, my lord.'

Carlisle's face turned red with rage and he looked set to explode. 'I don't know what you are going to use this . . . thing for but it looks diabolical, satanic even. What you are planning may even be treasonous, so I think His Majesty should be informed. Immediately.' He stormed off with the four warders trailing behind him, one of them muttering about all that being a bit embarrassing.

'He's still in Hanover,' shouted Newton, who had emerged from his quarters, woken by Carlisle's wrath.

'Is he?' asked Jenks.

'I have no idea,' said Newton, yawning and going back to bed. 'Well done, Phipps,' he said. 'Good man.'

It turned out that King George I wasn't in Hanover.

His Majesty arrived at the Mint the following afternoon accompanied by two aides, one of whom knocked on the door of Sir Isaac Newton's office. 'Might the King have a word?' said the man respectfully to a stunned Warden of the Mint. Newton rose from his desk. 'His Majesty is here?' he asked. 'Now?'

'He is,' said the man in German-accented English. 'Do you have a few minutes, Sir Isaac?'

The King was loitering almost timidly by the office door, waiting for an invitation to enter. 'Of course. Please come in, Your Majesty.'

Newton scuttled from behind his desk, bowed deeply and removed some books from a chair so that the King could sit. His Majesty, smiling, indicated that Newton should resume his seat.

'Do you speak French, Sir Isaac?' asked the aide. 'As you know, His Majesty is still getting to grips with the English language. But his French is perfect. Would you mind?'

'Of course not. It would be my pleasure, sir,' said Newton in French.

The King looked relieved. He was a very understated monarch, Sir Isaac observed. Wearing a plain brown coat, albeit finely made, and black boots, he looked more like a country gentleman than the nation's ruler. A long nose and pointy chin lay beneath a dark wig.

'The pleasure is all mine, Sir Isaac,' said the King. 'I have been meaning to call on you here at the Mint for some time, to compliment you personally on your excellent achievements in returning people's confidence in our sadly-abused currency.'

Newton looked pleased and thanked the King. 'You are, of course, very welcome here, sir. But I suspect there may be another reason for your presence today.'

'You see right through me, Sir Isaac,' chuckled the King. 'Why, I am here to see for myself the trappings of magic, witchcraft and paganism that are said to lurk in the bowels of my Mint. And, of course, to talk to those who are apparently intent on practising these dark arts in this ancient fortress.'

The King rose from his chair. 'May we go and see?' he asked.

The arrival of the King's coach had alerted the five scientists to the Royal arrival. After cursing Carlisle for his interference they had decided that if the King did pay them a visit they should present a tableau of scientific endeavour. Calvert and Jax pored intently over drawings and equations spread over a work surface. Allstein and Jenks tinkered needlessly with the equipment. Cooper swept up around them, whistling Waterloo Sunset by the Kinks. It was the first tune to pop into his head.

They too were surprised at the King's modest appearance and limited entourage. Just a couple of aides, a driver and a large man nursing a musket who was sitting atop the carriage.

Newton introduced the scientists to the King and asked if any of them spoke French. Jax was the only one to respond with a nod. 'Of course you do,' said Cooper.

His Majesty looked pleased.

'So what sorcery is being undertaken here?' he asked.

'No sorcery, Your Majesty, I assure you,' said Jax. 'An experiment to see if we can make the production of your coinage more efficient.' It was an explanation they had agreed with Newton should they ever be asked what they were doing by anyone in authority. Authority didn't come any higher than the King.

'This is an age of enlightenment, sir,' she added. 'In which people are not afraid to expand the boundaries of human knowledge, thanks to open-minded rulers such as you. The inventiveness of the British people will ensure that our country will one day soon lead the world into an era of industrial innovation.' She thought she had better avoid the word revolution. It tends to make rulers a bit jittery.

'A fine speech, my dear, but what does it do?' asked the King bluntly. 'It is made of no metal that I am familiar with, has a grey window that appears to serve no purpose and is connected to a windmill on the roof. You must admit, Sir Isaac, that this does all look rather . . . odd.'

'But not satanic, sir,' said Newton. 'Scientific. An experiment that we hope will expand our knowledge. In time,' he added, risking a discreet glance at Jax.

'Scientific!' said the King. 'What does this mean?'

'Think of it as a form of natural science, sir. Carlisle's scaremongering of witchery is a shabby attempt at revenge after my friends here unmasked him as a card cheat.'

The King walked around the device, his hands clasped behind his back. He looked genuinely interested. 'I am intrigued,' he said to Jax. 'We have long since put behind us the notion of witchcraft and it is my hope that one day accusations of that nature will be banned by law. We must cast aside such superstitious nonsense to stop people like His Lordship from using it for nefarious purposes.'

He walked around the device one more time. 'Interesting,' he said. 'Very interesting. Please let me know when you are ready to demonstrate your work. I would like to see it.' He nodded to indicate that his visit had concluded, climbed into his coach with his aides and left the Tower.

'How will you pinpoint your place and time of arrival,' asked Newton on one of his regular visits to the workshop. 'Will you not be seeking something that does not yet exist?'

'Well, Cambridge exists,' said Allstein. 'So that's one part of the problem we don't have to worry about.' He extracted his arms from a tangle of wires inside the Wells chamber. 'If you recall, Sir Isaac, the nature of our experiment was to take the idea that molecules could be in two places at the same time a stage further. Our aim was to move one of the molecule groups a few nanoseconds backwards in time and then cut the wave that joins the two. One group would exist in present time, the other in past time.'

Jax approached the two men. 'We don't know if the experiment would have succeeded but our presence here goes to show what little we know about the concept of time. If we can travel backwards, perhaps we can also travel forwards. Perhaps the place and time that we came from – and all the places and times before and after that - already exists in some form. A multiverse, if you will. That's our working hypothesis. So our first step is to see if we can tune our equipment to probe the future for recognisable sounds. For example, in the next 40 years Britain will experience an incredible Industrial Revolution, with powerful machines being used to make this country the world's leading manufacturer of a whole range of goods.'

'Then comes the building of vast metal ships,' said Allstein. 'Preparations for a great war, bombs falling in a second war, nuclear explosions, rockets sent up to explore space, noises from the future that we hope will enable us to lock into a time that is close enough to our own. Then all we have to do is fine-tune our original experiment.'

'And keep our fingers crossed,' said Jax.

'That's all there is to it,' said Cooper, nonchalantly throwing open his arms. 'By the way, the dynamo is whizzing around like nobody's business. Are we ready to flick the switch? See if we can get some life into this thing?'

They looked nervously at one another and huddled around the dynamo. Jenks asked Sir Isaac if he would do the honours. Newton slowly moved the power lever forward. They could hardly believe their eyes when a soft light emerged from the monitor set into the Wells chamber. And then five tiny LEDs glowed red. Jax leapt and clapped her hands.

'So this is the power of electricity,' said Newton, stepping back from the machine. 'A wonder indeed.'

The scientists looked pleased. Hugs were exchanged. Swear words were softly uttered.

'Let's not get carried away,' said Jenks, who was hopping up and down and already visualising a pint of Doom Bar being carefully poured at his local. 'Shall we try tuning this little beauty while we have the wind in our sails?'

Jax explained to Newton that future sound – if they could prove that such a thing existed – would be displayed graphically on the small screen. The louder the noise the higher the peak on the monitor. Newton looked puzzled. 'But,' he said. 'But . . . how will you detect sound that doesn't yet exist. If you will excuse me speaking plainly, it sounds simply ridiculous, my friends.'

'Well that's the quantum world for you, Sir Isaac,' said Cooper. 'It constantly makes a nonsense of everything we thought we knew. Who could possibly have believed that a bunch of molecules could exist in two place at once. It's preposterous!

'Before our little incident in Cambridge, we were on the verge of proving that an object could not only exist in two places but also in two different times, even though the difference was just a few nanoseconds.'

Newton said he was beginning to see. 'So sound waves cause a mechanical disturbance, for example in the air or the earth, which in turn agitates molecules. Your theory of temporal superposition tells us that molecules can not only be in two places simultaneously but also in different times. And your device is looking for echoes of sounds that will occur tens, maybe hundreds of years in the future.'

'Sounds simple when you put it like that, doesn't it?' said Cooper.

'No, it still sounds . . . how did you put it? Preposterous!' said Newton.

Allstein, who had been ignoring the chatter, leapt from the seat he had been quietly occupying in front of the monitor. 'Yeow!' he said. 'Take a look.' He turned a knob that he had fashioned a few days earlier from a piece of wood he had sawn from one of Newton's bedposts. The great man hadn't noticed. The knob was just below the monitor. He turned it anticlockwise.

'There's nothing there,' said Jenks.

'That's us, here and now. The sounds being produced around the city, the country are pretty low-level. There is just a line there but it's hardly anything. The world is quite a quiet place at the moment. A few small wars, some cannon fire, some building work. But if I dial forwards clockwise what do you see?'

'The line on the graph has moved up slightly,' said Jax. 'Industry is making Britain a little noisier. Is that what we're seeing?'

They watched fascinated as Allstein dialled through the future sounds of the earth, the loudest of which were the sounds of war, peaking on the monitor's chart. Atomic testing, which they decided not to describe to Newton. He had enough to take in. Other peaks suggested the grinding movement of the planet's tectonic plates, accompanied by earthquakes and tsunamis. There was a pattern to the peaks that suggested that they really were looking at the earth's history to come.

They felt sure that they could identify the period of World War II, culminating in the dropping of the atomic bombs over Hiroshima and Nagasaki in August 1945. There was relative quiet, then until peaks which probably indicated the wars in Eastern Europe and the Middle East, which they speculated indicated the early 2020s.

It was getting late and Newton had retired to bed. 'Are we just deluding ourselves,' said Cooper. 'Making unscientific assumptions about what's showing on that screen? Seeing what we want to see? We could just be picking up sounds from the river. Ships bumping into the quayside. New buildings under construction. Carts rumbling past the Tower. It could be anything.'

'It could,' agreed Jax. 'We could just be looking at random vibrations affecting the equipment. Which would be soul-destroying after everything we've been through to get this far.'

'Except,' said Allstein quietly. 'What's this? I've gone a little further forward and got this. It's very low down on the screen and I nearly missed it. There's a pattern, see?' he said pointing to an almost imperceptible pulsing line.

'Oh yes,' said Cooper. 'High low high low, low high, high high, low low low high high, high high high high high. And then it's repeated. It couldn't be coming from our wind turbine could it? Creaking round up there.'

"That's a strong possibility,' agreed Allstein. ' Let's take a proper look in the morning when we're all a bit fresher. It's been a long day.'

They were making their way to the workshop door when Jenks suddenly screamed at them. 'Bloody hell,' he said. 'Bloody, bloody hell and kick me up the arse if I'm being an almighty numbskull. But isn't this some sort of code?'

They gathered around him to look at the screen, peering at the faint line at the base of the monitor that appeared to be throbbing. Short blips followed by longer blips. Then short blips again. In a constant stream across the bottom of the glass.

'The sequences are repeating, I'm sure of it,' said Allstein.

'Could it be pile driving along the riverside?' asked Jenks. 'Or hammering in the forge?

They stared some more and Jax suggested trying to write down the sequence. 'Call them out as blips for the short ones and bleeps for the longer ones. Allstein had only called out half a dozen when Cooper shouted, 'It's Morse Code! It's got to be. Morse bloody code. Keep going.'

Allstein stopped when he felt the sequence repeating.

'Turn the blips into dots and the bleeps into dashes and let's see if it makes any sense,' said Calvert. 'Who knows Morse? Anyone?'

No one did.

Newton, half asleep, tottered into the workshop with a blanket draped over his shoulders. 'What has happened? I heard shouting,' he said.

Allstein turned to him. 'I think we're picking up a code. It sounds like Morse Code, which was developed in the early 19th century as a simple form of electric communication. But none of us knows it.' He explained that each letter of the alphabet was represented by a series of dots and dashes. The only letters any of them knew were dot dot dot, dash dash dash, dot dot dot for SOS.

'This sounds like something I may be able to assist with,' said Sir Isaac. 'Go to your beds and leave this puzzle with me. There will be logic to this code and although my grasp of logic has been somewhat tested recently, I am sure I will be able to provide you with a solution by morning.'

He took to his desk the paper Jax has scrawled on and ushered the scientists away to their lodgings.

Their red eyes and drawn faces the following morning revealed that none of them had slept well. They had begun to doubt themselves on the way to their rooms. Were they simply wishing that the sequence was code? If it was Morse it will have been generated in the future, which means that their technology was working. But what if it was simply a door rattling in the wind? When they walked into the workshop, Newton was fast asleep, head resting on his arms spread across his desk. Beneath his left hand was a neat rendering of the alphabet and beside each letter was a series of dots and dashes. Not only that, but he had also worked out a code for each number from 0 to 9.

And in larger letters at the bottom of the page – CAM30.

Jax's scream woke Sir Isaac with a start, his blanket slipping from his shoulders.

'Place and year,' she shouted. 'Sorry, Sir Isaac. You're a wonder, a marvel.'

'A genius?' offered Allstein.

'Yes, a bloody marvellous genius,' she bellowed, kissing the great man on the cheek and causing him to blush.

'Cambridge 2030. Do we agree?' she asked. 'Someone is sending us a message.'

'A message from the future,' said Newton. 'Logic evades me once more.'

'It's not just a message, though, is it?' said Cooper. 'It's the target we had been hoping for. A beacon to guide us home.'

Newton collected the blanket from his chair and headed for his sleeping quarters with a wordless wave.

The scientists spent the rest of the week working out how to reconfigure the equipment they had at their disposal to home in on the target they had been sent. It wouldn't have been easy even if they had had access to modern resources but they were some of the most respected quantum physicists in the world. If they couldn't do it, then no one could.

But they had their doubts, and expressed them often as they took the equipment apart, referred to their notes and equations and adapted the circuits and cabling to suit their new task of building what no one wanted to properly name. They simply referred to it as the TM.

The biggest doubter was Calvert. 'You know what we're doing is impossible, don't you? What we were trying to achieve in Cambridge was child's play compared to this. We were simply . . .' He chuckled at the word. ' . . . trying to prove that an object – a pea, for goodness sake – could exist in two places in different times. Temporal superposition as we grandly called it. Now we're trying to cobble together something from bits of that very same equipment that will be able to get the five of us – all of whom are considerably bigger than a pea – forward in time more than 300 years without blowing up one of the world's most famous buildings and scattering our own atoms to the wind.'

'Well, if you put it like that we should just pack it in,' said Cooper, reconnecting wires inside the Wells chamber. 'But personally I think this will definitely work.'

'Really?' asked Jax.

'Of course not,' said Cooper. 'It's utter madness, but it's giving us something to do. And if it works we will have invented a . . . '

'Don't say it!' shouted his colleagues as one.

'OK, OK. But the you-know-what prize would do wonders for our careers,' added Cooper. 'I'm done, let's test it.'

'How will you know if it's working?' asked Newton from the doorway.

'We'll switch on the dynamo and if these LEDs light up, we're in business. It won't provide the sort of power we need to fully activate it, but it will show that the system is configured according to our calculations.'

'And should, in theory, work,' said Allstein, pulling the lever connecting the dynamo to the unit. Four of the lights immediately glowed.

Cooper lay down on the floor, opened a service panel and examined the wiring. He looked for loose tags and pushed cables to make sure they were fully connected. Everything looked sound, he said, closing the panel door and standing. He tried tapping the unlit bulb gently with his knuckle. It shone. 'Phew,' he said quietly.

'We should now be able to focus on the device emitting the code,' said Jenks. 'The next problem facing us is generating sufficient power to get this up to full speed. I know we have considered a water wheel in the fast-flowing Thames but even with sufficient gearing this wouldn't be enough.'

'We're missing something very obvious here,' said Jax. 'We think our original experiment was hit by a surge in the electricity grid, perhaps caused by massive solar flare. Both unexpected occurrences overpowering our systems.'

'A little like a lightning strike, I would imagine,' shouted Newton from his bedroom.

The scientists stared at one another. 'Holy Frankenstein,' said Cooper. 'Why didn't we think of that?'

'You would have done,' said Sir Isaac. 'Eventually.' They heard him chuckle once more, seemingly getting the hang of this humour business.

They agreed that lightning occurred more frequently than the sort of major solar event they needed, and thunderstorms arrived with at least some warning. Jenks suggested that the wind turbine on the roof of the Mint could be extended with a metal rod to make it more likely to attract a bolt of lightning.

'That could possibly destroy the Royal Mint, killing everyone working . . . and living here,' said Jax, pointing towards Sir Isaac's quarters.

'You're right,' said Jenks. 'Which means we have to move everything away from here. To an isolated spot where the only people we're putting in danger is us. Let's talk to Phipps.'

He and Jax found the Ravenmaster talking to his charges and tossing dead chicks and mice into their cages. After their breakfast they would be released into the Tower's grounds where, wings clipped, they would hop and flutter about the place looking and acting like sinister comics.

Phipps was one of those men who seemed to know everything and everyone in this historic yet seedy part of London. And he would part with his knowledge for a few shillings to supplement his army pension and, surprisingly, to feed his passion for the theatre. 'I am a soldier through and through,' he said. 'But the battlefield changes a man. I've seen musket and cannon fire rip men's bodies to shreds and heard screams that still haunt my dreams. Brave men I served with have flung themselves into this very river or put a rope around their necks to escape those sounds. Me, I escape into the imaginary world of the stage. Comedies mostly, but if I'm with my lady friend, Mrs Comfrey, I'm also partial to a romance. And if Anne Oldfield is the lead so much the better,' he added with a twinkle in his eye.

'What a remarkable man you are, Ravenmaster,' said Jax with warmth. 'We already owe you much. We would never have succeeded at whist if you had not tutored us so well.'

'At which you cheated, of course,' he said. 'And mighty proud I was that you pulled it off so skilfully.'

Jenks asked Phipps if he knew of a building that stood alone, into which they could move their equipment.

'In case you blows it up?' he asked. 'I did wonder if you was going to end up demolishing our ancient fortress with your shiny metal boxes. I know it would be a great relief to the warders if you was to move elsewhere, and blow that up instead.'

He said he knew of just the building and he walked them through the Tower's grounds to Traitors Bridge and the edge of the Thames where he pointed across the water, churning at the turn of the tide. 'You see those new warehouses? Well just south of them are once-fine gardens that have gone to ruin and, I have no doubt, will one day be built on. In the middle of that rough ground is a brick shed that I would judge is plenty big enough for your needs. You could blow it to kingdom come and hurt no one – except yourselves, of course.'

He said some of his watermen friends would be able to ferry their equipment across for them or they could take it all by cart across the bridge. 'Which bridge?' asked Jax.

'There's only one, miss,' said Phipps. 'In case you haven't noticed it, London Bridge is right there.' And he pointed to a structure west of the Tower. Not just a bridge but a Gormenghast-like structure topped by four- and five-storey houses that, from a distance, looked like one of the grandest streets in the capital. 'That might be the safest choice,' said Phipps with a grin. 'Less chance of your stuff getting damp. I'll organise a cart and a driver. It'll just cost you . . .'

'A few shillings?' asked Jax.

'Correct, miss.'

As they walked back to the workshop, Jenks asked the Ravenmaster if he knew someone, a sea captain perhaps, who could forecast the weather. Phipps told him that there were few better at reading the signs of the sky than Captain Josiah Blades, now retired and living in a cottage overlooking the Thames in Southwark. He agreed to introduce them. Free of charge.

The following day, Phipps took the scientists to see the brick building he had told them about. It looked ideal. It was big enough for their equipment and remote enough not to cause too much damage – or alarm – if things went wrong. On the walk back, Phipps took Jax and Jenks to a small house by the waterside and introduced them to Captain Blades, who they found perched on a stool by his front door.

'Who's approaching?' he asked as the three made their way along the short path to his home. 'Just me, Captain Blades. Phipps from the Tower. I've brought some visitors who seek some insight into your famed knowledge of weather prediction and such like.'

'Tell them to shove off. I'm busy.'

The captain was busy leaning on a hefty walking stick, listening to the activity of the wharf. Listening because he was blind, his eyes milky white in a leathery face cured by the sun and wave-blown salt.

'They have money, captain,' said Phipps.

'Tell them to sit down then, man. What are you waiting for?'

'There ain't nowhere to sit but I'm sure they're just as happy standing.'

The small patch of garden in front of the house looked as though it had once been well tended. Just-discernible borders offered up small clumps of daffodils and old, leggy bushes but the patch had long since been annexed by choking weeds.

'The young woman may ask me anything she likes,' said Blades, smiling. His accent was Northumbrian.

'How did you know I was a woman?' asked Jax.

'Your tread on the path, more delicate than your companion, who I would say is of more mature years. Perhaps 60? Also, there is a pleasing lightness to your breathing, my dear.'

Jax smiled. 'We wish to know how we can predict the weather, captain. In particular the coming of a lightning storm. A few hours in advance would suffice.'

'I hear no jingling of coins,' said the captain.

Jenks apologised and dropped two shillings into the seaman's upturned palm. He seemed to weigh them. Despite looking disappointed, he tucked them into his jacket pocket. 'From where will you make your observations?' he asked.

'From the Tower of London, sir,' said Jenks. 'We are there as guests of Sir Isaac Newton.' He thought it would carry more weight than saying a garden shed.

'Oh him,' said Blades. 'When does your ship sail and what is its destination?'

'We need the information not for a sea journey but for an experiment on the effects of lightning,' said Jenks. 'It would be helpful to know when a lightning storm might occur. The Ravenmaster told us there was no one better at making such predictions.'

Blades blinked his ghostly eyes and sat up straighter on his stool. 'I first went to sea at the age of 14, listening and learning, putting up with the bullying and the baiting of ignorant men. I loved the sea. Everything about it. The mountainous waves, the invisible rocks. And I learned that if you wanted to survive you had to know what nature was going to throw at you. At first, if a storm was brewing I told the first mate. He told the captain and got the credit for it. So I started to bypass the first mate, and the captain began to realise that I had the gift. I could read the clouds, the direction of the wind, the surface of the sea, the behaviour of the birds. And not once was I shipwrecked.'

Phipps made a yawning motion with his hand over his mouth. He'd heard this story, word for word, many times before.

'I heard that, Phipps,' said the captain, pointing his stick menacingly at the warder. 'Lightning is a most powerful force, but also one that strikes at random, often at the nearest point to the heavens. A ship's mast, a church spire, a Beefeater's lofty opinion of himself. But there are signs you can look for. The formation of huge, puffed-up clouds, abrupt changes in the direction of the wind, a dark, threatening look to the sky and a sudden drop in the temperature. These things usually bring the sort of danger you're seeking for your experiment. But beware, lightning is a destroyer, a killer not to be toyed with by those who do not fully comprehend its might.'

The scientists promised that they would take every care and thanked the captain for his insight. Phipps apologised for the yawn. 'Late night guarding the nations treasures, captain. No offence intended, sir.'

It took a day to take the equipment apart and load it carefully aboard a cart, the process watched with interest by Newton, who perched himself on a chair in the corner of the workshop, occasionally asking questions about the purpose of a particular part or the materials from which it was made. From time to time he rose to scribble notes at his desk, often returning with more questions that the scientists readily answered. They all knew that without Sir Isaac's support, and steady stream of cash, they would not have reached this stage of their journey.

At first light the following day the cart, pulled by a knackered-looking mare and driven by Traddles Brown, a miller friend of Phipps, trundled across the Tower's drawbridge and into the teeming streets of the capital. An old sail was thrown over the equipment in case it rained, and to deter interest from others on the route. Jenks and Calvert sat beside the driver. Jax, Cooper and Allstein perched in the back.

It didn't take long to reach the City side of London Bridge. Newton told them that there had been a crossing there since Roman times, first wooden structures and then bridges, like this one, made of stone. But this was more than a bridge. It was also home to perhaps hundreds of people and a location for dozens of businesses, all housed in tall buildings rising up beside them and over them. For parts of the crossing it was more like passing through a tunnel.

'I hope there are no heads on spikes,' muttered Jax to Cooper. She had suddenly recalled from history lessons that the heads of executed people like Thomas More and Thomas Cromwell had once been displayed at the entrance to the bridge. The driver had heard her. 'No, miss, I'm afraid they're not here no more. But I can take you to Temple Bar if you'd like to see some 'eads,' said Brown cheerily.

'Perhaps another time,' said Jax, wishing she hadn't mentioned it. 'But thank you.'

The bridge was busy with horses, carts and people streaming across in both directions. It was slow going and they attracted little attention, the rich and poor they passed more focused on reaching their destinations safely than on this bulky, rattling cart.

It was another hour to the shabby gardens and the building they had dubbed the Bolt Hole, where they carefully unloaded their cargo and carried it inside. The place was about 40 feet square and had a pitched, pyramid-shaped roof over walls made from a poor-quality red brick that was flaking on the inside and outside. It had just one wide doorway, and pairs of arched windows high in each wall. No one would be able to see in. Jenks speculated that the building might have been used to store equipment for the gardens and allotments.

The following day Brown arrived with the wind turbine, broken down into its various parts, loaded on his cart. He helped them unload it and said he would be back in a day or so with the copper rods being made for them in the Tower's forge. Allstein was concerned that the turbine would attract unwanted attention but Jenks reminded him that without it they would not be able to test the equipment and tune in to their target place and date without the gentle power it generated.

'We can't leave anything to chance,' said Jenks. 'But it might be an idea to get Phipps and some of his colleagues to come over and provide us with a little security when they're not guarding the Crown Jewels. For a few shillings, of course.'

Ten days after arriving at the Bolt Hole the scientists had assembled, tested and tuned their equipment, clamped together ten lengths of solid copper to form a lightning conductor, attached it to the side of the building and wired it up to the power unit of their device.

'It'll never work,' said Calvert. 'Not in a million years. And if we do escape the 18th century, goodness know where we will all end up. Even if we survive.'

'Oh do shut up, John,' said Jax sharply. 'The science feels good, and we've done our best with the resources we have. But none of us should feel obliged to take this risk if we don't want to. Personally, I think it's worth it. I'm already planning my Nobel acceptance speech.'

'I don't like the odds either,' said Cooper. 'But it would be a shame not to give it a try now that we've got this far.'

Jenks, who was standing, hands on hips, admiring their work, said 'Let's look at it scientifically. Three things could happen. We get back home. We get fried by a lightning strike. Or nothing happens and we stay here making a life for ourselves.'

'There's another option that worries me most,' said Allstein. 'We get transported somewhere else. Like in front of a peckish Tyrannosaurus rex. Or into an Aztec city on let's-sacrifice-a-stranger day. Or just into the middle of the Atlantic Ocean on a particularly choppy afternoon. I've had nightmares about all of these things, but I'm still willing to give it a go.'

'So, John, what do you say?' asked Jax.

'I liked living in Bigby,' he said meekly. 'It was peaceful. But OK, I'm in. Just for the record though, my money's on being frazzled.'

Newton made sure they had daily supplies of food and drink, and even delivered it himself one day, arriving as a passenger on Brown's cart. The scientists slept in the Bolt Hole, taking turns to keep an eye on the weather during the night.

Days went by with nothing but calm overnight skies bedecked with fluffy moonlit clouds. The thought occurred to them that they could be waiting weeks for the weather to break. But then . . .

Cooper was on watch at about 3am when a rumble rattled the slates on the roof. He was suddenly more alert than he had been for days. But he waited before rousing his colleagues, keen to be sure of what he had heard. Then . . . there it was again. Unmistakable in the black stillness. Another deep and threatening rumble, miles away, like the stirrings of hell. He burst out of the door to look at the sky, the noise waking the others. There was a gust of chill wind, and he saw tall, fast-building clouds rising steadily to block out the moon. And, in the distance, a brief, startling white flash that cast a supernatural spell across the city.

They stood outside the Bolt Hole, every heart pounding as realisation struck. Within minutes their experiment could see them dead or back home. Or somewhere else entirely. They were the experiment.

Calvert had suggested that they should stand close together on one side of the device so that if it worked – which it probably wouldn't – they would have a better chance of arriving in the same place.

Outside, the wind turbine cranked urgently. The dynamo lit up the screen. The tuning was checked and the faint, bumpy Morse Code line at the bottom displayed what they hoped was a message from home. The scientists stood and waited, silently, unable to find any words to express what was going through their minds as the storm approached. It crept towards them from the east like destiny, with earth-shuddering cracks and splashing rain suddenly whipping at the building's tiles like the devil himself was searching for them.

Within minutes the vast storm was upon them. Dazzling light and ear-splitting sound coincided. They were at the heart of a mighty maelstrom. The five huddled together, hoping that the roof would hold, that their copper conductor would attract a bolt and not the roof, which could be ripped away at any second.

Amid the thunderous symphony of natural power that surrounded them a deafening crack shook the building to its foundations. Lightning struck the ground nearby. Electricity sizzled in the air.

Then suddenly . . . silence.

But not total silence.

The sweet song of a blackbird. A whisper of breeze through long, dry grass. A gentle splashing fountain.

Cooper was first to wake. He was slumped against a wall that had retained the warmth of a day's sun. It was night and a fingernail of moon flicked off and on behind a scattering of slow clouds. He quickly realised that he was naked and looked around to check if anyone could see him. He was alone. It must be late. There was no sign of the Bolt Hole. The ground was dry. He stood shakily, made sure he wasn't injured and then dashed to the only area of natural cover he could see in the dim light, a clump of small trees and bushes about 50 yards away.

Jax woke up face down in an area of dry grass. She too was unclothed. Cooper saw her stand up and let out a piercing whistle, beckoning her to the copse. He looked away as she got near and the two of them stood back to back, amongst the foliage.

'Well this is embarrassing,' said Jax.

'What? It's bloody brilliant. We aren't dead!' said Cooper. 'And we're together. Which means the others might not be far away.'

Allstein burst into the bushes. 'I heard you whistle,' he said.

'I woke up in a pond, for goodness sake.'

'Nice soft landing then,' said Cooper, trying not to look at either of his naked colleagues. The three of them stood facing outwards in an embarrassed triangle. 'Who's that?' said Allstein. 'There's someone walking round and round that fountain, looking a bit drunk. I think it might be Jenks.'

Cooper whistled but got no reaction. 'Someone needs to go and get him,' he said.

'Well I'm not going,' said Jax. 'Quick, he's walking away from us.'

'Bloody hell,' said Cooper, sprinting away from their hiding place and quickly reaching Jenks, who appeared disorientated. Cooper grabbed his arm. 'Come on, Will, we're over here,' said Cooper.

'Who the hell are you, and why haven't you got any clothes on?'

'None of us have any clothes on, Will.'

'Oh. Are we in one of those nuddy colonies,' he asked with a vacant smile.

'Yes, that's right. We just need to go and sign into the clubhouse. But quickly, before there's a queue,' Cooper said, trying to keep the panic from his voice. They reached the sanctuary of the bushes where a semblance of realisation appeared on Jenks' face. 'I know you guys, don't I? But I don't think I've ever seen you naked before.' At which point his memory sprang into red-faced life and the four snapped away from one another, looking up into the leafy canopy.

'This is looking good, so far,' said Jax. 'Four of us have ended up in the same place, although we have no idea what year it is, and . . .'

She was interrupted by a male voice beyond the bushes. 'Help! Can anyone hear me?' The low volume of the voice suggested it was emanating from someone who needed assistance but in as discreet a way as possible.

Cooper sidled over to the edge of the bushes. 'Is that you John?' he said as loud as he dared.

'Tom? My God, Tom? I'm stuck in a tree with no clothes on. I need help to get down.'

The four in the bushes looked at one another. Their faces showed that none of them fancied the job of helping down a naked man, particularly one that they knew pretty well. Cooper relented. 'Daniel and I should go. We're the tallest,' he said. 'Just don't look.' Allstein nodded in reluctant agreement and the two of them trotted in the direction of Calvert's voice.

He was halfway up an ancient oak tree. He could struggle down a little further but then there was a ten or twelve foot drop to uneven ground that would have been dodgy in footwear let alone bare feet.

'See if you can get to this lower branch,' said Allstein. 'I'll stand underneath and you can balance on my shoulders. Tom can help you to the ground from there. Are you hurt?'

'Just a few grazes. Are the others here?'

'In the bushes over there. We're all safe,' said Cooper. 'For the moment. But we probably need to find out where we are and what date this is, and get our hands on some clothes. Before daylight preferably.'

Once they had retrieved Calvert from the tree and scuttled back to the safety of the bushes they stood in a circle, backs towards the middle, each of them sensing the embarrassment of the others more acutely than pain itself.

'There was a narrow, low-down window near to where I came to,' said Cooper. 'It might lead to a cellar or storeroom. If we can get it open, we might be able to find some clothes.'

'Dear God, yes please,' said Jax with feeling. 'This is . . . excruciating.'

'I'll go and have a look. If I need help I'll whistle,' Cooper said. He dashed off into the darkness, bending low, commando style. The opaque glass in the window was reinforced with a fine metal grid but there was a space between the hinged top edge and the frame that he thought might give if he had a lever of some sort. He looked around and spotted a metal plant marker in a nearby flower bed.

'What's he doing?' asked Allstein.

'Gardening, by the look of it,' said Jax. 'No, he's pulled something out of the ground and is levering open a window.' She heard a faint crack as the hinges gave way. 'He's in. I hope he hasn't caught himself on anything sharp.' The men winced as one.

'He's throwing stuff through the window. Now he's putting the window back in the frame. He's a bloody hero,' said Jax.

Cooper's arms were full of clothes when he got back to the copse. But joy turned to despair when they found they were all 18th century. Breeches, waistcoats and long-tailed coats. Leather boots and curly grey wigs. And not good quality at that.

'It'll have to do for now,' said Jenks. 'Where did you find them, Tom?

'They spilled out of a wicker basket I fell on from the window. They were all I could find. Sorry, folks.'

They started to get dressed, sharing out the items that best fitted each of them. When they were done they finally turned round to face one another. A motley assemblage of 18th century roughs and nobles.

'We may not be home, but at least we're all still alive,' said Jenks.

They decided to continue hiding until it became light and they could assess where they were. They knew there was one large building nearby but couldn't be sure that they were still in London. They made themselves as comfortable as they could and waited. And dozed. It had been an exhausting night.

'I think my phone's dead,' said a young woman standing a few yards from the bushes. 'You haven't got a charger, have you?'

The words didn't register with Jax immediately. Then suddenly they did. She scrambled to her feet and peered through the foliage. 'What was that?' said the young woman with the dodgy phone. 'Just a bird or something,' offered her female companion. 'Or a fox.'

'Or a flasher. Let's get out of here, it's creepy,' said the first young woman.

Jax shook her friends awake and held her finger to her lips. They stood and looked out. At the Science Park, people in 21st century casual clothes, men and women on bicycles, shiny commercial buildings and laboratories. Modernity. Their world. Their time.

Only one thing stopped them from celebrating. Walking into their laboratory, the one they thought they had destroyed, was Daniel Allstein and Will Jenks.

The long, numbing silence was eventually broken by Jenks saying, 'Ohhh, shit! We're too early. It hasn't happened yet.'

'But how come we're here, and they're here,' said Calvert.

'Shouldn't that be impossible. Isn't that a time paradox or something.'

'Nobody has done this before, so perhaps time doesn't know what the bloody rules are. And we look ridiculous. These must be the theatre group's costumes. The lovies will be livid.'

Cooper had been unusually quiet. 'Why don't we just go up to the lab and explain . . . to ourselves. We know for a fact that they're not only brilliant physicists but reasonable people. And whether we like it or not, they are part of all this. They're us.'

Jenks said while all that was strange to hear out loud, it was also very true. However, it might be more prudent to involve a go-between. Someone of this time who would believe their story and make the introductions a little easier. 'No one will take us seriously if we showed up looking like this,' he added. 'If I was me . . . I mean the me over there . . . which I am, I know that . . . I would struggle with any sort of explanation that would result in there being two of me. Does that make any sort of sense?'

'None whatsoever,' said Calvert.

'Who have you got in mind as a go-between?' asked Allstein.

'Haven't a clue. But it needs to be someone credible, preferably from our field,' replied Jenks.

'I know someone who will take us seriously,' said Cooper.

They looked at him expectantly. 'Angela Hawkins,' he said. 'She's a physicist here working on a big Government project. She's got a bit of a . . . thing for me. Took my picture once when she thought I wasn't looking.'

'I know Ange. I didn't know she was short-sighted' said Jax. 'With a bit of work I can make this costume look more 21st century. Untuck the blousy white shirt, wrap a belt around it to make it look like a skirt over trousers. Even the boots work. How do you think I should approach this with her? I don't want to come across as deranged.'

They agreed that it would be best to invite Angela into their hiding place to try and explain what had happened. After that she should go over to the laboratory to see their doubles for herself.

Angela was analysing the results of an experiment on her computer when Jax walked into her office. It was the first time Jax had been to Angela's lab.

'Jax! This is a nice surprise,' said Angela. 'Is there something I can help you with?'

Jax had thought of her approach on the walk over. 'There is actually,' she said. 'My colleagues and I have stumbled across a paradox we think you might be interested in. Indeed, we could really do with your help in trying to explain it. I hope I'm not being too abstruse but all will become clear if I show you. Do you have half an hour?'

'Are you OK, Jax? You sound a bit . . . strange.'

'Oh, I'm feeling very strange, and when you hear what we've got to tell you you'll understand why. Tom Cooper will be there,' she added as an incentive.

'Then what are we waiting for?' asked Angela almost leaping from her chair.

'This all sounds very mysterious,' said Angela as they passed the group's lab. 'Where are we going?'

'Just follow me, and prepare to be more than a little surprised.'

Angela stopped when they reached the bushes. 'What the . . . ?' she said.

'Please trust me, Ange.' Jax took the young scientist's arm and led her through the foliage to a small clearing where she saw Jenks, Allstein, Calvert and Cooper looking uncomfortable and utterly ridiculous in 18th century stage costumes. They removed their wigs and hats.

'Hello Angela,' said Cooper.

'Hi Tom,' she replied. She knew she was blushing and was glad the dim light was hiding her red cheeks.

'I expect you want to know why we're all hiding in here looking like this?' said Jenks.

'I'd be absolutely fascinated to know,' she said. 'You're all very serious scientists, so I'm sure you will have a logical explanation. Are you planning a surprise for someone?'

'Pretty much. Though it's something of an unplanned surprise,' said Jax. 'Can I ask you to do something weird. But not creepy. Would you mind going over to our lab and then come back here and tell us what you've seen. Try not to act surprised.'

'Okay,' said Angela, drawing out the word. She turned with a worried expression, wondering if the five physicists had somehow been driven mad by the secret experiment that everyone on the park seemed to know about. She walked quickly to the lab and went straight in. Less than two minutes later they saw her sprinting across the grass to the bushes. She was wide-eyed and breathless.

They stood in silence for several seconds, allowing her to digest the information. 'You're all there. And you're all here,' she said slowly, as if to herself. She wobbled and Cooper helped her to sit on the leaf-strewn ground.

'It was caused by our experiment, Angela,' said Calvert. 'And we need to explain it all to you so you can help us. If you're willing, that is.'

Before she had time to respond Jax blurted out a question. 'What's today's date, please Ange?' she said urgently.

'The date? June 9th. Is that important?

'Oh no,' said Allstein grimly. 'It's today. It happens this afternoon.'

They gathered at Angela's small flat. She drove Jax, Jenks and Allstein there, while Cooper and Calvert jogged, arriving puffing and sweaty in their bulky costumes. For a couple of hours they took turns in describing their 18th century experiences, patiently answering Angela's questions. She was particularly intrigued by the way they had reconfigured their equipment to affect a return.

'I wonder who built the beacon that helped you back? That was quite a brainwave,' she said. 'Even if you did arrive a little earlier than intended.'

'That was just down to the way we tuned into the beacon,' said Jenks. 'Our equipment just wasn't sensitive enough. But it got us this far. Now all we've got to do is stop them – us – from pressing the button, otherwise we fear there will be this constant loop. Them going back in time, us returning, in a cycle that lasts for goodness knows how long. We have to find a way of pausing the experiment for a day without alerting them to the problem.'

Angela asked why it would matter if their doubles knew what had happened.

'We've discussed this at great length,' said Jax. 'We don't think time travel is a good idea. Any one of us could have died back in the 1700s. Tom arrived there in the middle of a fast-flowing river, for goodness sake, and fought in sea battles. The smallest thing we do back there could change future events dramatically, and even though we tried to be careful we don't really know if our presence in the past has affected anything now.'

'Apart from duplicating ourselves, of course,' said Cooper. 'Going back in time was an unfortunate mistake. But returning here was controlled and could be refined and repeated. We don't think that's wise. If we made ourselves known to our doubles, the story might get out, and indeed one of them/us might decide to make a name for themselves/ourselves as the inventor of time travel.'

Jenks looked at Angela with concern. 'We believe that our accident may have occurred because of a power surge caused by something like a giant solar flare. Do you know anyone with the sort of knowledge and authority who can warn them that such a flare is going to happen today, just to get them to delay the experiment by 24 hours.'

'I do know someone, as it happens,' said Angela. 'My friend Joel is an astrophysicist on the park. But what if he doesn't believe there's going to be a solar flare?'

'He will have to lie,' said Allstein. 'Would he be prepared to do that?'

'Oh god! He might if I make it worth his while,' said Angela. 'If he does manage to convince them, what will happen to you guys if the experiment is delayed? Will you still be here? Will you just go back? Will you just vanish?'

'We don't know,' said Jax. 'We've thought about it but there's no way of knowing. It's one of the reasons we don't want this experiment to go wrong and for time travel to be developed into something that could change the world in unpredictable and disastrous ways. If an unhinged dictator got their hands on the technology goodness knows what damage they could cause.'

Angela nodded. 'Don't worry. He'll do it.'

'I think I'd like to go home,' said Jax. 'There's a key under Terry the gnome. It'll be nice to get out of these clothes.'

'Yep, me too,' said Calvert. 'I was wondering how I would get in but I remembered my neighbour has a key.'

'Mine too,' said Jenks.

Cooper and Allstein said they would have to break in somehow and hope their neighbours didn't call the police.

Angela thought they looked weary and offered to drive them, but all said they would welcome the walk.

Angela spotted Joel pushing his bike to the building where his lab was located. She couldn't recall seeing him actually ride the thing, a flashy, expensive-looking model he had probably bought to make himself look more sporty, she thought. He was pleased to see her and instinctively pulled in his stomach, releasing it when she told him she needed an urgent favour. He liked Angela – a lot – but she did have a habit of making his life more complicated than it ought to be.

'I need you to go over to that lab and tell the guys there that there's going to be a powerful solar flare today and that they should seriously consider shutting down any experiments they don't want fried,' she said. She had been running and was panting. He quite liked it.

'How did you know about the flare?' he asked.

'You mean there really is going to be one?'

'Yes but nothing out of the ordinary,' said Joel. 'It shouldn't affect anyone's experiments.'

'This is important, Joel. I can't explain but I will make it up to you if you can just persuade them that this flare is going to be a biggy and that they should just shut down for the day. Tell them you're warning everyone. Please, Joel.' She looked as if she was about to cry.

'It's really that important?' he asked. She nodded, tears now filling her eyes. 'Hold my bike. Don't get it dirty.' Angela thought he looked quite heroic as he strolled purposefully towards the lab.

The sun burned down on the Science Park on June 9th 2030. But the aircon was operating silently and efficiently in the lab as William Wilberforce Jenks, Daniel Allstein, Tom Cooper, John Calvert and Esmerelda Fortescue-Jackson sat down for a mid-morning meeting with coffees and pastries.

'If this solar flare is going to be as big as this Joel character says shouldn't we disconnect everything and reset for tomorrow,' asked Jax. 'We don't want to risk all this being cooked. I think I'd cry for a week.'

Cooper looked as though he was going to respond but took a bite of his iced Danish instead. 'Have you ever heard of a solar flare warning before?' he asked eventually. 'It seems very odd to me. And who was that guy, anyway.'

'He seemed to know what he was talking about,' said Calvert. 'I looked him up and it's definitely his field. It is a bit frustrating though, having to sit on our hands when it's all ready to go.'

'It's tempting,' said Calvert.

'I agree,' said Jenks. 'It is. Personally, I think we should go for it.'

The body language around the table suggested that

everyone was in agreement. They didn't know Joel from Adam and had no reason to believe his warning. They finished their drinks and stood fretfully around the lab. They would have been nervous without Joel's warning but his advice to pause until the flare had passed had racked up the tension a couple of notches.

Jenks moved towards the monitor's touch panel on which five red-lit buttons were displayed. He pressed the first and turned it green. Calvert touched the second, Cooper the third, Allstein the fourth. Jax's finger was hovering over the final button when, at 4.46pm a wave of what felt like static electricity swept through the room. The hairs on their arms and necks stood up. The coffee machine, photocopier and kettle hummed and zinged for several seconds. Car alarms sounded across the park. Their watches stopped.

'Woah,' said Jax, withdrawing her finger. 'Did you feel that?'

'It made my teeth itch,' said Cooper. 'I've never felt anything like that before, and we were that close to pressing the fifth button. We might have wasted years of work.'

'It could have frazzled the lot. Shut it down,' ordered Jenks. 'This can wait another day. We should have listened to that guy.'

Bigby – 1719

Eli Graves was driving his weather-racked cart along the track towards the north-south road, his head-drooped horse plodding the dappled route with a slow, rhythmic tread. Eli was enjoying the familiar symphony of grasshoppers, birdsong and sissing leaves when his ears detected something else, something unfamiliar on this lonely trail.

Footsteps. Footsteps crunching the dry surface of the path.

His horse, Clarence, halted without being asked and looked up, alert.

Two men stood before them. A tall, elderly, keen-eyed man dressed in ground-skimming black robes and a cap. He was holding a long walking stick. Beside him was a shorter man with a weather-worn face dressed in a red uniform of some sort.

'Are you, by any chance, Eli Graves the carpenter?' asked the older man, who had spotted the beautifully-crafted wooden buckets in the back of the cart.

Clarence snorted and directed his ears towards the man's slow, droning voice. 'I am,' said Eli. 'And who might you be, sir.'

'My name is Newton, and this is my friend, Ravenmaster Phipps. We have travelled from London to visit your fine village with news of Master Calvert and Miss Jax. Is Bigby far?'

'My goodness,' said Eli, flustered and excited at the same time. 'Oh my goodness. The village will be filled with delight at your visit Sir Isaac. Truly thrilled. I will drive you there myself, good sirs.' He surprised Clarence by clumsily turning his cart around on the narrow road.

Eli's sudden return to Bigby caused a stir and half the village turned out to see what had brought him back. Elbowing her way through the throng was Enid Whipple, her whole body charged with the thought that she might once again be called upon to exercise her medical skills.

'What's wrong, Eli?' she shouted. 'Are you unwell?' she added, half in hope. Then she noticed the carpenter's passengers.

'No, Enid, I have not been weller. I have in my cart Sir Isaac Newton, no less. And a man called Phipps who looks after ravens, which I never even knew was a job,' he said, his voice rising excitedly as he completed his explanation standing in his cart. 'Sir Isaac Newton, everybody. Come to us in Bigby. And he has news.' The swelling crowd muttered. Some clapped, although others couldn't fathom why.

Phipps smiled broadly at their reception, wondering if he had ever been greeted in such enthusiastic fashion in his life before. Newton rose to stand beside the carpenter and gestured for the crowd to quieten. Parson Perkins arrived, puffing and apologising for being late for whatever this was.

'Ah, parson. I have heard much about you,' said Newton. 'Would it be possible to have some refreshment before gathering the villagers for a meeting in the church?' Perkins said he would be honoured and helped Sir Isaac from the cart. 'And might we invite Mistress Whipple and Seth the blacksmith to join us?' asked Newton.

Enid looked at Seth, standing tall at the back of the crowd, and beamed like a lighthouse. She shoved her way through the throng, grabbed Seth by a powerful arm and hurried to catch up with the parson.

There was standing room only when the four of them walked into the church an hour later and sat in chairs facing the expectant congregation. The pews were full and villagers were standing in rows three deep at the back. Perkins introduced Newton and told the villagers that Master Phipps was a Yeoman Warder at the Tower of London, and by all accounts a most resourceful man. He had been charged with ensuring that Sir Isaac got to Bigby safely. A Beefeater in Bigby. Newton stood and waited for the clamour to subside.

'I am here to honour a promise I made to Master Calvert and Miss Jax. You took them both to your hearts, and I know that they carried all of you in theirs. They asked me to let you know what happened after Seth delivered them to the Tower of London and, you will all be pleased to hear, reunited them with their three colleagues.' There was a cheer at the news that they had all made it safely to London.

Newton related their tale, highlighting the ingenuity they employed, the faith they had in one another's skills, the determination that inspired others to help them. The deception that allowed them to shame one of the country's best card players, a nobleman no less, and the exposure of his bag of names. This brought the biggest cheer ever heard in the church.

He also told them about their dangerous final experiment at the Bolt Hole, where they put their future and their lives in the hands of one of nature's most ferocious forces.

'What I cannot tell you is what happened after lightning struck the Bolt Hole,' he said. The congregation sighed as one. Newton held up his hand to quieten them. 'Phipps and I went there the day after the storm. The building was all but demolished. Their equipment was there and I ordered it destroyed. But there was no sign of our friends. And . . . no bodies.'

People spoke to their neighbours, not knowing what to make of this news. Newton stilled them again. 'This means that they did not die there, my friends. And if you were to ask me where I think they are, I would say . . . home.'

There was another great cheer. Perkins slapped his hands on his thighs and stood, shouting and clapping along with his parishioners. Enid dried her eyes on the edge of her grey pinny. She rose as Newton approached her.

'I have something for you, Mistress Whipple. Master Calvert asked me to give you this letter, a reply to the one you sent him. I have heard much about you. About your kindness and wisdom. And it has been the greatest of pleasures to meet you.' Enid did an involuntary curtsy. 'Thank you, Sir Newton. I've never had a letter before. I hope it don't make me cry.'

She hurried out of the church and perched on the cemetery wall, staring at the letter before sliding a finger beneath the seal and unfolding the paper.

Dearest Enid, it began. Well, that set her off straight away and she had to dry her eyes again before continuing.

Dearest Enid,

I wanted to reassure you that I have not been eaten by lions and have been well looked after by Sir Isaac Newton and the friendly Beefeaters here at the Tower of London.

My stay in Bigby was extraordinarily special, particularly the time I spent getting to know the wise and resourceful woman that is Enid Whipple. The village is very lucky to have you, although I expect the "old hag at the inn", as you call her, would rather you had joined me in London.

I have missed your company and your sage advice, but would it be ungentlemanly of me to say that I have not missed your plum brandy? It always took at least 24 hours for my taste buds to recover. Seth likes it though and says it is an acquired taste.

Bigby will always have a place in my heart, as will you, Enid. And I thank you for your kind letter of invitation. If I don't die in

our experiment, or if it fails, I will return to Bigby. I can think of no other place I would rather see out my days.
Your friend,
John Calvert

Enid wanted to share her first ever letter with someone. So she took it to the parsonage, where Newton and Phipps had been invited to stay for the night. Perkins welcomed her and showed her into the drawing room, where a fire was blazing, despite the warmth of the day.

There were beads of sweat on Newton's brow as he tossed sheet after sheet of paper into the flames. 'What is it you're doing, Sir Newton?' asked Enid.

Newton paused and mopped his forehead. 'I learned so much from Master Calvert and his colleagues during their time with me, and I made notes on everything. I felt it was my duty to record what I had learned. Not to publish, you understand. It was never my intention to take credit for the knowledge and work of others. I wanted to be able to remember . . . remember all the remarkable things I heard of the future.' He looked at the page he was about to burn.

'I showed them to Parson Perkins, and we agreed. Our time is not ready for such ideas and we cannot risk upsetting the natural order of things. The natural order of time.' He flung the final sheets onto the fire. 'But I will remember. Until, perhaps, I cannot.'

Cambridge – 2030

The experiment having been abandoned for the day, Calvert walked up the five steps to his Edwardian townhouse with the door key in his hand. But he didn't need it. The door was open a few inches and the light was on in the hall. He pushed the door closed behind him and called out to ask if anyone was there. He walked cautiously from room to room, bracing himself to tackle an intruder. When he got to the top of the stairs he came across a pile of clothes that looked as though they had simply fallen from someone's body – a pair of long black boots, breeches, an embroidered 18th century coat, a waistcoat and a long grey wig. Beside the heap were the house keys his neighbour kept for him. He picked up the keys, stepped over the items and checked the rest of the house. There was no one there. He collected up the clothes and spotted a label in the back of the coat. Park Drama Group.

Puzzled, he called Jax. She had found a pile of discarded clothing just inside her front door. Plus the keys she kept under Terry. It looked as though someone had let themselves in and stripped naked in the hall. Cooper, Jenks and Allstein also reported finding drama group costumes in their homes but no sign of any damage or theft. They arranged to meet in the Eagle pub.

'Should we call the police?' asked Jenks.

'And tell them what?' said Cooper. 'That a bunch of amateur dramatists have broken into our homes and left their clothes there? It's too weird for words. And, anyway, the only homes broken into it seems were mine and Daniel's. Smashed glass in the back doors.'

'It gets weirder,' said Calvert. 'I asked my neighbour who he had given his key to. He said it was me. In fancy dress.'

'Same here,' said Jenks. 'He swore it was me.'

Jax looked worried. 'My neighbour said she saw me looking under Terry for my key when she was making her kids' tea. I was dressed oddly, she said.'

'So, to summarise,' said Jenks. 'Someone has entered each of our homes, three of them using a key that they knew how to access, dumped a pile of theatrical costumes and vanished. And all this happened just before we got home ourselves.'

'You've missed a significant point here,' said Jax. 'The people looked like us. What the hell is going on?'

On her way to work the following morning, Angela stopped by Jax's flat to make sure she was OK. 'Hi, Ange,' said Jax, still in her pyjamas and a robe. 'What are you doing here?'

'Just wanted to make sure you were all right after yesterday.'

'Oh yes, the solar flare. Thank you so much for getting Joel to warn everyone about that. Could have saved years of work. I'll go and thank him when I get in,' said Jax. 'You look worried, Ange. You OK?'

'Er, yes, fine. Bit of a strange day eh?'

'And it got stranger,' said Jax, holding up a black bin bag. 'When we got home yesterday afternoon all five of us found these old costumes dumped on us. From the drama group. A prank we think. What a bunch of oddballs.'

'Goodness. Would you like me to return them for you? I know a couple of the members.'

'Great,' said Jax. 'Look, I have to get dressed. I'll see you later at the park. Let's have a coffee.'

Angela took the bag to her car, sat in the driver's seat and cried. Cried for the people she had met yesterday. Who are, in some weird way, the same people she will meet today. Cried for all they had gone through to survive in the past. Cried for their bravery and ingenuity in getting back and preventing a temporal loop from happening time after time.

But need she be sad? The brilliant scientists she had spoken to among the trees and bushes in the Science Park yesterday were the same brilliant scientists who would arrive at their lab today, weren't they? Well, not entirely, she felt. They had not experienced and survived life in 1719. Or found ways of contacting one another in an age of quill pens and sealing wax. Or met Isaac Newton. Or found a way of building a time machine powered by wind and lightning. And they would never know of all these achievements by their other selves, who had simply stopped being when the giant solar flare put the world back onto its axis. The only reminder of their existence were five piles of shabby theatrical clothes.

But that's not entirely true, she suddenly thought. She knew of their existence. She knew their story.

Joel had his feet up on his desk and was reading a thriller when Jax strode into the lab. 'I'm not slacking, honestly,' he said defensively. 'Just waiting for some figures to run through a new program. What can I do for you?'

'I hear you like doughnuts,' said Jax. 'It's a thank you for the heads up on the solar flare yesterday. You're a life saver, or an experiment saver anyway.'

'To be honest, it was much stronger than I'd anticipated. An

X15-class. Surprised me as much as it did you,' he added with honesty. 'Thanks for doughnuts though.'

Mrs Carter was in her kitchen making a batch of scones when she felt an irresistible urge to drive to the Science Park. She had no business there, she had long retired. But for some reason she simply couldn't put her finger on she just had to go to the park.

She slid her Audi TT into a parking space and found herself standing outside the lab from which her friend Tom Cooper was regularly mailing her back-up drives. She hadn't been here for months but it had attracted her today like a magnet and she had no idea why. She just stood there with a puzzled look on her face, with no intention of going inside because she wouldn't be able to offer a sensible explanation as to why she was there.

Mrs Carter was about to leave when she was joined by a young woman carrying a coffee in a refillable mug who stood beside her. 'Are you looking for someone?' the young woman asked. 'I work on the park. Perhaps I can help.'

'No, my dear. No one. I don't really know what I'm doing here. I know it sounds strange but something just drew me to the park today. I worked here years ago but I feel a bit foolish now, just standing here, staring at that very dull looking building where some of my friends work.'

'It is very ordinary, isn't it?' said Angela. 'But extraordinary things go on behind boring walls like those, don't they? I'm Angela.'

'Mrs Carter,' said the older woman. 'They do indeed, Angela.'

Angela looked at her properly for the first time. 'Felicity Carter?' she asked.

'Yes,' said Mrs Carter. 'Have we met?'

'No, I would have remembered,' said Angela. 'I know about you, of course. You inspired me to be a scientist. I was the geeky kid in the school. While my contemporaries lived their lives on social media I lived mine in New Scientist and Physics World, constantly Googling the long words and finding that they would stick and make sense. Your published papers were always so exciting and unstuffy. And the ideas you put forward . . .' Angela stopped abruptly. 'Sorry, I sound like a giggly schoolgirl.'

'I'm so pleased to hear that. It means a lot,' said Mrs Carter. She detached her gaze from the building. 'I think I'll take a look at the sculpture trail while I'm here, although rusty metal isn't really my sort of thing.'

'Mind if I come with you?' said Angela. 'There's one that's a bit different and I'd like to know what you think about it. It's just behind the lab here.'

The skinny, upside down pyramid with twinkling LEDs looked to be in a very awkward place. Too close to the building and difficult to find in an overgrown tangle of council-grade broom and red robin. 'I only noticed it yesterday,' said Angela. 'It's not on the list of exhibits and is completely different to all the other sculptures. I was quite drawn to it.'

'I wonder who it's by,' said Mrs Carter. 'It seems to have some writing on it but I'm not getting snagged up in that shrubbery to find out what it says.'

Angela knew what the words said. They were the names of five scientists who had disappeared yesterday, leaving nothing behind but a pile of clothes, and without knowing that this was the beacon that had guided them home. They had no idea who had built the beacon. And neither did Angela. But she knew what it was. She couldn't take her eyes off it. Mrs Carter asked her if she was alright.

'Yes, I'm very alright. Very alright indeed. But I do have an urge to tell you a quite unbelievable story, Mrs Carter. If you have time.'

Steven Scott lives on the Norfolk coast with his wife Linda. They have three grown-up daughters and three grandchildren. He failed his GCE O Level Physics exam so anyone planning to build a time machine should probably ignore most of the science in this book.

OK, all of it.

He did alright at History though.

Printed in Great Britain
by Amazon

46251849R00158